"I love you, Micah," Carrie said

"I think it's only fair to warn you that if I stay here I'll do everything in my power to make you love me, too."

"I don't love you, Carrie," he said very softly.

"I don't believe you," she said equally softly.

"I was married once. I failed miserably as a husband."

"I loved unwisely, as well. I wouldn't want to believe I'd lost my only chance at love because of it."

"Some things are given only once." Micah couldn't keep the bitterness from seeping into his voice. She heard it.

"We can all be lucky enough to love a second time."

She was very close. Her lips were only inches from his. With a little sigh, she lowered her head and kissed him....

ABOUT THE AUTHOR

"Every American of our generation has some experience with Vietnam," says the two-sister writing team of Marisa Carroll. "We wanted to look at Vietnam from a slightly different angle. For example, we thought it was time for something to be written about women veterans." This germ of an idea eventually grew into The Saigon Legacy. This second book of the trilogy, Micah's story, is the authors' fourth Superromance.

Books by Marisa Carroll

Don't miss any of our special offers. Write to us at the following address for information on our newest releases.

Harlequin Reader Service
901 Fuhrmann Blvd., P.O. Box 1397, Buffalo, NY 14240
Canadian address: P.O. Box 603,
Fort Erie, Ont. L2A 5X3

Refuge from Today

MARISA CARROLL

Harlequin Books

TORONTO • NEW YORK • LONDON
AMSTERDAM • PARIS • SYDNEY • HAMBURG
STOCKHOLM • ATHENS • TOKYO • MILAN

For Marsha Zinberg,
with respect and affection,
and for Ellen Lupu,
bravely into the breach

Published November 1990

ISBN 0-373-70426-7

CHAPTER ONE

IT WAS ONE HELL OF A LONG way to the ground.

Micah McKendrick checked the safety lock on his climbing belt, leaned back in the harness and looked down over his shoulder. His friend and research assistant, Reuben Henry, waved back at him from the forest floor one hundred feet below. The gesture was typically Reuben, composed of equal parts reassurance and impatience. They'd been climbing this same tree for twelve seasons, and Micah knew Reuben's moods and quirks better than his own. His friend made a cup of his hands and hollered loud enough to wake the dead.

"Jeez, hurry it up, Micah. The wind's pickin' up damn fast."

As if to lend credence to Reuben's words, another gust of wind sent the huge platform of twigs and sticks ten feet above Micah's head swaying precariously. The bald eagle nest was a fitting ornament for the magnificent Michigan white pine in which it rested. An enormous skeleton bleached by the sun, the dead tree wore the nest like a crown of thorns. The wind gust subsided as quickly as it blew up. The mournful sigh of the dead branches faded away; only the sound of his own ragged breathing filled Micah's ears. Overhead storm clouds raced along in tattered disarray, allowing fitful May sunshine and bright blue sky to show through the gaps. The day was cold and damp, changeable, typical spring weather so close to Lake Superior.

Above him the occupants of the nest squawked and fussed, unaware of his presence, interested only in the fact that dinner was being withheld. Higher still the parent birds circled endlessly above the nest, creeing loudly, shrill cries of distress.

Micah didn't even glance up. Bald eagles would not attack an intruder at their nest as hawks and owls do, but would only call down to their young until the disturbance was past. Their actions weren't dictated by cowardice or disregard for their young but by a defense mechanism perfected by nature over thousands of years. A mated, reproducing pair of bald eagles were of far more importance in the scheme of things than an unfledged chick, whose chances, especially in this day and age of pesticides, habitat destruction and poaching, were slim, indeed.

He pulled an old pair of leather gloves from the back pocket of his jeans and unlocked his safety belt. Free-climbing the last few feet to the nest, Micah grasped the edge, hanging for several seconds as he strained to get over the lip, then hoisted himself into the nest. Once past the lip, he tied himself in with a rope hanging from his belt. The huge, shallow bowl of twigs and branches was sturdy, if uncomfortable, having been added to over five nesting seasons by the parent birds. Reaching for the hooked stick attached to his belt, Micah attempted to snare the occupants of the nest, two chocolate-brown eaglets, still sporting wisps of white down, which had removed themselves as far as possible from the bearded human intruder in their midst.

"Come on baby, come here fella," Micah crooned, his low, harsh voice mellowed by a tenderness he wasn't even aware had seeped into his words. "It's all right. Won't hurt a bit." One of the parent birds, the female probably, from the large size of the shadow that passed across the nest, made a tentative strafing run, still far above. Micah didn't even flinch. His mind was on his work. He kept talking to the frantic chick he'd snared, drawing the screeching, gawky youngster close enough to snap a numbered, riveted tag around the yellow talon.

The eaglet reciprocated by gouging Micah's wrist above the cuff of his glove with its razor-sharp beak. Micah swore and released the bird. The wind sent the nest swaying in another dizzying arc before he managed to snag the second youngster, a male. He tagged this one with a minimum of wasted effort, avoiding a repetition of the gouging the chick's sister had given him.

He gave the pair a final assessing glance, gauging their weight and state of health with a practiced eye. He jotted down a few quick notes on the contents of the nest in a small pocket notepad. The pike and walleye jawbones, the rabbit fur and the remains of a water snake in evidence were all typical prey of the big raptors at this time of year.

Micah stuck his notebook back in his shirt pocket. It was time to go. If he disturbed the sanctity of their nest for too long a time, the parent birds might give up their anxious vigil and not return. He didn't want to push his luck. He'd need it all to get safely back on the ground.

He hung from the edge of the nest for several seconds while he searched with his feet for a safe purchase on the tree trunk. His battered climbing irons caught and held, sinking into the dead wood with a hollow thud. He started down, free-climbing without a harness, his heart hammering in his chest. Only a fool wouldn't be afraid of a climb like this one. Only a fool or a man who didn't care what happened to his life. The tree was getting more dangerous to climb every season. He probably should have let Reuben do it again this year. Reuben was twenty-five or thirty pounds lighter and damn near ten years younger. But he was also scared to death of the wind.

And maybe, just maybe, Micah admitted as he started down the trunk searching for hand- and footholds among a myriad of broken-off branches, he wanted to impress the second observer watching him from below. Doug Simpson, his brother Simon's new stepson, stood several feet away from Reuben, watching with apparent disinterest as Micah negotiated the hazardous climb.

He still wasn't sure how he'd allowed himself to become responsible for the Amerasian teenager. Him, a man with no wife or children of his own, no experience with teenagers, especially a teenager with problems. Doug was seventeen, a real hard case, if you believed what he told you. Except that Micah didn't believe him. Maybe that's why he'd agreed to let him spend the summer up here after he'd been suspended from school. Micah owed his very life to the boy's mother, Annie Simpson McKendrick. Taking Doug under his wing for a season was the only way he could repay her for defying the corrupt Vietnamese official who had held him hostage and making sure he wasn't left behind to rot in a Saigon jail the year before. He'd do his best for the boy.

His climbing iron bit into the soft wood, skidded and held, jerking his attention back to the business at hand. Just because he had a dozen seasons of climbing and tagging behind him, didn't mean he was immune to accidents. Hell, he was forty-four years old, and pretty beat up into the bargain. Someday he was going to have to turn his job over to someone younger. Just as, in the same way, he was going to have to stop avoiding the future to keep the past at bay. With middle age staring a man in the face, he couldn't live only for the here and now much longer, even if that was the only way he was able to get through the nights.

REUBEN KNEW SOME PRETTY good cuss words, Doug had to give him that. He listened appreciatively as the older man punctuated Micah's descent with a flurry of interesting and colorful four-letter words and phrases. It wasn't that Reuben was a wimp or anything like that. Just yesterday Doug had watched him climb a tree almost as high as this one and never look down. But yesterday had been cloudy and overcast without a hint of wind. Today was different and Reuben hated wind. He'd learned that much about Micah's friend in his two weeks stuck up here in the boonies. There wasn't much to do but listen to the men talk. At least Reuben talked; Micah seemed only to listen.

He was even beginning to think he could get into being a wildlife biologist like Micah, spending his time outdoors, working with bald eagles and ospreys and peregrine falcons, learning what made them tick. And not from books and old, dead, stuffed birds like in biology class at school. Micah worked with real, live birds. Yeah, it wouldn't be bad at all.

Doug caught himself grinning. A frown quickly replaced the errant smile. You couldn't be a wildlife biologist, not a real one with a college degree like Micah, if you didn't even have a high-school diploma. And thanks to that one night of cruising and drinking with Emil Fraser and Marty Benson back home, he wouldn't ever get one. It wasn't fair. Just because two years ago three seniors had been driving and drinking and got themselves killed after a football game, it didn't mean the school board had to make an example out of him and poor old Fraser and Benson.

Doug looked up, shading his eyes against the sun, watching Micah's descent. Doug's jaw was set in a hard, obstinate line. Those guys had such good grades they didn't even have to go to summer school, let alone face flunking a whole year. What were his mom and Simon thinking, expecting him to spend another year in that school with kids that were barely old enough to drive? So he'd told them he wasn't going to go back to school in the fall. He was a man and he'd made his own decision. Only he'd just never expected his mom to look so sad or cry so hard...or get so mad and practically kick him out of the house.

Micah was two-thirds of the way down. The lowest branches of the big tree were so far above the ground that he'd had to climb a smaller maple nearby and throw a weighted rope across a big limb of the pine, crossing hand over hand before he could climb the nest tree. Doug caught himself wondering if he had the guts to take on something like that dead tree. Reuben didn't seem to mind if anyone knew he was scared. But then he was a lot older. He'd been in the Vietnam War. You could admit you were scared when you were so old it didn't matter anymore. It wasn't like being seventeen and having to prove you were a man to the whole world.

"Hell and damnation!" Doug knew Micah was in trouble before Reuben started to yell. A branch, solid enough on the upward climb, broke off under his weight. He skidded, his climbing irons finding little purchase in the rotten wood. He made a grab for another limb just above where his rope was tied off, snagged it and spun around, coming up hard against the trunk of the pine. He hung there a long moment. Reuben already had his climbing irons buckled in place. Doug never remembered seeing anyone move so fast. Reuben was mumbling and cussing and praying under his breath, all at the same time. He sprinted up the trunk of the big maple as Doug ran over to the base of the dead pine. He didn't know what he could do to help if Micah fell the rest of the way to the ground, but he just couldn't stand there like a dummy and watch it happen.

Reuben was still yelling but Doug couldn't understand what he said over another gust of wind that rattled the new green leaves of the maple and sent the dead branches of the pine moaning like lost souls. Micah's voice was deeper than Reuben's. It carried better on the wind.

"I'll make it. I think I cracked a rib or two." Reuben made sweeping gestures with his hand. Micah shook his head. "I'm okay. We've gotten out of tighter spots than this."

Doug wondered what he meant by that, but he didn't have much time to think about it. Micah flipped a length of his climbing rope over the rope strung between the two trees, snapping it to a second loop on his belt. His movements were slow and awkward, not like the unhurried, easy way he usually worked. He set off, taking most of his weight on his right side, letting the rope support him when he had to use his left arm. Doug was never sure, afterward, how he did make it safely back to the ground.

"Hell, Micah, did you poke a rib through your lung?" Reuben's usually ruddy face was almost as pale as Micah's beneath his tan. Reuben had been cussing and encouraging, both at the same time, all during Micah's descent.

Micah didn't answer, only shook his head no.

"You sure?" Reuben didn't seem convinced by the denial.

"I'm sure." Micah's voice was drawn tight with pain. "Just cracked a couple, like I told you." He allowed Reuben to take his gear and throw it in the back of the twenty-year-old Jeep that, thankfully, Doug realized, they'd been able to drive in close to the nest tree. Yesterday they'd banded a chick in a nest on a little island in the middle of a lake an hour's walk from the car.

"I damn sure hope so," Reuben said, shaking his head as he settled a grim-faced Micah into the passenger seat. Doug clambered into the back. Reuben's next words echoed his own thoughts. "I sure as hell don't look forward to hauling you into Doc Sauder's office while Rachel's working there. She's going to have my butt in a sling for letting you get yourself banged up, sure as my name's Reuben Henry. You just see if she don't."

CARRIE GRANGER HEARD the commotion before she saw the men who were causing it. Or two men and a boy, to be precise, she decided as they came through the door. She looked up from the three-year-old copy of *National Geographic* she was holding, but not reading, to watch the drama unfold. The boy came first. He was wearing a gray hooded sweatshirt, a black T-shirt and jeans that had definitely seen better days. His hair was brown and wavy, long in the back, and pulled into a short ponytail. There was a pronounced Asian cast to his features: Japanese, Korean or Vietnamese, Carrie couldn't be sure which. His eyes were brown, his expression troubled, his attention fixed on the two older men who had followed him into the waiting room.

One of them was doing all the talking, although yelling was probably a more accurate description of his volume and tone as he called for the receptionist, the doctor and his nurse. He was about her own height, five foot nine, or maybe an inch or so taller, with a ruddy complexion, a shaggy mane of ginger-colored hair and blue eyes set deep in his head. Wrinkles fanned out at the corners of those blue eyes. He looked as if he might laugh easily and often. He wasn't laughing now.

Neither was the taller man he supported with an arm around his shoulders. Carrie, being tall herself, always noticed height first. He was a big man, not fat, but broad-shouldered and hard-muscled. A man who worked with his hands for a living, like her father and uncles, she would guess. He was also, obviously, in pain. It showed in the grim set of his jaw, evident even beneath his neat, dark beard; in his narrowed blue-gray eyes as they swept over the room, meeting hers for a fraction of a second before moving on, leaving her strangely uneasy and concerned; in the way he held his left arm pressed tightly across his chest.

"Doc! Rachel! Get out here. We need help. Micah's had an accident." There were four other patients sitting on worn leather chairs in the small waiting room. Micah's hard, dark gaze had passed over each and every one of them. Only Carrie was singled out for a second quick, assessing glance. She dropped her eyes. The door to the exam room and the inner offices of the rustic one-story clinic swung open. Dr. Rex Sauder's receptionist, Marie, a friendly woman in her late middle years whom Carrie had already met, bustled through.

"What's all the hollering going on out here, eh?" she asked, ending the question with the evocative monosyllable Carrie had heard so often since coming to the Upper Peninsula of Michigan.

"Micah busted a couple of ribs on a climb. Where's Doc?"

"Doc's right behind me, so calm down, Reuben Henry." Marie gave the injured man a long, penetrating look. "Come on back, Micah. You look like you could stand bein' off your feet for a spell."

Carrie liked the name Micah. A good, strong, old-fashioned name. It suited this man. Carrie was very aware of names these days, the way they seemed to belong to the people who bore them, or the way they did not.

A small, childlike figure in a dark skirt, pale pink blouse and long white lab coat emerged from the doorway behind Marie. She went immediately to Micah's side. "What happened? Are you badly hurt?" She had a beautiful contralto voice. She laid her hand on Micah's arm, looking up into his harsh face, her own elfin features drawn tight with anxiety.

"Banged up a couple of ribs, that's all. Honest." The corner of his mouth twisted up into a rueful smile that never quite reached his eyes. He was a man who didn't smile easily or often, Carrie guessed. The woman who did merit his smile must be very special indeed.

"I thought you were going to let Reuben climb the nest tree today." She laid her hand gently on his injured ribs. A muscle twitched in his cheek but he made no sound of pain, nor did he flinch from her light, exploring touch.

"Wind's blowing, Rachel," he said, tilting his dark head toward the man who still supported him as if that explained everything. Evidently it did to Dr. Sauder's nurse. She smiled and shook her head.

Rachel. Carrie liked that name, too.

"Reuben always did have more sense than you."

"X ray's all set. Bring him on back." The doctor's voice came from somewhere out of sight.

"I suppose once I get in there, Doc's going to read my pedigree, too." Micah started forward, moving slowly, stiffly, favoring his injured ribs.

"Did you really expect anything else?" Rachel opened the door to the examination rooms, smiling up at Micah as she did so.

They made a handsome couple. Both were in their early forties or so, Carrie guessed, although she was a terrible judge of age. Both had dark hair and blue-gray eyes. The contrast between his height and rugged strength and her petite femininity made Carrie more aware than ever of her own less than sylphlike figure and above-average height.

"Looks like the eagle man went and almost got hisself killed this time," the toothless old woman sitting next to Carrie said, chuckling with unholy glee. "I've said time and time again, if God meant birds to wear little bracelets and teeny tiny radios on their backs, then He'd 'a' made their nests a lot closer to the ground so's crazy men like that wouldn't fall and knock their brains out trying to get to 'em."

"Eagle man?" One thing she'd learned in the weeks she'd been staying in the Munising, Michigan area was that after a long, cold winter of being isolated in their homes by blizzards and raging ice storms off Lake Superior, most people liked to talk. To anyone. About anything.

"Sure. Him. Micah McKendrick, the eagle man. He lives way the hell and gone back on Blueberry Lake. About forty miles south o' here."

"Blueberry Lake." Carrie liked the sound of that name, too.

"Yeah, they say things is pretty screwed up over there. Everything's at sixes and sevens. Him gettin' his ribs banged up good and proper ain't gonna help any, far as I kin see."

"That's a shame." It didn't take much encouragement to keep the old lady talking. The memory of a fleeting glimpse of blue-gray eyes kept Carrie's own interest piqued.

"One of them college boys who usually help with all the computer stuff they do out there—he knocked up his girlfriend and had to stay down below, make an honest woman of her, 'stead of traipsin' all over the countryside chasin' down birds and wiring them up to this thing and that." Carrie felt a tight little pain around her heart at the woman's heedless words but tried to ignore it.

"Course *she* came to help, but that didn't do him much good neither."

"She?" Carrie couldn't seem to help herself when it came to acquiring information about Micah McKendrick.

"Yeah, that little one, the nurse. Rachel Phillips is her name. Practically the same day's she got here, oh, I guess it must be goin' on a couple o' months now..." She considered the passage of time, then shrugged and went on, "Doc's real nurse, Maggie LeSatz, had to leave. Her daughter was in this real bad accident in Detroit. Gonna be laid up for six, eight months. So Mrs. Phillips stepped in to help Doc out. Not that she ain't a good nurse. She is. Just a might strange and standoffish is all."

"Miss Granger." The receptionist, Marie, stood in the doorway once again.

"I'm Carrie Granger," she said, rising from her chair, her hands going automatically into the pockets of her shapeless oversized sweater, pulling it away from her body.

"Six weeks? Dammit, Doc, I can't be laid up for six weeks." Carrie stopped halfway down the short hallway leading to the interior of the ranch-style, log-sided clinic. Micah McKendrick's incredulous voice came from the cubicle directly ahead of Carrie, but it was the short, bald figure of Dr. Rex Sauder who appeared in the combination office-treatment area onto which all the other rooms opened. His back was to Carrie and Marie.

"I said no climbing for six weeks and I meant six weeks." He was making notations on a chart as Carrie followed Marie into the open area. He ignored Micah's tone, which was more angry growl than speech, talking over his shoulder as he scribbled more notes on the chart. "Make me mad and it'll be eight weeks."

Carrie caught a glimpse of the teenage boy sitting in a chair against the far wall, still silent but no longer quite as sullen and frightened-looking as before. The ginger-haired man they called Reuben was leaning against the foot of an unused exam table, his arms folded across his chest.

"Rachel, those X rays ready yet?" Rex Sauder raised his voice to carry across the room.

"Two more minutes. They're in the fixer." Rachel walked out from behind a small partition near the boy's chair. The tight, drawn look of anxiety had receded from her fine-boned features. She smiled slightly in Carrie's direction when Doc turned his back and Carrie realized suddenly that the other woman was very pretty. She smiled back. Micah McKendrick's injury was evidently not serious. She was glad to know that. "Marie, why don't you put Miss Granger in treatment room three...."

"In six weeks the nesting season will be over. We're already ten days behind schedule because of all the rain." Micah McKendrick strode into the already overcrowded room, his red and black plaid flannel shirt in his hands. He was pale beneath his tan, his eyes storm-cloud dark with pain, but except for an ugly red abrasion on his left side and a bloody gouge on his right wrist, he appeared to have no other visible injury. His attention was fixed unswervingly on the doctor. He didn't seem to notice Carrie as she stepped back, closer to the maple-paneled wall.

"Doc, aren't you going to tape those ribs or anything?" Reuben jerked upright from his lounging position against the high black exam table. "I mean, you're just going to let him walk around like that with two busted ribs?"

Rex Sauder snapped the X ray into a lighted display rack against the wall. He studied it closely for a long moment, Reuben peering over his shoulder. "We don't tape busted ribs anymore. It decreases lung capacity, makes it harder to breathe, maybe even masks some symptoms later on. Nope. Let the ribs heal naturally. If it hurts, don't do it." He switched off the bright light behind the X ray and turned to Micah.

"You're going to be mighty sore for a week, ten days. I'll give you a prescription for some pain pills and Rachel can see that you get some extra rest. Sleep sitting up in a chair if it helps." Micah opened his mouth to protest again but Doc forestalled him. "And what can we do for you, young woman?" he asked, turning his attention to Carrie. Penetrating brown eyes stared out at her from behind an old pair of black horn-rimmed glasses.

"I . . . I have an appointment for a checkup."

"We'll be with you in a moment." He pushed the heavy frame of his glasses higher on his nose. He was a small, rotund man in his sixties, bald as a baby, his round features puckered into a perpetual frown. "Any more questions, Micah?"

"Yes." The word was forced out, short and sharp. "How the devil am I supposed to get my work done if I can't even manage to dress myself?" He was struggling into his shirt, favoring his left arm, annoyance and pain both easy to read in his face.

"I'll help." Rachel moved forward quickly, easing the heavy flannel shirt across his back, dealing with the stubborn buttons in the blink of an eye. "There," she patted his chest, her small, delicate hand seeming smaller than ever against the broad expanse of tightly stretched material.

"You're working too hard as it is, Rachel," Micah said. "I'm not going to ask you to log in three or four more hours every night on that damn computer even if I could simplify the program enough for you to use it."

"I'm a fast learner. Just think where I was eight months ago."

Micah smiled again, as reluctantly as before. Some private communication passed between them. "You're one in a million, Sis."

Carrie's heart gave a little jump of surprise. Micah McKendrick and Rachel Phillips were brother and sister, not lovers, as she'd half supposed.

"You can't do this alone, Micah," she said so softly that Carrie, who had excellent hearing, barely caught the words.

"I won't." He made an attempt to tuck his shirttail into his jeans with one hand but soon gave up with a disgusted grunt. "I'll put in an emergency call to Ann Arbor tomorrow. Maybe Bill Haines at the University Raptor Center can dig up a grad student who's even slightly interested in raptor biology to help out for a few weeks. I just sure as hell hope he sends someone who can understand that damn computer."

"Excuse me." Carrie heard herself speak and was astounded. "I've worked with computers at a university in Ohio for the last six years. I'm good and I could use a job."

"Do you know anything about raptors?" Micah asked, turning towards her for the first time.

"I know they're birds of prey. Eagles, ospreys, hawks..." She let the sentence trail off into silence. That was really all she did know about the big hunting birds, and she wasn't about to make herself look ridiculous before this stern-faced man by pretending to know more than she actually did.

"We also do some work with falcons." He exchanged a quick assessing look with his sister. Carrie studied their faces more closely, seeing numerous subtle similarities that she'd missed before, similarities that spoke of a closer bond than shared ethnic characteristics.

"You'll have to live at the compound. Blueberry Lake is pretty isolated," Rachel said. Rachel seemed to be studying her as intently as her brother. Carrie stood a little straighter. "There aren't any other women at the compound. When we work late here I sometimes stay overnight in town. Does that bother you?" She gave Micah a saucy look that seemed out of character for her, but made her all at once more approachable, less remote. "Does it make you nervous knowing you'll be alone with my brother?"

"Does the idea of being alone with three men bother you?" Micah broke in, impatient once again.

"No." She lifted her chin and gave him back look for look.

"Is there a man in your life?" Micah's tone was blunt.

"No." Carrie could be blunt as well.

Micah looked slightly taken aback, as though he hadn't realized he was being rude. "Good. There's very little time for socializing during the nesting season." He looked her over carefully, head to toe, as though making a decision. Suddenly, irrationally, Carrie was disappointed he wasn't looking at her as a woman instead of a potential employee. She fought down the urge to smooth her hand over her dark blond, French-braided hair. Instead, she kept her hands in the pockets of her sweater and refused to drop her eyes from Micah's storm-dark gaze.

"I don't have any commitments that will interfere with my work." *No commitments for the length of time she'd be involved with Micah McKendrick.*

"What's your problem physically?"

"What?" Carrie blinked.

"This is a doctor's office." Micah continued to hold her gaze captive with the intensity of his blue-gray eyes.

"I . . . I've just been feeling a little run down lately. It's nothing, really. Spring fever, I suppose. Actually, I was just about to leave when Marie called me back. I've forgotten a very important appointment." She looked away. She wasn't a very good liar.

"Okay." He accepted her excuse at face value. "You've got the job. If you want it. I can't pay much and there are no fringe benefits whatsoever. It's an internship, really. For graduate students in raptor biology, but you'll have to do. Room and board are included," he added as an afterthought.

"I understand." Her mouth was suddenly very dry.

"It's a deal, then." Micah held out his hand. It was large and hard and callused. Her hand disappeared in his. He was very strong. "Can you find your way out to Blueberry Lake?"

"I'll find it." Carrie felt it was important to prove her competence to this strange, hard man from the very beginning.

He nodded curtly. "Be there by 8:00 a.m."

"Ten." Rachel's tone was quiet but firm. "We're all sleeping in tomorrow."

Micah opened his mouth as if to refute the statement.

"Ten," Rachel repeated firmly. "It's my day off, so I can help you settle in." She smiled one of her rare, beautiful smiles.

"Thanks."

"Are you sure you don't want to see the doctor today?" There was no censure or impatience in her tone.

Carrie hadn't even noticed when Doc had left the room but he was gone. Reuben and the teenager whose name she didn't yet know were making ready to leave also.

"I know it's inconvenient but I do have another appointment." Micah was still watching her. She didn't look his way again.

"Don't worry. Marie can reschedule you. But if you are feeling unwell I wouldn't put it off much longer."

"Thanks. I won't." She couldn't. Just as she couldn't put off facing the future any longer. Carrie turned and hurried outside into the cold, fitful May afternoon. What had she gotten herself into? She needed a job, yes, but not this job. She had enough money saved to see her through the summer. Her friends, Joe and Denise Hartman, had promised her she could stay with them in Marquette as long as she wanted, as long as she needed, to plan for all the to-morrows that lay ahead.

Tomorrows when she would have another human life besides her own to be responsible for. Because she knew in her heart that she wasn't anemic, or run-down or even depressed. She was pregnant. She knew and understood the changes in her body, although she'd tried long enough to deny them and, lately, in the past few days, the first faint movements within her womb.

The truth was that she was twenty-eight years old, unmarried and pregnant. A story as old as time and men and women and love affairs that should never have been. Only when it happened to you, it wasn't an age-old story. It was something very real, very imme-diate, and very, very frightening.

CHAPTER TWO

"DOUG, GET THE TOOLBOX from the shop and take it over to Carrie's unit. I'll check with Rachel and see if the new curtains are ready to hang." Reuben's scratchy tenor voice disturbed the song sparrow in the cedar tree outside the door. It also disturbed Micah, at work at his desk.

"What's going on now?" he asked, without looking up, as Rachel walked into the big, high-ceilinged main room of the cabin, her arms full of material. "Reuben's out in the yard yelling at the top of his lungs."

"They're helping Carrie hang new curtains," Rachel answered, choosing to ignore the decidedly bad-tempered growl in his voice.

"She's wasting her time trying to fix up that shack when there's plenty of room for her right here." Or there would be as soon as he moved his stuff out. The two-story log cabin was picturesque but a little short of usable living space. The main room was dominated by a huge stone fireplace that took up most of one wall and rose all the way to the peak of the ceiling. Opposite that, a small loft topped the two bedrooms. An even smaller kitchen and a no-frills, thirties-era bathroom completed the floor plan of the house.

"I don't think many brand-new employees would have the nerve to take their boss up on an offer to turn him out of his own bedroom." Rachel picked up one of the faded yellow and white polka-dot organdy curtains she had carried down from the loft above the bedrooms. "Did you know Mom has stashed Great-grandmother McKendrick's cradle up there? When do you suppose she brought that up here?" There was no longer any laughter in Rachel's soft, hesitant voice. It was filled with sorrow and loss, longing for what could never be again.

She was thinking of her son, Micah realized with a jolt of pain around his heart, a child of violence, conceived in captivity, born into a world too harsh and violent for its small spirit, dead and buried in a lost corner of the world seven thousand miles away. He knew it was the pain of that loss that had driven her to seek refuge with him shortly after Simon and Annie's marriage.

Micah turned away from the scene of blue sky and green pine trees beyond Carrie's small cabin that he could see through the open screen door. His usually harsh voice was low and scratchy with seldom-expressed emotion. "She brought it one summer about four years ago, right after Simon's divorce. Just before she and Dad sold the hardware store and bought the condo in Florida. I think with you still missing in Southeast Asia, me holed up here and Simon single again, it somehow meant the end of her hopes for a house full of grandchildren."

"I thought that might be the answer." Rachel smoothed her hand over a fold of the curtains she'd laid carefully over the back of the couch. "The

McKendricks aren't a very lucky family. We've all lost our dreams one way or another, haven't we?'' She looked up and smiled, a tight little twist of her lips that held no happiness or joy.

"Just some of them, Sis." Micah came forward, awkwardly, to rest his big, callused hand on her shoulder. She nodded and turned away.

Micah looked helplessly at the back of her head; her dark, night-black hair, like his own and their brother's, lay like silk against her nape. Only seventeen months separated Micah and Rachel in age. They'd always been close as children, but that was half a lifetime ago and more than half a lifetime in experience, in suffering and loss.

"You're right," Rachel said. "Look at Mom and Dad. They've got five grandchildren now that Simon and Annie are married."

"More than enough." Micah's tone was dry. "One of them has even spilled over onto us." He squeezed her shoulder and grinned. He didn't smile often, and the muscles of his face felt stiff. Rachel smiled, too, so he figured he'd come close enough to the real thing to fool his sister. He felt her square her slim, delicate shoulders, saw the shadows of the past recede from her blue-gray eyes and stepped back as she picked up the armload of old curtains.

"How are you and Doug getting along?" She turned to face him, searching his face for a more truthful answer than he might want to give.

"We aren't," he admitted, running his hand through his hair. "The boy doesn't want a father confessor."

"And you aren't sure you're cut out to be one."

"That's about it."

"You'll find a way to get through to him." She sounded so certain that Micah might have believed her himself if he hadn't known his own track record on relationships.

"You've got more faith in my abilities than I do." Micah picked up several file folders and and a floppy disk. He held open the old-fashioned wooden screen door for her to precede him out of the cabin.

Doug appeared in the doorway of the toolroom at the near end of the lab building, carrying a small red toolbox. He let the metal door slam shut behind him, startling the blinded osprey that resided permanently in the first flight cage behind the building. She began a raucous creeing that signaled distress.

"Will that boy never learn?" Micah muttered as he watched Doug disappear into Carrie's cabin. Rachel's hand on his arm was a reminder, feather light, a fleeting touch.

"He is just a boy, Micah. Remember that."

"He's almost a man. He's made a man's decisions about his life. He's going to have to learn to live with them."

Bright laughter spilled out of the doorway of Carrie's small cabin, one of three relics of a bankrupt tourist motel that Micah had moved onto his property two years earlier to house visiting ornithologists and professors he wasn't encouraging to stick around the compound any longer than necessary. The one-room cabins were watertight, rodent free, and supplied with electricity and running water. Beyond that, the amenities were somewhat lacking. That hadn't stopped Carrie Granger, though. She'd been working at fixing up the place ever since she'd moved in a week ago.

Carrie walked out onto the tiny front porch of her cabin to shake a dust mop. She was smiling, laughing, as she called back over her shoulder. The sight of her gave Micah a jolt in his middle, just as it had the first time he'd seen her in Doc's waiting room. Women didn't usually affect him that way, especially tall, skinny ones who didn't have enough meat on their bones. Her voice was light and gay but not giggly or affected. When she talked business, she sounded as though she knew what she was talking about. And when she asked him questions about his birds, they were intelligent, probing and to the point. He had to admit he liked that in a woman: strength and intelligence and knowing her own mind.

If you got right down to it, he liked the way she braided her hair, too, although he had no idea how she accomplished the intricate French braid that kept all but a few stubborn wisps of fine dark blond hair confined against her head. He liked her intelligent, warm brown eyes—

Doug bounded out of the cabin and pitched a bucket of dirty water almost at his feet.

The half grin that had stolen undetected across his hard, bronzed face transformed itself into a scowl. What was the kid up to now? He didn't have time to waste on silliness and neither did any of the others.

"You scared hell out of the osprey, slamming the door to the toolroom that way. Don't let me catch you doing it again." *Damn, it was back.* That low, menacing growl in his voice he'd never even noticed was there before. The kid heard it, too, and his head came up, anger flaring briefly in his brown eyes before being overtaken by his usual sullen apathy.

"I'm sorry, I forgot. It won't happen again."

"See that it doesn't." At least the kid had some spirit. That was good. And some control over himself. That was even better. "When you're done here, the osprey needs to be fed. There are three perch carcasses thawing in the lab. She'll probably only want two but if she's hungry, she'll take a third."

A little of the heavy sullenness in Doug's almond-shaped eyes lifted. "I'll get right to it. Just as soon as I help Carrie finish up inside."

"Never mind, Doug. We're almost done." Carrie rested the ancient dust mop on the rickety floor-boards of the cabin porch and smiled at the teenager. "Thanks for all your help."

"You're welcome." With a last darting glance at Micah's stern profile, Doug walked away in the direction of the lab.

"We brought the curtains I was telling you about." Rachel broke the silence that stretched out after the teenager left.

"Thanks. We can hang them right now...unless there's something that you need me for...." Carrie indicated the file folders and floppy disk Micah carried in his hand. She never knew quite how to act around him. He was so remote, reserved, complete within himself. Possibly it came from spending so much time here alone. Possibly it was because he had no interest in her as a woman, or as a person, whatsoever.

"No, I don't need you. Go ahead and finish what you're doing." He turned on his heel but Reuben's voice from inside the cabin stopped him.

"Hey, boss, I could use a hand with this curtain rod."

Micah looked as if he wanted to refuse his friend but could not. Reluctantly, it seemed to Carrie, he handed the folders and floppy disk to Rachel, who added them to her armload of curtains, and walked past Carrie into the cabin without a second glance.

"We might as well join them. I've never known a man to put a curtain rod exactly where you want it unless you're standing right there giving directions," Rachel said with a smile that was between her and Carrie alone.

"I heard that." Reuben stuck his head out of the open door of the cabin. His ginger-colored hair was standing up in spikes around his head, giving him the look of an overgrown gremlin. "Don't bad-mouth the hired help. Especially when it's free."

"Not exactly free," Carrie reminded him. "Didn't I promise you and Doug homemade pizza tonight?" She liked Reuben. He was straightforward and uncomplicated with no dark, unexplained facets to his personality. She wasn't about to let her taciturn and very complicated boss's presence on the scene put a damper on her newfound friendship with his assistant.

"Well, now you did do that. And I suppose you'll be including Rachel and our esteemed leader in on the party too, now that they're pitching in to help."

"Of course..." Carrie felt herself begin to stutter. She'd had every intention of asking Rachel to be one of the party, but she hadn't considered including Micah in the festivities because she was certain he'd refuse the invitation. She took a deep breath to begin again. "You've both very welcome. Tonight. Here. About nine."

"How are you going to fix pizza here?" Rachel looked around her, plainly curious. Sometimes, Carrie thought, she appeared as innocent and open as a child about things. At other times she looked as if she had seen and experienced more of life than a woman twice her age. At this moment the child-Rachel stared out of her expressive blue-gray eyes at the bright red and blue plastic plates and cups that sat neatly alongside canned goods on the two wooden shelves that did duty as Carrie's kitchen cupboards, at the colorful old quilt Denise had insisted Carrie take for her bed, at the bright red, blue and yellow plaid throw she kept in her car and that now graced the back of the lumpy armchair in the corner. Although the dreary little room was much improved in looks, the only means of cooking food remained the two-burner hot plate on the counter by the sink.

Carrie felt her cheeks grow warm with embarrassment at Rachel's continuing questioning gaze. Micah wasn't looking at her, thank goodness, seemingly concentrating on making sure the curtain rod above the window was as straight as humanly possible, but she felt him listening just the same. "I was going to ask if I might borrow the use of your oven."

"Of course you may use the oven," Rachel said, smiling again. Carrie smiled back, though she knew Rachel suspected something was wrong. Rachel hadn't pressed Carrie to reschedule her appointment with Dr.

Sauder, but sometimes, when she thought Carrie wasn't looking, she would watch her with the evaluating gaze of a trained nurse. "I'd be honored to attend. I can't answer for my brother, however." This time her smile held a hint of mischief that matched the glint of devilry in her eyes. Expressive eyes, blue-gray as a summer sky after the rain had passed, eyes exactly like Micah's, Carrie realized with a start, except that Micah's showed no emotion at all.

"I'm busy." He must have heard how curt the words sounded but did nothing to soften their impact.

"If you finish up earlier than expected, the invitation still stands." Carrie drew herself to her full height and looked her employer straight in the eye. Or would have, if he'd been facing her. Instead, she stared straight at the back of his night-black head, the gray scattered through it only serving to highlight the darkness of the rest.

He turned with a jerk that must have hurt his healing ribs. "Thanks," he said awkwardly, handing the screwdriver to Reuben. "I'll keep that in mind. This window's finished." Without another word, without meeting Carrie's eyes, he picked up his paperwork from the white enameled metal table where Rachel had laid them and left the cabin.

"I'm afraid my brother's not a very social animal." Rachel smoothed her hand over the yellow and white organdy curtains once more. She looked sad and concerned.

"I remember a time when he used to be." Reuben, too, looked unusually subdued. "But that was a long time ago and a lot of miles away." He stared off into the distance for a moment. Just a hint of the sky-blue waters of the lake could be seen from the window above the sink. The only other window in the cabin, the one where Micah had been working, was a small one beside the door. It looked out over the compound toward the lab and the back of the main cottage, almost directly in line with the window of Micah's bedroom. "He was a real party animal before the bad times, before Elaine . . . died."

"What did Elaine look like, Reuben?" Rachel asked, surprising Carrie with the question. It seemed a strange thing for a sister to ask, but Reuben didn't seem to notice anything unusual about the query.

"She was a pretty little thing, not much taller than you, with fiery red hair and freckles. 'Freckles everywhere,' Micah used to say. They fell in love and got married before Micah went back to Nam for that third tour. Sort of a whirlwind romance, you might say." Reuben stopped, embarrassed, and finished tightening the screw in the rod above the kitchen sink. "All set to go." He handed the slim gold-colored rod to Rachel, who immediately began gathering one of the curtain panels on it. Her slim, blunt-nailed fingers were shaking uncontrollably.

"Were they happy together?" Her voice was soft, hesitant.

"They didn't have much time together after the war ended—" he paused "—not at the end, anyway." Reuben looked uncomfortable, as uncomfortable as Carrie felt listening to the stilted conversation. Rachel finished sliding the soft white organdy onto the rod and handed it back to Reuben.

"I never met her, you know. Or Simon's first wife, either." She shook her head and there was a world of meaning in the bewilderment the gesture conveyed. A heartbeat later Rachel seemed to notice the uncomfortable silence in the cabin for the first time. "Oh dear, I've forgotten again. I'm sorry, Carrie. It must seem strange to you that I've been asking such personal questions about my brother in front of you. It's just that where I've been—" she broke off for a moment, took a quick little breath and then went on "—where I've been living it isn't impolite to ask such personal questions unless you mean to cause mischief by learning the answers."

"I see," Carrie said, but she didn't. She'd gathered the second set of curtains onto the rod for the window beside the door. She handed them up to Reuben, who'd moved the stepladder he'd been standing on across the room, being careful not to lift her arms so high that her shapeless old pink T-shirt lifted up to reveal the gentle swell of her belly.

"It's all so different here." The faintest hint of something—surely it wasn't panic?—sounded in Rachel's voice. Her expression had tightened, highlighting small lines around her eyes and mouth, making her look her age for the first time since Carrie had known her. "Are you sure you can finish up alone?"

"Don't give it a second thought. Are you okay? Are you feeling unwell?"

"I'm fine. Truly I am. I just have...things to do." Rachel walked out of the open cabin door, into the bright but still-cool afternoon sunlight without another word, just as her brother had done before her.

"Rachel got left behind when the Americans pulled out of Saigon in '75," Reuben said, his voice tight as he slid the curtain rod into its brackets. "You deserve to know what's goin' on around here if you're goin' to be workin' with us, and there ain't no one else gonna tell ya. We all thought she was dead until about a year ago. Then Micah got word she was still alive and went after her. He'd have brought her out, too, but Rachel got sick and missed the rendezvous and before they could make their way out of the jungle, they got picked up by a Vietnamese army patrol. It was their brother, Simon, and his new wife, Annie, that got them back safe and sound.

"Rachel's been trying to get her life together ever since, but the damned reporters and book publishers and, worst of all, them Hollywood pretty boys are always after her to give them her life story. Hell, she's been through enough, what with all them years wasted in that Stone Age village, her husband gettin' killed in the war..." He stopped and hesitated a moment to look long and consideringly at Carrie. Something in her expression, in the compassion that caused her eyes to fill with tears, must have satisfied him. "...losin' her baby and all." His Texas drawl was growing more pronounced as his words grew more impassioned.

"Losing her baby?" Carrie could barely get the words past the sudden tightness in her throat.

"Yeah." Reuben tossed the screwdriver he'd been wielding so expertly into the small tool chest on the table and slammed the lid. "Some damn bastard at the labor camp raped her and got her pregnant. She managed to get away, but not long after that the baby was born—but too little and died. He's buried over there somewhere in a little corner of the jungle, lost, just like so many of our guys." He looked down at his work-roughened hands. "We're all doin' everything we can to make it easy on Rachel."

Carrie put her hand on his, suddenly wanting to show her support with more than words, even if her memories of the war Reuben remembered so vividly were little more than hazy recollections of television footage of riots and guns and helicopters filled with scared-looking armed and helmeted soldiers not so many years older than herself. "I'll help, too, if I can."

"She needs a woman friend." Reuben looked embarrassed by his show of emotion. "It'll do her good to have you around." He picked up the small stepladder and hooked it over his shoulder, taking the toolbox in his other hand. "I just wish there was someone to help the other McKendrick around here that needs it."

CHAPTER THREE

"REUBEN." MICAH'S VOICE close behind her made Carrie jump in her seat. She'd been concentrating so hard on transcribing the data in the field report she was transferring to the computer disk that she hadn't heard him come into the lab. She turned in her seat to see him standing alongside the inclined table on which was spread out a topographical map of the Upper Peninsula with the location of each and every known raptor nest marked by a red dot. "We haven't tagged the chick in 24 Alpha."

"I'm tied up today, boss. Flyin' into Marquette to have the plane inspected, remember?" Reuben stood up and pushed his chair back from his desk with a screech of wooden legs on the linoleum floor. Carrie shivered and lifted her hand to push back a straying wisp of damp blond hair. It was getting warm in the small office at the front of the lab building, but she didn't dare take off her sweater, not with Reuben and Micah both in the room.

"No, I didn't forget." Micah's low, gravelly voice affected Carrie on some basic level just below the threshold of conscious thought, as it always did. She shivered again. "That last recon we flew over the nest makes me think that chick's just about to fly. We can't afford to lose this one. No chicks in that nest for two seasons. Now an apparently healthy fledgling. Maybe there's something up there to tell us why."

"I'll get at it first thing tomorrow." Reuben stretched his arms above his head.

Micah swung around. His shoulders and back were taut with impatience, possibly anger, but Carrie knew him well enough already to know his face would be free of expression. "Damn it, Reuben, I don't want to wait till tomorrow. Did you listen to the last weather forecast?"

"There's a front comin' through. I don't have to hear no weather forecast. My bad knee's been achin' since last night. If you're in such a hurry, take the boy with you. Let him climb." Micah swung around to face Reuben once again. He moved so quickly it must have caused a streak of pain in his half-healed ribs, but not a sound escaped from his lips.

"Let the boy climb?"

"I can do it."

Now it was Carrie's turn to shift in her seat. Neither she nor Micah had seen Doug enter the room from the door leading to the lab and the big flight cages behind the building.

"I've been climbing with Reuben." He squared his shoulders, the usual sullen frown stealing across his features. It was almost as effective a mask of his true feelings as Micah's habitual shuttered gaze. "I've been practicing with the eagle stick and the rivet gun. I can do it."

Micah said nothing. Silence stretched out in the room. From a long way off Carrie could hear the creeing of the blinded osprey. She glanced at the clock. Eleven-thirty. Time for her morning feeding.

"It's the easiest climb we've got," Reuben said in a very ordinary voice that belied the tension in the room. Carrie folded her hands in her lap and waited. She was holding her breath and didn't even realize it for a moment or two.

"I'll make the climb." Micah's voice was as hard and level as ever, but Carrie thought she detected just a hint of uncertainty beneath the steel.

"Doc said six weeks, no climbin'. It's only been three. Don't push your luck."

A muscle twitched in Micah's cheek above the dark line of his beard. He shoved his hands in his pockets and turned back to the map table. He didn't look at Doug or Reuben. "Fix Doug up with some climbing gear. We'll leave right after lunch."

"I'll be ready." Doug shoved his hands in the pockets of his jeans in unconscious imitation of the older man. He wasn't as well-schooled in hiding his true feelings. A look of triumph mixed with anticipation and nervousness crossed his face.

"Put my gear in the Jeep, too." Micah didn't look at Doug again, but Carrie saw disappointment replace the anticipation and was angry at Micah for causing the boy more pain.

"Yes, sir." Reuben's expressive voice betrayed only a hint of dismay. Micah's, as usual, held no emotion at all.

Carrie prepared to go back to her transcribing with a barely suppressed sigh. What had happened to Micah to make him the way he was? She'd never realized how much she depended on the inflection in another person's voice for clues to their feelings and inner thoughts—not until she'd met Micah McKendrick, a man who guarded his speech as closely as he guarded his emotions and the secrets of his past.

"DO YOU WANT TO COME ALONG?" Micah addressed the back of Carrie Granger's dark blond head. For the hundredth time in the three weeks she'd been working for him, he found himself wondering how she managed the intricate braiding of her hair without help. Her hands paused above the keyboard. Her fingers were long and narrow, her nails short and bare of any polish. She turned to face him.

"Come with you?" She sounded amazed he'd asked. Her brown eyes met and held his reluctant gaze. Her eyes were a deep, rich chocolate shade of brown. Her gaze was level and straightforward. Micah wanted to look away but he could not.

"Would you like to ride out to 24 Alpha with us? Watch Doug make his climb?" He stopped, coughed and cleared his throat. "I . . . I thought you might like to get away from the compound for a few hours. See how we work."

"Thank you. I'd like that." She continued to hold his eyes with her own for another moment or two. Automatically Micah found himself reinforcing the barriers he kept around his emotions and his expression. "I'll be ready anytime you are. Do I need to wear anything special?"

"Sturdy shoes and a ton of bug spray." Reuben's voice broke the spell, the power of her dark eyes, that seemed to be holding Micah in thrall.

"You probably won't need that heavy sweater," Micah added. "It's warming up very nicely this afternoon."

This time it was Carrie's turn to look away, down at her hands, at the clock on the wall, anywhere but into his eyes. Micah was surprised at the action but he recognized its origin only too well. Carrie Granger was afraid. She, too, had something to hide.

"Thanks. I'll remember to find something lighter."

"Okay." He turned to Doug, relieved to have finished the conversation. He usually avoided women like the plague. Those he did deal with he had no trouble keeping at arm's length. Somehow he sensed deep within himself that Carrie Granger was going to be quite a different story. "You might as well learn the right way to tag an eaglet and evaluate a nest. Maybe it'll help make sense of some of my notes."

"I doubt it," she said, but she was smiling. Micah found himself almost smiling, too. Almost.

"Doug, go feed the osprey and then we'll all break for lunch. I don't want Reuben flying too late. The weather's likely to turn at any minute. Can't trust early June weather this far north. Too much can happen with a front coming down from Canada across Lake Superior. The water's still damn cold. Makes for a lot of unstable air."

"I appreciate your concern," Reuben said dryly. "Or is it your airplane you're worried about and not my valuable hide?"

"A little of both." Micah walked to the door and turned the handle. "I'll pick you two up in forty-five minutes," he said, indicating Carrie and Doug with a nod of his head. "Be ready."

RACHEL WATCHED THE JEEP with her brother, Doug and Carrie inside pull out of the compound just as she'd watched Reuben take off in the small, aging Cessna pontoon plane a few minutes earlier. She could have gone with him into town, done some shopping or gone to a movie, but she'd declined. It was nice to have some time for herself. Time alone. She seemed never to be alone anymore. There was always someone or something making demands on her time. Not that she resented having so much to do, but there seemed to be so little time for her, for Rachel, alone, anymore. And that was what frightened her. She hadn't found herself yet, not really, and the emptiness in her heart and soul terrified her. Perhaps there was nothing left of her, deep down inside where it counted. Nothing left of the girl she was, of the woman she might have been. Of the mother she should have been.

Babies.

They had been on her mind a lot lately. She suspected they were also on the mind of Carrie Granger.

"KEEP YOUR BELT TIGHT and use the safety rope. There's no glory in falling forty feet onto your head." Micah gave one last tug at the safety belt snapped around Doug's slim waist. "Take your time. This isn't a race."

His voice was level and controlled but lacking the gravelly harshness Carrie so often noticed in his speech. He had a nice voice, she decided, a low, rich baritone that set the nerves at her nape to tingling. She wondered suddenly what he sounded like making love to a woman, saying all the things men say to their lovers in the night. The image of Micah McKendrick with a woman in his arms, a tall woman with braided blond hair, flashed across her mind. Was he as emotionless and controlled in his lovemaking as he was in day-to-day reality, or did the fires that she sensed burned deep within him flare into life when passion beckoned?

"Grab that branch and I'll boost you up." Micah's curt instructions cut into her thoughts and she was grateful for the interruption. She had no business thinking of him that way. No business thinking of herself that way, as part of a pairing, a joining, not now, perhaps not ever again.

He bent at the waist, making a stirrup of his hands, his shoulders straining the thin flannel of his gray and black plaid shirt. A momentary shadow of pain crossed his face, a tightening of his muscles—the only indication that lifting Doug into the lower branches of the half-dead pine had placed any strain on his healing ribs.

With a grunt and a scramble that sent a shower of pine needles and small cones raining down on Micah's head, Doug worked his way up the tree. Situated on the crest of a small knoll a mile from Lake Superior, the eagle nest was wedged in a big branch near the top of the lightning-struck red pine, about forty feet off the ground. "A piece of cake," as climbs went, Reuben had assured Carrie when she'd asked him about the nest before they left the compound. "The boy's good. I've been coachin' him for a week," he added to reinforce his statement.

"Don't spook him. Move slow and easy." Micah still hadn't raised his voice but his words carried easily on the still, warm air. An errant breeze rustled the leaves in the maples behind Carrie. "Just get the tag on him. We'll worry about statistics later." Micah stepped back from the base of the tree, lifting his hand to shade his eyes from the bright June sun. Doug climbed steadily, competently, it seemed to Carrie's untutored eye. He grabbed the lip of the big nest, hung suspended for a heart-stopping moment, then scrambled over the edge.

Relieved, Carrie tipped her head back and watched intently as, overhead, Doug made a lunge for the young bird, snaring him with the homemade "eagle stick." With a crow of pride he flipped the angry nestling onto his back and snapped the riveted tag home. Hanging precariously over the edge of the big, sturdy nest, he called down to Micah. "There's an unhatched egg up here." His voice cracked with mingled excitement and exhilaration. "Should I bring it down with me?"

The eaglet took advantage of Doug's momentary lapse of vigilance to wiggle out of his grasp, its five-foot wingspan knocking him back against the restraining straps of his climbing harness. The indignant bird squawked and flapped its way across the nest, balancing comically on the edge, teetering back and forth while Carrie held her breath, and then launched itself into the sky.

"Damn!" Micah swiveled on the heel of his heavy work shoes, trying to keep the half-falling, half-flying youngster in sight and at the same time make sure Doug was not injured or in danger of falling from his own perch at the edge of the nest. "Don't let that bird out of your sight," he called over his shoulder to Carrie, then made a cup of his hands and yelled, "It's okay, Doug, come on down. Take your time. We'll find him."

Carrie barely heard his last words. She'd already marked the spot where the young eaglet had entered the heavy ground cover of the second-growth forest. How often had she heard Reuben speak of the importance of getting to a "jumper" as quickly as possible? Micah's first duty lay in getting Doug safely down out of the tree. Hers lay in finding the baby bird. She didn't bother to tell Micah what she was doing, didn't bother to consider the consequences of leaving the small clearing at the top of the knoll to plunge into the forest with no compass and no path to follow. She just started running.

A hundred yards into the woods she had to stop, the stitch of pain in her side making her short of breath. The baby kicked inside her, hard and insistent, as indignant as the young eagle. "Having a bumpy ride, sweetheart?" she crooned softly, trying to catch her breath. She'd started talking out loud to the baby when she was alone, trying to bring the reality of life growing within her into sharper focus. *A baby. Her baby.* A baby about whom she had so many unresolved feelings, who forced her to ask herself so many questions.

Would he be tall and blond as she was? Would he have straight, reddish-brown hair and a beaked nose like his father? Would he look like Evan Walsham's family? Or her own? Carrie sighed and looked down at her softly rounded belly beneath the oversized T-shirt and shapeless blue windbreaker she wore.

In that case, in both cases, actually, she'd be staring at a stranger, for she knew her biological parents no better than she knew her lover's.

The farther she went into the undergrowth, the more disoriented Carrie became. The sunlight filtering down through the branches of tall maples and oaks was distorted and fragmented with a pale green cast that made her think of being underwater. Dead leaves were thick on the ground, muffling her footsteps. It had rained during the night and everything she touched was damp. Her shoes were soon soaking wet, her jeans streaked with loam, her hair pulled loose by grasping branches. She stopped to rest, half-sitting, half-leaning on the fallen trunk of a big oak.

Carrie looked around her, fighting down a sudden attack of panic. She had no idea where to go, how to find her way back to the small clearing on the knoll with its distinguishing lightning-scarred pine and its woven crown of twigs and branches.

She was tired. Her back hurt and she was all at once very frightened, indeed. She'd heard stories of old people and very young children wandering off into these same woods and never being heard from again. Tears of weakness and fatigue pricked behind her eyes.

She was tired of being strong and fearless and making her own way in the world. She was afraid of the responsibility of raising a child by herself. She was afraid of a future that she couldn't see.

With a sniff Carrie stood up. She wasn't going to sit there until the sun went down and it got too dark to see where she was going. Feeling sorry for herself would accomplish nothing. Giving up would accomplish even less. She just needed a moment to orient herself, to find the sun and check her direction.

Trying to remember the way she'd come, Carrie walked around the big fallen log she'd been sitting on and stopped dead in her tracks. The quiet around her was intense, yet filled with life. For the first time she saw the pale pink blooms of trillium and the twilight purple of violets, the delicate lavender of a wild orchid. And she saw the baby: a fawn so new his dappled coat was still damp. His eyes were enormous as he stared at her from his nest of matted fern and soft dead leaves. Above him, larger ferns acted as a protective screen, hiding him from view. Carrie sank to her knees to stare in wonder at the fragile new life, oblivious of the faraway echo of her name.

Large, liquid brown eyes followed her every move. Instinct ruled the tiny creature. He didn't move, although fear caused every muscle under the soft, spotted hide to quake. Carrie looked around, searching for signs of the doe, but only a blue jay's raucous call from a nearby tree disturbed the peace of the forest.

"Poor baby, I scared you, didn't I? Don't worry. It's all right." Her voice had taken on a crooning note but she didn't recognize it herself. She only knew she spoke as a mother always speaks to her baby. "I'm going to have a baby, too." Although she'd told herself that over and over, for the first time she actually believed it. And for the first time she knew, without reservation, that she could never deny the child growing within her. That for better or worse, she would keep her baby, love him, bring him up to be the best human being that he could be.

Tears pricked behind her eyes again, more insistent than before, tears of happiness as well as apprehension. "I have to leave, little one, I have to find my way back to Micah," she whispered, not really hearing what she said, only speaking from the heart. "I probably scared your mother away, crashing around here like the bull in the china shop." She wrapped her arms around her middle and rocked back and forth. "I'll go. In just a minute I'll go, but you are such a pretty little thing, and I really am afraid of being alone."

"DAMN THAT WOMAN," Micah swore under his breath as he turned in time to see Carrie Granger disappear into the undergrowth. "She's going after that jumper on her own." He continued to watch Doug's descent from the nest tree but his thoughts were on the young bird, and even more so on the woman who'd gone after it. She'd be lost in five minutes. Hell, she probably already was.

"Take it easy, kid," he hollered as Doug's climbing iron slipped and skidded on a damp patch of bark. Micah was so angry his ears buzzed. Or was he angry? For so many years he'd automatically interpreted any strong emotion as rage, shutting it down immediately, never giving it a chance to take control, that he'd become accustomed to feeling very little at all. But now the churning urgency inside of him refused to go away.

"The mother bird's sighted her young one," Micah said, pointing to the big raptor circling some distance away. Doug skidded the last six feet down the trunk as he spoke. Micah went down on one knee to help the boy unfasten the heavy leather safety belt and battered climbing irons. "Can you head off in that direction without getting yourself lost in the woods?" He didn't take time to look at the teenager's face. He just kept talking. If the boy wanted to be treated like a man, take on a man's responsibilities, then he shouldn't expect a lot of mealymouthed soft talk.

"I think so."

"If you're not sure, don't try it, just stay put right here," Micah said, rising abruptly. This time he did look at the boy. Doug's eyes were wide with fear. His hands trembled but his voice was steady.

"I can look for the eaglet without getting lost," he said forcefully.

"Okay. Take off. Got a watch?"

Doug nodded.

"Head due west for ten minutes. If you don't spot the bird in that time, turn around and come directly back here. Do you understand?"

"Yes."

"That's an order, not a suggestion." Micah reinforced his instructions in a voice that brooked no further argument.

"I understand." Doug glanced down at his watch.

"Then get going. Carrie took off into the woods after the jumper. I'm going after her."

"She hasn't got a very good sense of direction." Doug's face grew concerned. Micah was so used to seeing the sullen, I-don't-give-a-damn frown marring his features that he just stared at the boy for a heartbeat or two. Doug's perception surprised him. But his conclusion about Carrie's woodsman's abilities matched his own.

"I was afraid of that."

"Good luck," Doug said, moving toward a small break in the heavy undergrowth at the edge of the clearing.

"Thanks." Micah spun on his heel and headed off in his own direction. He picked up her trail almost immediately and found his heartbeat slowing down, his breathing returning to normal, but the feeling of urgency and the need to find Carrie remained foremost in his thoughts.

Micah stopped abruptly when the clear trail of broken branches and disturbed leaf clutter ended, grew confused and petered out in front of a tangle of spindly poplar trees three hundred yards into the woods. He stayed still, a listening, waiting addition to the forest. He seemed as tall and unbending as the huge oaks around him. Off to his left the noisy atonal scolding of a blue jay caused him to swing his head in that direction. He moved again, much slower now, but angling his way steadily toward the disturbance that had alerted the nervous bird. He skirted upthrust roots of a big fallen oak to find Carrie kneeling on the forest floor, a tiny newborn fawn in its nest only a foot or two in front of her. Her fingers were pressed against her lips; her shoulders were shaking. She was crying and Micah didn't know what in hell to do about it. *Elaine had cried so much, for him, for herself, for all they'd shared and lost. He heard her sobs sometimes, still, in the middle of the night.*

"Carrie!" She jumped as if he'd frightened her. He hadn't meant to yell but it was too late now. She turned, startled, her eyes wide with fear. She recognized him and the fear was replaced by wonder, and a radiance so strong it rivaled the sun.

"Shh," she said, smiling. "Look, a fawn." Her tears were as soft and bright as crystal rain on her cheeks. Later Micah would realize that combination of smiles and tears, sunshine and shadows, was his undoing.

"What's wrong?" he said, too loudly, because the blue jay screamed again. The fawn lay without moving but tremors ran under its soft hide.

Carrie stood up, too quickly, and took a stumbling step backward just as Micah moved forward to help her. She came up against him and spun around. His arms came out to steady her, nothing more. He didn't know what to say, what to do in the face of her obvious distress, but he couldn't remain silent.

"Damn it, Carrie, why'd you take off like that?" His tone was scolding, berating, one more way to keep his distance from her. If he treated her like Doug, like a kid, then he'd be less apt to make the mistake of thinking of her as the grown, desirable woman she was.

"I'm not lost," she insisted valiantly, but her apprehensive brown eyes made a lie of the words.

"Not anymore, you aren't. God, don't you know people wander off in these woods every year and some of them are never found?"

"I . . . I've heard that." Carrie's warm brown eyes caught his, held him prisoner. Before he could help himself, Micah pulled her close. He felt the softness of her skin even through her jacket, the curve of her back against his fingers. Her hands were between them, holding her away from his body, but he could feel her warmth, smell the heady mixture of soap and shampoo and something much harder to describe, faint and alluring, the scent of Carrie, herself. Micah moved his hands from her back to her shoulders, upward to cradle her face between his palms. He made himself look at her. *Would he see fear in her eyes?* "I didn't touch him, Micah, the fawn. I know enough about wild animals not to do that. But what about his mother? Will she come back for him?" There was no fear in her expression, only compassion for the tiny deer.

Having Carrie in his arms threw him off balance. It had been a long time since he'd held a woman in his arms, a long time since he'd felt the hot, fierce prompting of desire and need. He didn't want to feel them now but his body refused to obey his mind. She was trembling and her pulse beat high and fast under his splayed fingers but not with fear. "Micah, no," she said, sensing his intention before he did. She shook her head, made a muffled little sound of protest, then closed her eyes and accepted the touch of his mouth on her own.

"Carrie, my God." He didn't know if he said the words aloud or merely heard the echo inside his head. She tasted of mint and spice. Her lips were warm, her breath sweet against his mouth. She kissed him back, tentatively, hesitantly, her response full of reluctant passion and banked fire. He wanted more of her and moved to pull her closer, to mold her slender curves to his own hard length. She sensed that need, too, and with a muffled cry of denial, pulled out of his arms.

Micah let her go. He wouldn't hold her against her will. *She was afraid of him.* He had only fooled himself by imagining her response. His body was tight with need, tight with holding back, but he stepped away. She had closed him out in the blink of an eye. She had retreated as quickly, as completely, as he was prone to do if any woman dared try to breach the defenses he'd erected around his emotions. Now he was

on the outside of an emotional wall as strongly constructed, as zealously guarded as his own, but he remembered only the nightmares of the past and let it
color his perception of the present.

"The fawn?" Her words were slurred a little in her
haste to speak. She ignored the kiss they'd shared as
though it had never happened. At least she hadn't run
from him in terror; although she might still do so if he
moved too fast.

"The little guy will be fine. The doe will come back
as soon as we leave." Micah didn't know how to react
at this point. She'd turned the tables on him, shutting
him out, and it was an uncomfortable and frustrating
experience.

"Are you sure?" She sniffed, but one last crystal
tear rolled down her cheek.

Micah reached out very slowly and wiped it away
with the pad of his thumb. He couldn't have stopped
himself from touching her if his life depended on it.
"I'm sure," he said gruffly.

Carrie caught her breath, her great brown eyes still
brilliant with unshed tears. For a long heartbeat she
was still, then with a deep, shuddering breath she
turned to look at the fawn once again. "He seems...so
alone."

"His mother is nearby...I promise you."

Carrie looked up into his face once more and nodded as if satisfied by his answer. "I believe you." She
turned away, shoving her hands into the pockets of his
old blue windbreaker before she squared her shoulders as though settling the weight of a heavy load. A
stray breeze sent wisps of dark blond hair dancing
around her cheeks. "Micah?" She didn't turn around.

Her voice was small and fragile-sounding in the silence of the forest. "About the kiss . . . I don't . . ."

"Don't mention it." His words were curt. He did nothing to soften them. "I'm the one who should explain. I apologize. I'm not in the habit of taking advantage of my employees. It won't happen again."

"I know that . . . that's not what I mean. I think I should tell—" She broke off abruptly. Doug's excited voice, calling Micah's name, came from not too far away.

"Over here," he shouted back, and wished the boy in Hades. What had she been going to say? She didn't act frightened of him anymore, but then she wasn't trapped in his arms. He wanted to tell her not to be afraid of him but he could not because the words were a lie. "Carrie." He owed her a warning, even if it cost a piece of his soul to say the words.

She didn't give him a chance to say any more. "Don't blame yourself. It was only a kiss. Nobody's fault." She gave him a wavery, sad little smile and veered off in the direction of the shout.

Micah cursed and started after her. He knew she'd felt something for him back there in the woods and he couldn't let it go any further. She was better off being afraid of him. It was safer. Because if she trusted him she would want to get close. And if that happened and the demons inside of him broke their bonds, it could cost her her life, just as it had Elaine.

DOUG PLOWED THROUGH a screen of some willowy type of bush that was tough as the dickens to get through. His T-shirt was stained and torn from collisions with hanging branches and wild raspberry canes.

The darned eaglet wrapped up inside his sweatshirt was squirming around furiously. Whoever said if you covered up a bird's head it would go to sleep sure didn't know what he was talking about. His arms ached. He had scratches and bruises in places he couldn't even see, let alone show someone else, and he was tired as blazes. But he'd found the eaglet and that was all that mattered. Micah was going to have to give him credit for that. It had to at least cancel out the screwup he'd made letting the bird get out of the nest in the first place. Maybe Micah would even tell him he was sorry.

"I thought you said you could find your way around in the woods. You're ninety degrees off-track." Doug nearly jumped out of his skin when he squirmed through the last of the whiplike branches to find Micah standing right in front of him, black, straight eyebrows pulled together in a frown.

Doug felt like he'd been kicked in the chest. "I found the eaglet," he said, holding up his cloth-wrapped burden. "I thought you'd be glad."

"Let me take a look at him."

If Micah was going to apologize, he sure didn't act like it during the next few minutes. He took off for the clearing so fast Doug and Carrie practically had to run to keep up. She gave Doug a watery smile and a thumbs-up sign but it didn't help. Not that he wasn't glad to see her safe. If Carrie had gotten lost Micah would have blamed him for that, too.

"He looks fine," Micah acknowledged grudgingly after he examined the young eaglet beneath the nest tree. Above them in the calm, bright afternoon sky, the parent birds wheeled and circled, crying for their lost young one. "You did a good job of getting him back here."

Doug nodded and picked up his climbing belt from the ground where he'd dropped it before taking off to hunt for the jumper. "I'll get him back up in the nest." He was tired and hot and the scratches on his face and arms hurt like the devil. The last thing he wanted to do was climb that tree again, but it had to be done and he was man enough to know that, no matter what Micah thought of him.

Micah was still kneeling on the ground, wrapping the young bird back up in Doug's sweatshirt. He narrowed his eyes against the brightness of the sky behind Doug. The eaglet was as quiet as a mouse. Doug just stared but he thought maybe it was more Micah's hands smoothing its feathers than the covering on its head keeping the bird quiet.

"Be careful with him," he said. "Keep him on his back and he'll stay quiet on the way up." This time Micah didn't make it sound like an order. He was talking as if Doug knew what he was doing. It helped a little but it didn't completely erase the sting of his earlier bad temper. "Bring down the unhatched egg and take note of anything else you notice that's interesting or unusual in the nest."

"I will." He wasn't the only one with problems. Micah had some of his own, too. Doug bent to strap on his climbing irons. He wondered what had been going on back there in the woods when he'd come across Micah and Carrie. He'd caught sight of them once before he walked into those stinking willow bushes. It looked to him as if they'd been kissing. And Carrie had been crying, or he missed his guess.

"Be careful, yourself," Carrie said, interrupting his thoughts.

Doug stood up straight and smiled at Carrie. She was a great lady, smart, like his mom and Rachel. And she made great pizza. "I will."

She smiled back but the smile never reached her eyes. Her eyes were sad. Doug thought he might know why. Carrie Granger was going to have a baby. The stepmother of one of his school friends had just had a baby and he knew the signs. It didn't show much now but before too many weeks, it would. He'd bet money Rachel had guessed Carrie's secret, too. But not Micah. He didn't have a clue.

It was all pretty complicated, he decided, as he started for the base of the tree. Grown-ups could be just as dumb as kids. All the time he'd been out risking his neck to find Micah's darned jumper eaglet, they'd been kissing in the bushes. He'd just about had it with all of them. The more he thought about it, the angrier he got.

Some of the guys he'd met in town wanted him to go out cruising with them tonight. A couple of them had quit high school and they had good-looking cars and money to spend. Why should he bust his tail being Micah's whipping boy when those guys had everything going for them with no education to speak of? It didn't matter that they weren't the kind of guys he'd spend much time with back home. It didn't matter that Micah and Carrie or any of the other grown-ups he knew wouldn't approve of them. It was time he started making that kind of decision on his own.

Micah handed him the trussed-up eaglet and told him once more to watch himself on the climb. What did the guy think he was, stupid or something? Of course he'd be careful. He wasn't about to fall and bust a couple of ribs the way Micah had.

"I'll be careful," he said. Yeah, tonight he'd give those guys a call. No more excuses, no more holding back. Tonight he was ready for anything.

CHAPTER FOUR

CARRIE COULDN'T GET Micah's kiss out of her thoughts. Every night for the better part of a week she'd lain awake in her small, dark cabin until long after midnight, reliving the moment. A hundred times she'd recalled the touch of his mouth on hers, the taste of him, the unexpected silky texture of his beard. He was a strong man, yet his kiss had been oddly gentle, questioning. The knowledge that he was as unprepared, as unwilling for what passed between them to happen as she was, did nothing to inhibit the electric jolt of need and desire that had coursed through her body, arching her spine, pulling her closer to the hard length of his body—and to disaster.

A thousand times since that moment she'd flinched in distress as her mind's eye conjured up a vision of how quickly he'd broken off that kiss, backed away from her, tuned her out. What had happened to her, to them, in the silence of the forest with the small, terrified fawn at their feet? Had they both gone a little mad? Or was it that there was something about her now that marked her as an easy touch? Was she so needy that it showed even to a man as indifferent to women as Micah McKendrick?

As unflattering and uncomfortable as that conclusion might be, it did explain her own response. Had her involvement with Evan Walsham left her so unsure of herself that she was at risk of falling for the first man who came along, just to prove to herself she was still a loving and desirable woman?

She didn't want to believe that was the case. But if it was, Carrie decided with characteristic forthrightness as she sat up and swung her legs over the side of the narrow iron bed, she'd certainly chosen the wrong man. Micah, except for that one unforgettable and astonishingly sensual kiss—that moment of weakness on his part and near insanity on hers, given her situation—had left her strictly on her own. Why? She was trying to understand her own feelings, but what prompted Micah's actions? She knew so little of his past. His wife was dead and Reuben had hinted at problems in their marriage. Did Micah feel responsible for Elaine's death? Did those regrets haunt him still? She thought perhaps they did.

Carrie wandered barefoot over to the window by the front door and pushed aside the thin yellow and white curtain. Moonlight flooded the compound. It was a beautiful night, still and quiet, cool, but no longer cold now that they were almost in the middle of June.

She liked it here. She felt safe and secure, despite her uncertain emotions where Micah was concerned. She was making friends with Reuben, and very tentatively with Doug. She trusted and admired Rachel, although she couldn't say they were close. She marveled at the older woman's apparent resilience, her determination to build a future for herself on the shattered remnants of her life.

She still hadn't found the courage to tell anyone her secret, although she knew her time of waiting, of limbo, was by necessity coming to an end. She'd made another appointment to see Dr. Sauder the following Monday. Rachel would know then and Carrie would have no choice but to inform Micah also. She smiled into the darkness, a wry little twist of her lips. Sometimes if you couldn't face a problem head-on, a flanking maneuver worked just as well.

A very faint light came from Micah's window, but Carrie didn't know if it was the reflection of a night-light through an open bedroom door, or if he was still awake, reading one of the technical journals he seemed always to have with him. She leaned her head against the window frame, tired but not sleepy.

The red glow of the digital alarm clock on the shelf above the sink told her it was after two. The growling whine of a four-wheel-drive engine on the stretch of roadway that looped into a curve about a hundred yards behind her cabin alerted her to the fact that one of the other inhabitants of the McKendrick compound wasn't in his bed.

Doug was making a habit of late nights. Once she'd caught a glimpse of the boys he'd started running around with when they drove into the compound to pick him up. She hadn't liked what she saw. The gang—it seemed the only appropriate word—of youths were all older, rough-edged, harder-looking than Doug. It worried her that he should be spending so much time with them. It worried her that he and Micah should be so much at odds. The boy needed guidance, not lectures or cold silence; anyone could see that. Or could they? It was certainly obvious Micah wasn't prepared for the responsibility of raising an almost grown child any more than she was a baby.

Carrie frowned as she watched Doug walk up the driveway into the compound. His course was erratic, his gait unsteady. She didn't need an expert on raising teenagers to inform her that he'd had too much to drink. Finding Doug in that condition would be the last straw as far as Micah was concerned. That was reason enough, to Carrie's way of thinking, to interfere—for Doug's own good. She pulled a pair of old gray sweatpants on under the knee-length plaid flannel shirt she wore to sleep in, stepped into her shoes and walked out onto her rickety front porch.

Doug was almost past her cabin, heading for his room at the far end of the lab building in more or less a straight line. "Doug. Wait up a minute." She kept her voice pitched low and not too loud, but he jumped like he'd been shot.

"JEEZ!" HE SPUN AROUND so quickly he stumbled and almost fell flat on his face. *Great, that was all he needed.* "Carrie, is that you?" It took a moment to focus on the figure coming at him from the dark shadows of Carrie's cabin. It didn't look like her somehow, with her hair all loose and wispy around her shoulders. It was brighter, more golden that it seemed when it was braided, almost like moonlight come down out of the sky. *Boy, he must really have a snootful if he was starting to spout poetry—almost. And God, she was pretty standing there.* He hadn't noticed how pretty or how young-looking she was until just that moment, either.

"I couldn't sleep," she said, sounding like she didn't want it to seem she'd been spying on him. "I heard the engine. It's awfully late, you know."

"I know," he said, and regretted how sullen his voice sounded. Carrie had never been anything but great to him. It was just that he felt like such a jerk tonight. He didn't like himself very much at the moment, either.

Carrie tugged at the blue and green flannel shirt she was wearing. "Doug, have you been drinking?"

There probably wasn't much use in denying it. He had a real buzz on but he could still think pretty straight. "I had a few beers with the guys, that's all."

"Oh. Are they twenty-one? Did they buy it for you?" She seemed as if she wanted to say more, like: "Don't you know it's illegal to drink in this state until you're twenty-one?" but she didn't.

"Hank Kisabeth. It's his Bronco you heard. He was twenty-one last month. But that doesn't make much difference up here. They all know each other. Sometimes guys sell them stuff anyway."

"I know," Carrie said, shaking her head. "I grew up in a small town, too."

"Where?" Doug heard himself ask and was surprised. He felt a little dizzy. If he looked up into the sky, the stars would all be dancing around. He kept his gaze fixed on Carrie, instead.

"Hamler, Ohio. You couldn't have ever heard of it. Only seven hundred people live there."

"Jeez. There were seven hundred kids in my junior class—" Doug snapped his mouth shut. The last thing he wanted to talk about, to think about, was getting suspended from school.

"I know a little bit about what happened, Doug," Carrie said quietly. "I know you don't want to talk about it but for what it's worth, I think you should go back to school."

"Yeah, well, so does everybody else. Everybody except me." He shoved his hands into his pockets. He turned around and started walking. She followed him.

"Doug, I'm sorry. I didn't mean to preach."

He walked a little faster. She was having trouble keeping up. He remembered she was going to have a baby, even if she still hadn't told anybody. Angry with himself, he slowed his steps. "Don't worry about it. It's over and done with. I'm going to stay here, maybe. Look for a job. Hank said his uncle could get me something to do. I'm a pretty good short-order cook, and during the day I can work with Hank, remodeling summer cabins and stuff." It sounded like a pretty lame plan and they both knew it. Carrie didn't start ragging on him, though. She only nodded her head and kept on walking beside him.

"Do you think you'll like living up here in the winter? I hear it gets pretty rough."

"It can't be much worse than Chicago."

"No, I suppose not," she said, but she didn't sound like she meant it.

"Look, it's pretty late. Don't you think you should be back in bed? I appreciate your coming out to see if I was all right and everything, but you don't have to baby-sit me all the way to my room."

"Oh." She stopped walking. "I'm sorry," she said again, as if it had only just occurred to her she was acting like a guy's mom when she didn't have any right to.

"Just 'cause a guy had a couple of beers doesn't mean he's gonna be an alcoholic or anything."

"You're under age." Carrie's voice was low but easy to hear.

"Lots of kids do it."

"I know." She looked past him as if he weren't there. As if she were looking at someone else. "My best friend in high school died because a drunk driver hit her car one Saturday night."

"Jeez. I'm sorry." He couldn't think of anything else to say. "This is the first beer I've had since—" he decided he might as well come right out with it "—since I got kicked out of school."

"Was that the reason you were suspended?" She didn't look like she was going to lecture him, so he told her.

"Yeah. It was the dumbest thing I've ever done." Except for what he'd been doing tonight. He wasn't about to tell Carrie he'd been out spotlighting deer, because it was illegal. She probably didn't even know what the term meant, anyway. He hadn't, either, until Hank suggested it. You hook up a powerful spotlight on your car, he'd explained, and drive around in the woods until you see a deer. Then you shine the light in its eyes and while it's too scared to move, you shoot it. Carrie wouldn't like that. Not one bit. Especially after the way she'd carried on about the fawn she'd stumbled across in the woods the other day. Anyway, he'd only gone along because he didn't want the other guys to think he was chicken. And because Willie Jenks, the one guy of the bunch he really liked, needed the meat to help feed his brothers and sisters, so it wasn't really as bad as poaching. He just didn't realize how crummy he'd feel watching a poor deer stand there, too scared to run, while some drunk took potshots at it with a high-powered rifle. He was lucky tonight. Hank missed the first shot and his brother, Leon, laughed so hard he knocked the light a little sideways so that the deer got away. It didn't help him feel much better, though.

"You could go back to school." Carrie was still talking.

"No." There he was yelling at her again. "I'm not going back and repeat the eleventh grade with a bunch of kids nearly two years younger than I am." He stopped and took a deep breath. "Come on. Let me walk you back to your cabin. It's so damn dark out here you can barely see your nose in front of your face, even if the moon is out."

"I can get back to the cabin without any help."

Now she sounded mad at him. *Women.* Jeez, what were you supposed to do with them? "No, you can't. My mom taught me better manners than that."

"I'd like to meet your mother someday." She was trying to be friendly again.

"She's great," he had to admit. "My getting kicked out of school really made a mess of her and Simon's honeymoon. He's a pretty good guy for a stepfather. He's a spy." Carrie swiveled her head in his direction, her eyes wide with surprise. Doug nodded, pleased to have given her a shock. "He won't admit it, of course. He says he works for the Census Bureau, but you can tell."

"How?"

"Just things." He shrugged, not finding the words he wanted. "People he knows. Stuff he knows about."

"I see." Doug looked at her sharply to make sure she wasn't laughing at him. Turning his head so quickly made him dizzy again.

"He's just about as mad at me as my mom is but he won't say anything because he's not my real dad." He snorted, trying to hold back a laugh that was a lot more nasty than he'd intended. "Except my real dad wasn't my real dad, either."

"Doug..." Carrie stopped walking and put her hand on his arm very lightly. "You don't have to tell me anything you don't want to, just because I cornered you out here."

"It's okay. I'm used to it. I'm an *Amerasian war orphan*, you know," he said, putting italics around the words with his voice. "There are thousands of us out there. My sister, Leah, found out who her real mother was because the woman recognized my mom when my mom went back to Vietnam last fall. My brother, Chad, knows his mom was a prostitute and his dad was an American GI. Do you know the only thing I know about myself?" He reached out and put his hands on her shoulders. She was almost as tall as he was but her shoulders were slim and felt fragile under the pressure of his hands. She didn't say anything, just looked at him with big brown eyes. "I was the only person who didn't get killed when my village was bombed. The only one." He shook his head. "Can you imagine what it's like not to have a single living person know who you really are?"

"Yes," Carrie said very quietly. "I can. My mother deserted me when I was seven. She never told me who my father was. I have no idea where she came from or who her family was."

"Jeez, I'm sorry." Doug let his hands fall to his sides. He felt like a jackass. A jackass who was going to be sick all over his shoes. He was never going to drink anything again if it made him run off at the mouth like this.

"It's okay. It was a long time ago. I'm twenty-eight, you know," she said with a shaky little laugh. "I was adopted by a great couple. I love them very much." She was silent a moment, thinking. "Have you talked with anyone else about how you feel? Your mother?"

"Nah. I don't want her to feel bad. I thought about asking Rachel once if she remembered anything about when I came to the orphanage. That was how she got left behind in Vietnam, you know, trying to get all the kids and the nuns rescued when the Americans pulled out of Saigon. Simon couldn't get there to help us and Micah was in Laos."

"I remember reading about Rachel in *Time* magazine," Carrie said with a funny little smile. "I never expected to meet her, or to be living in the same place with her."

"Life's strange, ain't it." He was feeling a little better. Maybe he wasn't going to be sick . . . just yet. "Anyway, I just couldn't do it. She's so small and, you know, fragile-looking. So sad sometimes. I don't want to remind her of what happened later. And then sometimes when she looks at me in that sad way of hers I wonder if she isn't thinking that maybe I look like her son would have. . . ." Doug slammed his fist against his thigh. "Cripes, I shouldn't have said that."

"It's all right. I know about Rachel's baby."

At least he was sober enough not to blurt out anything about his guessing Carrie was going to have a baby, too. "Yeah?" he nodded, accepting her answer. "It makes me feel funny. You know. I can't talk to her like . . . I can to you. And I can't talk to Micah at all. Maybe getting messed up as bad as he did in the war makes it hard to be around other people . . . you know what I mean?" Probably it was the beer in him but he really did think Carrie understood. Imagine her not knowing who her real mom and dad were, either. It was fate or something. She didn't think he was weird because he wondered sometimes who his real parents were, even when he loved the ones he'd been given more than anything. He wondered if he could tell her about the deer poaching?

"Carrie, what if you . . ." They were almost at the door of Carrie's cabin. From just off to their right the crash of a metal garbage can hitting the side of the lab building slammed into Doug's brain with the force of a shell going off under his feet. "Jeez, what was that?" They both turned toward the sound, only to be confronted by a pair of roly-poly black bear cubs, wrestling with an upended garbage can, minus the heavy cement block that usually weighted down the spring-loaded lid. The bear cubs were frustrated by their inability to open the container and bleated their dissatisfaction into the night air.

"We've got to get out of here." Carrie grabbed the sleeve of Doug's jacket and tugged. "The mother bear will be somewhere close by. We can't stay here." She started pulling him toward her cabin.

He dug in his heels. "No. The door's so flimsy even those cubs could knock it in without even half trying.

We'd be trapped." He couldn't take his eyes off the cubs. They were cute, fat and black as coal in the moonlight. They also smelled. He wasn't any Daniel Boone, but it didn't take a mountain man to figure out that you were too close to a bear—any size bear—if you could smell it. "Let's head for the house. Wake Micah up. He'll know what to do about them."

This time it was Carrie who balked. "No." The word came out in a strangled rush.

The cubs abandoned their attempt to open the garbage can and started squealing even louder as they in turn became aware of the strange and frightening human scent. There was no time for a long, drawn-out discussion of which way to run. Doug reached out to grab Carrie by the arm and steer her toward the main house, but she was already moving toward her cabin. His reflexes weren't too good after four beers. He grabbed and missed. There wasn't anything he could do then but follow her, even if it meant running right past the cubs.

They almost made it. Carrie wasn't more than three or four yards from her porch when something big and bulky detached itself from the darker shadows at the edge of the woods and ambled into the clearing.

Another bear. A big one. Doug and Carrie skidded to a halt. They were too far from the porch and too close to being in direct line between the mother bear and her bawling cubs. The she-bear stopped, swinging her head to identify the source of danger to her offspring. Her eyesight might not be so good but her nose was great. Doug knew the exact moment she got their scent. She gave a low, hair-raising growl and reared up on her hind feet, yellow fangs glinting in the moonlight. Doug reached down and grabbed a short piece of two-by-four that Reuben had been using to mend the railing of Carrie's porch and left stacked in a pile alongside the path to the lab. Then everything seemed to happen at once.

The cubs squealed louder, the she-bear roared and hit the ground running. The explosion of a shotgun going off splintered the cool June night, and Doug had one very long second to wonder how it would feel to get his head bitten off by an angry mother bear before Carrie latched onto his shirttail with both hands and dragged him over backward with her onto the porch of her cabin.

CHAPTER FIVE

MICAH LOADED ANOTHER SHELL into the chamber of the shotgun. The peace of the June night was shattered beyond repair. The crows in the trees behind the clearing that he'd fired above took off into the dark sky, spiraling upward with shrill, angry cries. The bears had already disappeared into the woods, unharmed.

Micah was glad he hadn't had to kill the female bear to keep her from attacking Carrie and Doug. He'd seen enough of killing and dying, of violence and destruction in his lifetime. He'd lost all interest in hunting. For too many years the game he'd hunted from the sky had been human beings, like himself. For a few tense moments he stood waiting in the moonlight but nothing moved along the dark perimeter of the woods. Micah lowered the shotgun from his bare shoulder, snapped on the safety and headed across the compound toward Carrie's cabin. He hadn't gone ten feet when he stepped on a stone, reminding him he was barefoot. No shirt. No shoes. He'd fallen asleep while reading and was wearing just his jeans.

"What the devil's going on here?" Lights were coming on in the lab. The commotion and gunshot had awakened Reuben. He was probably cussing up a storm. Micah was glad he was a hundred yards away.

Rachel was also awake. He heard the back door of the main cabin open and close. The dancing beam of a flashlight skipped across the ground toward them. These facts registered at the periphery of Micah's awareness, but most of his attention remained focused on the troublesome pair in front of him.

"Bears," Doug said, stating the obvious. He rose to his feet, swaying slightly before bending over to help Carrie up.

The boy was drunk. Anger sang through Micah like a sweet poison that would soon turn acid and eat into his nerves. He tightened his grip on his emotions automatically, set his jaw and rounded on Doug. "Where have you been? Who got you drunk?"

The boy ignored him. He leaned closer to Carrie, who was still half-lying, half-sitting on the rough plank floor.

"Answer me." Micah couldn't remember the last time some punk kid had had the nerve to defy him like this.

"Carrie, are you all right? I didn't hurt you or anything, did I? I landed right on top of you, I know I did." Doug swung his head in Micah's direction, anger and chagrin blazing from his almond-shaped brown eyes. "Help her up," he ordered, his voice cracking on the last word. "Can't you see she might be hurt? I fell on her. Maybe I hurt the baby." He went down on his knees beside Carrie.

"Baby?" Reuben came to a halt beside Micah, still tucking in the tail of his shirt, his gingery hair standing up here and there on top of his head. He sounded incredulous.

"Doug." Carrie's protest was a mere whisper of sound.

Micah felt as if he'd been jabbed in the stomach with the butt of his own gun. He could tell by the shocked and accepting look on Carrie's face that what the boy said was true. He forced himself to look at Carrie, although in the moonlight it was too dark to see much. In any event, he didn't need to see her. Every line of her figure, every delicate curve of her face were in his thoughts a thousand times a day, a hundred thousand times each night. Her breasts were small and full, the gentle swell of her hips and the sassy curve of her bottom left him tight with need, the slight roundness of her stomach as she'd arched against him that day in the woods...

Carrie Granger was pregnant and he'd never suspected a thing.

"Don't just stand there like idiots." Rachel's voice was matter-of-fact, no nonsense. "Help her to stand."

"I'm sorry, Carrie." Doug sounded miserable and all at once very sober. "I didn't think. I just said it." He was already helping her to her feet. When Micah stretched out a hand to help her in spite of his warnings to himself, she ignored him.

Rachel moved past him, stepping up onto the porch. She looked small and ethereal in her long, pale pink nightgown, her hair loose on her shoulders. Carrie's hair was loose, too, Micah noticed, although he didn't want to. It was the color of moonlight on water, soft silvery gold, as feathery as thistledown as the night breeze stirred the curls around her cheeks. His fingers itched to reach out and touch it, to thread themselves through its silky layers. Rachel's question brought him out of his thoughts with much the same effect as a bucket of cold water in the face.

"Are you and the baby both all right?" she asked. Her voice was concerned but slightly detached, professional, as though she, too, couldn't allow herself to get too close.

"I'm fine." Carrie brushed at the seat of her pants. "We both are," she said more quietly. She kept her gaze firmly anchored on Rachel's face.

"How far along are you?"

Carrie took a deep breath, squared her shoulders and let her eyes touch on each of them in turn. Each of them but Micah. "I'm going to have a baby sometime in November."

Micah found his voice at last. "Why didn't you tell me this when I hired you?"

"Would you have given me the job if I had?" She still wouldn't look at him. She fixed her eyes somewhere about the level of his chin.

His silence was evidently answer enough. She did raise her eyes then, and her chin, confronting him, challenging him—asking him for understanding? He couldn't be sure. *God, it had been so long since he'd had to deal with a woman, any woman, let alone one who churned up his insides and turned his brain to wood.*

"This isn't the kind of job for a . . . woman . . . for someone in your condition. The work's too hard. It's dangerous."

Damn it, why did she have to affect him like this? He couldn't think straight when she was near him under ordinary circumstances. Now look at them all grouped around him, waiting for him to spill his guts, let them all see what a bombshell she'd dropped on him. "It's better if you leave." He wasn't going to give any more of himself away than he had to.

"I get the picture," Carrie said in a clear, hard voice that only just missed convincing him she wasn't going to cry.

"Look. I'll give you the rest of your month's salary...so you have enough money...." He hadn't thought about her financial circumstances before. Hell, he'd tried not to think about her at all, for all the good it had done him.

"I don't need it." She looked scared, defiant and incredibly sexy standing there in an old plaid shirt, her hair loose on her shoulders, tears sparkling like diamonds in her eyes. "I have friends and family. I don't need your charity."

"It's not charity." Micah snapped his mouth shut on the words. He wasn't about to argue with her. Especially in front of an audience. He already felt like enough of an idiot. From the looks on Rachel's and Doug's faces, they agreed with his assessment of himself. Reuben was still standing behind him, but he didn't have to be able to see his friend's face to register his disapproval, as well. "Take all the time you need to get your things together. If everything won't fit in your car, Reuben can load it in the Jeep."

"Thank you." Her tone was every bit as gracious as some royal duchess. "I'll be ready to go first thing in the morning." He hadn't thought she'd leave so soon. He caught himself from saying so just in time. Micah ran his hand through his hair. If he didn't get away from her soon, he'd be asking her to reconsider, telling her they could work something out...until the baby came. A stranger's baby. Micah hardened his resolve.

Perhaps his indecision had shown on his face because he thought she was having second thoughts, as well. At least for a heartbeat or two. She stood a little straighter, smiled at Reuben and said, "I don't think I'll need the Jeep, but I could use some help packing up my things."

"You just holler whenever you're ready, Carrie. I'll be right there. I've had enough commotion for one night," Reuben said, still in a disapproving tone of voice. "I'm goin' back to bed. C'mon, boy." He motioned for Doug to follow him.

"Okay." The teenager looked doubtful. "I'm sorry."

"Don't be." She smiled even more brilliantly at Doug than she had at Reuben. "I'd planned on telling everyone Monday, anyway." Doug nodded, walked down the steps and followed Reuben in the direction of the lab building without another word.

"Would you like some company, Carrie?" Rachel asked.

"No, really, I'm fine."

"Then I'll say goodnight." Micah knew Rachel was looking straight at him but he didn't acknowledge it. Rachel flicked the switch on the flashlight and set off to follow the yellow beam of light back to the main cabin. All the years of deprivation and lack of medical care she'd endured in Laos and Vietnam had left her night vision slightly impaired. She didn't like to drive at night or walk where she wasn't sure of her footing.

"I'm going to take a look around the yard before I turn in," Micah said. "If you hear me outside again later, don't let it bother you."

"I won't." Carrie's voice was as cold as a winter morning. She turned around, opened her door and disappeared inside, closing him out of her life.

"IT'S AGAINST THE LAW to fire a woman because she's pregnant, you know." Rachel wasn't surprised to find Micah getting dressed. She'd expected him to go back to check the compound and the birds in the flight cages, especially the injured goshawk whose wing she'd helped him set only two days before. It was like him to see to the comfort of the others in his care before his own. He was dedicated, thorough and stubborn to a fault.

"Don't start in on me, Sis." Micah shoved his hands into the sleeves of his shirt while he talked. He didn't bother to button it, just rolled the cuffs halfway up his arms and bent over to drag his shoes out from under the bed. "I didn't fire her. I laid her off. Permanently."

"It's discrimination. She might file a grievance." Rachel had done a lot of reading over the winter, catching up on the world around her, familiarizing herself with changes in the way things were being done. Micah looked up from the chair where he was sitting while he tied his shoes.

"I don't need a lecture on fair employment practices, either." Rachel hid a smile. She knew he was trying to decide if she was serious or not.

Her brother deserved so much more than he was getting from his life. Her imprisonment had been real

and physical. Micah's was of his own making, his own
determination to cut himself off from the pain and the
joy of feelings of the heart and soul. The war had
scarred men like Micah emotionally just as surely as
it had maimed and killed so many others.

She thought Carrie Granger might be the woman
who could unlock the door of Micah's solitary cell, a
woman of substance and courage who could wage the
siege necessary to break down the walls around his
heart. Perhaps she'd been wrong, given what just
happened between them, but she didn't think so, not
yet, anyway.

"Maybe she'll sue you."

"I've got three hundred and eighty-seven dollars in
the bank. Think that will be sufficient compensation
for her mental anguish?" Rachel didn't flinch from
the venom in his tone, although angry men still caused
her to tremble in unreasoning fear.

"I'm sorry. I won't tease you anymore."

"It's okay, Sis." He sighed and ran his hand over his
chin. It had taken her a long time to get used to his
short, neat beard. Now she liked it. "I'm just not in
the mood to see the joke."

"There isn't any joke, Micah. Carrie's alone and
frightened."

"Aren't we all?" She couldn't be certain she'd heard
him correctly. "She lied to me." There was no mis-
taking his words this time.

"She lied to herself." Rachel moved fully into the
doorway, blocking his exit. She didn't think Micah
realized how easy it was to read his expression in the
dim room. The light was coming from behind her,
over her left shoulder, highlighting the harsh planes

and angles of his face. He thought himself safely seated in shadow, unobserved, so his habitual mask of indifference was laid aside. She did nothing to alter his faulty perception of the situation. If only she could reach him, give him back confidence, in his humanity, in his self.

"Maybe she did. It doesn't change anything as far as I can see. It's late, Rachel. Go back to bed so I can make my rounds and get some sleep, too." He stood up. "You don't have to worry, I'm not going to fly off the handle and do something stupid."

"Why should I think that?" His statement surprised her.

"Come on. Don't tell me Mom didn't fill you in on my life in the years you were gone."

"I know they weren't easy for you." She chose her words carefully. What was going through her brother's mind? What nightmares of the past haunted his dreams as they did her own?

"It was hell," he told her bluntly. "I can't remember big chunks of it, but I'm not going out there and strangle her because once upon a time I tried to kill my wife."

Rachel was aware Micah's inability to tolerate the massive doses of tranquilizers the doctors at the Veterans' hospital had used to treat his insomnia and depression had led to violent outbursts, leaving him so mixed-up in mind and spirit that he'd been confined to the hospital's psychiatric ward for almost eighteen months.

"Micah, don't talk like that." His tone was so bitter, so resigned, it frightened her. "That was the medication. Surely the doctors made that clear to you."

"They didn't make it clear to Elaine."

"Her overdose was an accident." Somehow she had to make him believe that.

"Who told you that?"

"Mom." Elaine had been too young and unprepared to deal with the problems Micah had brought home with him from Vietnam. She had taken too many sleeping pills by mistake. It was a tragic, terrible coincidence. An accident, Frances McKendrick had insisted when she informed Rachel of the circumstances surrounding Micah's retreat to the north woods.

"What else did you expect her to say?" he asked wearily. There had been others who said Elaine had killed herself deliberately because she was scared to death of her husband, terrified of further abuse. God help him, Micah was one of them.

"It wasn't your fault."

"That's what the doctors said. I'm sane, or cured, or whatever passes for it." He stood up, walked toward her. She let him pass, watching in silence as he left the cabin. No one would ever know the truth of what happened to Elaine that fateful night. It haunted Micah still. Yet Rachel would trust him with her life today, and she would trust him with Carrie's life and the life of her unborn baby.

THE MOON HAD SET BEHIND the trees. In less than an hour it would be dawn. The grassy space beyond Carrie's cabin was silent and deserted. She could no longer see the dark figure of a man moving quietly, surely, around the compound. Apparently Micah had given up his lonely vigil and gone back to his bed.

What did he think of her now that he knew her secret? What did they all think of her? Everyone had
been too stunned by Doug's bombshell to have asked
any personal questions, yet surely they all must wonder at the circumstances of her pregnancy? That would
be the last straw, baring her soul, reliving the pain and
betrayal of her affair with Evan Walsham for Micah
McKendrick's benefit. The sooner she could leave the
compound, the better. Carrie turned away from the
window and began folding her clothes into her suitcase.

She couldn't go back to sleep so she might as well
make use of this last hour of the night. Keeping busy
was far better than lying awake, staring into the darkness, waiting for dawn and all the decisions that would
rush at her in the daylight, demanding to be made. She
was a fool to have put off telling Micah and the others. Now what had happened last night would probably cause yet another misunderstanding between
Doug and the older man.

Poor Doug, it wasn't his fault. She would leave him
a note telling him so and rely on Rachel's intercession
to keep Micah from jumping down his throat. If only
she'd had the courage to reveal her condition from the
first.... There was no use going over it again and again
in her thoughts. What was done was done. She had to
go forward now, for her own sake and for the sake of
her baby.

She had a little money in the bank. Enough to get
her through the winter. She could go back to Joe and
Denise's, at least for a while. Her parents would take
her in when the baby was born and in the spring she
would begin searching for another job, a new place to

live, to begin her life again. She wasn't destitute, or lacking in skills. She wasn't being turned out into the snow to freeze or starve like some poor Victorian serving girl who'd given in to the master's base needs and suffered the consequences. Except that at the moment that's just how she felt—alone and deserted and scared to death.

Carrie folded a sweatshirt and laid it neatly in her suitcase. She really didn't need Reuben's help to load her car. She didn't have all that many things to call her own. She didn't want to see anyone again. She would have to face Rachel at Dr. Sauder's on Monday, but by then she would have regained her composure and her equilibrium.

Stealing away in the night was a cowardly thing to do but she couldn't say goodbye. She was too close to leaving pieces of herself behind with these people. She was too close to crying over Micah McKendrick and losing something that never really was, or ever could be.

Five minutes later she slipped along the path to the lab in silence, little more than a dawn shadow herself. In her hand she carried a note for Doug. She pressed the code on the digital lock and wondered for a brief moment if Micah would change the combination once she was gone. The green light flashed. She opened the door and walked inside, turning to the right, toward the door that led to the short hallway where Doug's and Reuben's rooms were located. She hadn't taken two steps in the darkness when the light above her work station flashed on and Micah's voice came out of the shadows surrounding it.

"What in blazes are you doing in here at this hour of the morning?" He sounded exasperated, resigned, wary. That she could interpret the inflection of his words surprised Carrie a little. He must be very tired, too, to have let his guard slip so far.

"I...I have a note for Doug. I wanted to slide it under his door." She smoothed her hand over the front of her shirt in an automatic, protective gesture and saw his eyes fasten on the slight roundness of her stomach for a second before he looked hastily away.

"Can't it wait until morning? You got banged around pretty good. You ought to be resting."

"I'm fine. I landed on my backside and got the breath knocked out of me, that's all. I have something I want to give Doug now. It's important." It shouldn't be so hard to tell him she was leaving. After all, he wanted her gone. He was the one sending her away, but it made no difference; the words stuck in her throat and refused to be spoken.

"You can deliver your message in the morning." He was still carrying the shotgun. It rested casually in the crook of his arm, looking as if it belonged there. He was a strong man, patient, attentive to details, knowledgeable about nature and its creatures, a born hunter and provider. He set the gun aside when he saw her staring at it. "The boy's had a rough night. Let him get a little rest. You can talk to him later."

"I won't be here when he gets up. That's why I'm leaving a note." She raised her eyes to his. At five-nine, Carrie didn't often have to tip her head to meet a man's gaze head-on. It always disconcerted her that she had to do so with Micah. His blue-gray eyes were shuttered and unreadable, telling her nothing of what he might be thinking. "I want to leave at first light."

"You don't have to do that." He spoke so roughly Carrie jumped. She took a step backward without thinking, then stood her ground.

"I'm aware of that. Still, it's what I want to do."

"Carrie. Damn." Micah smacked his fist on the edge of her metal desk. "It's all that damned kid's fault, carousing around, getting drunk with a bunch of punks...."

"How can you possibly blame my pregnancy on Doug?" She was so tired she couldn't think straight and his words made no sense to her whatsoever. She didn't think she could bear to tell him the whole sad story of her affair with Evan tonight ... or ever.

"Your pregnancy?" He looked and sounded almost as confused as she felt. "That's not what I'm talking about. Or maybe it is." He ran his hand across his beard and raked his hair back from his forehead. The thick, dark waves laced with silver settled back in place almost at once.

"Don't take your anger at me out on Doug, please." She made a pleading little gesture with her hand. "He needs your understanding, not your contempt." That she might be asking for the same things for herself from this taciturn, enigmatic man didn't occur to her. She was only grateful that he didn't seem to be going to ask her about her past.

"I didn't intend to." He moved forward so quickly Carrie didn't have time to step out of his way. "Don't go." He reached out, took her arm in a grip that held her solidly but painlessly, then released her quickly, as if her skin had burned his hand.

"You fired me." Some of the hurt and anger she felt must be visible in her eyes, audible in her voice, but Micah paid no heed.

"Rachel says you have grounds to file a complaint with the government if you want. Maybe even sue me for everything I've got." He smiled then. "I'm warning you ahead of time, it isn't much." His smile was stiff, frayed a little around the edges, as if the muscles were reluctant to form the unfamiliar expression. "I'm trying to tell you I want you to stay."

"I don't know." Deep in her heart it was what she wanted, and she couldn't be positive her exhausted imagination hadn't dreamed up the words.

"Are you planning on returning to the baby's father?" Micah's face was stony with the intensity of his control.

Carrie knew for certain she hadn't imagined those words. "No!" She couldn't help herself; the word just exploded out of her mouth. She took a deep breath and tried again. "This is my baby, do you understand? Mine alone. His father doesn't figure in any of my plans for the future." She raised her chin, defying the tears of self-pity and sudden panic that pushed behind her eyes and tightened her throat.

"I think you've made yourself clear on that point." The hand that rested on her work station relaxed a little but Carrie didn't notice.

"Micah, what are you getting at?"

"I want you to stay. I need . . . your help with my work."

"You just got finished telling me you could get along just fine without me." When she was tired she was obstinate, even though she wanted to stay with him more than anything in the world.

"Where will you go?" He changed the subject too suddenly for Carrie's slowed responses.

"I . . . don't know exactly. . . ."

"Do you have other employment?"

"No. . . ."

"Then I don't see any problem." There was a lot to be said for a steamroller approach. Carrie couldn't form her objections quickly enough to voice them. "After you see Doc Sauder, we'll work out a new schedule. You can rest all you want. Take naps—" he shrugged helplessly "—do whatever it is pregnant women are supposed to do."

"I'm capable of doing what any other twenty-eight-year-old woman does. Within reason." Carrie felt a little healthy exasperation begin to burn away the threat of tears. *Men, they were always so darned helpless when it came to dealing with pregnancy.*

"Twenty-eight?" The slight, reluctant smile came and went. "You look much younger." Carrie couldn't think of anything to say. Seeing that his left-handed compliment had taken the wind out of her sails, Micah pressed his advantage. "Then it's settled. You'll stay." Reaching forward, he plucked the note from her fingers, tore it in half and dropped it in the wastebasket. He picked up the shotgun, cradled it in his arm and motioned toward the door. "I'll walk you back to your cabin."

He was so close she could smell the scent of his skin, the faint but pungent odor of gunpowder and the spicy tang of pine in the air when he opened the door. It made Carrie think of their time alone together in the woods, although she didn't want to. It made her remember his kiss and what it did to her body and her heart, and she didn't want to remember that, either. She could not afford to cloud her mind or her emotions with hopeless longings for a man she could never have.

"Carrie." Micah stopped walking, touched her arm to turn her toward him slightly. Dawn was coming up fast in the east. Eerie streamers of mist rose off the lake. The light was faint, yet sufficient to see his face. As always, his expression gave nothing away, but the frightening emptiness she'd so often encountered in his eyes was gone, replaced by something very much like sadness and terrible remorse. His hand moved toward her as if he wanted to touch her, to hold her and, dear Lord, she wanted that, too. "I meant what I said the other day in the woods. I won't interfere in your life any more than I already have. And you won't have to worry about any unwelcome advances. I meant that, too."

She wanted to tell him his kiss had been anything but unwelcome, but common sense, or perhaps it was cowardice, kept her silent on that point. "I know that." About one thing more she could speak the truth. "I'm not afraid of you, Micah McKendrick."

In the space of a heartbeat the frightening mask of emptiness clamped down over his face, giving him the look of a statue carved in bronze. "Never think that, Carrie. For your sake and mine, never let yourself feel safe around me."

CHAPTER SIX

"FINE. FINE." Rex Sauder patted the slight mound of Carrie's stomach beneath the soft cotton exam gown. "A good healthy heartbeat." He nodded, pleased, as he draped his stethoscope around his neck. "A good healthy mother, too, even if you have put off coming to see me for too long. When did you say you think you conceived?"

Carrie named the date, sitting up as he directed, her feet swinging free over the edge of the high exam table.

"You're sure?" He cocked one white eyebrow in an inquiring gesture.

"As certain as I can be." Carrie didn't try to avoid his kindly gray eyes, but she wasn't really looking at him, she was looking into the past. Until she'd met Evan, become intimate with him, her body and its cycles hadn't taken up much of her thoughts. Now, of course, her woman's body and how it functioned were of major importance.

"Okay, that date is close enough."

Close enough. What she'd shared with Evan had been close enough to love to make her believe it was the real thing. They'd spent their first weekend together very early in the new year and she'd truly thought it was the beginning of forever for them. Three months later the university offered to extend

Evan's visiting professorship for another year and he told her he was married and that his wife would be coming from their home in California to join him. Just like that, as though he hadn't lied to her, or omitted the truth, for the entire time they'd gone together. He had been contrite, apologetic and almost as bewildered by his infidelity as she was. He'd never intended their affair to go so far, he said. He cared for her very much but he was still in love with his wife. He wanted to try to make his marriage work. This was goodbye.

It was a scenario that replayed itself hundreds of times a day around the world, she supposed. Except that this time it had happened to her and it had not seemed ordinary at all. It had hurt, hurt badly. And it still did.

"I take it this pregnancy wasn't planned?" The doctor busied himself with the small computer terminal on the stainless-steel counter. Carrie was a little surprised to see how competently he managed the program. He caught her watching him out of the corner of his eye and smiled, a bit ruefully. "My nurses refuse to transcribe my handwriting any more than they have to. I hate to admit it but I'm getting kind of partial to this thing, myself." He punched another key with a flourish. "Okay. Let me see what we've got here and I'll work up a profile for you."

"No, my pregnancy wasn't planned." Carrie was grateful for the time his rambling commentary gave her to collect her thoughts and order her emotions. She might as well get used to talking about it. Her baby wasn't a secret from anybody anymore.

"Were you using any kind of birth control?"

She colored slightly. "Yes. But . . ."

"Product malfunction?" The doctor allowed himself a slight smile. He looked so much like a mischievous gremlin that Carrie couldn't help but smile back, even though her memories lay heavy on her heart.

"Yes."

"It happens a lot more often than people realize." He factored in a number of other details, punched a button and waited for a printout. "Everything looks good so far, as I said. When your blood work gets back from the lab we'll know a lot more." He walked over to stand in front of her, the top of his head level with her eyes. "I'd like a blood workup on the baby's father, also, if that's possible." He must have seen a reflection of her pain in Carrie's eyes because his words were suddenly serious.

"I . . . don't know. . . ." She hadn't seen Evan or spoken to him since the day in late winter that she'd told him she was pregnant and that she was quitting her job at the university, leaving town as soon as possible. She didn't even know why she'd told him about her pregnancy at all except that she felt she must.

"So that's how it is." The doctor rubbed his bald head reflectively. "Well, we can probably get by. As long as we're sure there isn't any Rh problem, or any other inherited diseases in your family history."

"I'm an orphan, Doctor," Carrie said, raising her chin as though to ward off any slight. "I don't know anything about my family history."

"Then I do suggest you contact the baby's father as soon as possible. For the child's sake, as well as your own."

"I . . . will." She didn't want to talk to Evan again. Not now, not yet. She wasn't ready to deal with any demands he might make on her or the baby. If he cared enough to make any demands at all.

"Good. Get the results to me as soon as possible. Rachel will make up a list of the tests I want. Rachel," he hollered over his shoulder, "get in here." Micah's sister had quietly and discreetly left the room as soon as the doctor had finished his initial exam. Carrie was grateful for her thoughtfulness. It was harder to talk about Evan and the facts of her pregnancy than she'd thought it would be. "Marie can make you an appointment for an ultrasound scan test next week. That way we can get a good look at the little fella and maybe come closer on your delivery date. Right now I'm guessing the end of October."

Carrie was surprised by his pronouncement. "I . . . the book said it would be the middle of November, perhaps even Thanksgiving."

"Books." The doctor snorted. "I've been delivering babies for thirty-five years. I say the end of October. And right now my guess is that it's a boy."

"HE'S RIGHT ABOUT THE SEX at least half the time," Rachel said with one of her rare, engaging smiles as she walked back into the exam room in time to overhear the physician's last statement. "Doctor, Mr. Amos is waiting for you in number one." The cantankerous old man had been fussing and fuming over the delay for the past twenty minutes. He was beginning to get on her nerves.

"I'm coming. I'm coming. Babies are a lot more interesting to talk about than Jake Amos's faulty plumbing."

"Shh," Rachel warned with another smile. "He'll hear you."

"Let him get another doctor then." He turned and marched toward the door, throwing a last comment to Carrie over his shoulder. "See you next week, young lady. Be here. And do what I said about those blood tests."

"Blood tests?" Rachel made it just enough of a question that Carrie could answer or not as she chose.

"Dr. Sauder wants me to contact my baby's father and have some routine blood tests done."

"It's a good idea." Rachel let Carrie proceed at her own pace. She didn't feel comfortable enough with the younger woman to try to force any confidences yet. Confidences exchanged with Carrie Granger would involve either her pregnancy or her relationship with Micah. Rachel knew both subjects were too close to her own heart to discuss dispassionately.

"I don't want to talk to the man." Carrie set about putting on her clothes as Rachel handed them to her.

"Do you want to talk about him?" She held her breath. She hadn't volunteered anything of herself in this way in so long. What would she do if Carrie turned down her offer to listen and advise? Rachel didn't know what had passed between Carrie and Micah that night after the bear cub invasion of the compound, after the scene outside Carrie's cabin. She was only glad something had. She still felt somewhere deep inside her that Micah and Carrie would be good for each other, a way out of the darkness for her brother, a chance for completeness for Carrie—and her child.

"There isn't much to tell." Carrie pulled the string on her gray sweatpants, frowning at the snugness as she tied a loose knot over the gentle swell of her belly. "He was a nice guy and I started to fall in love with him. I did make love with him. And then he told me he was married, but I was already pregnant. Pretty stupid, huh?" Her head emerged from the neck of her pink oversized sweatshirt, her brown eyes rueful and full of pain.

"Not stupid. Natural and human. And you have a baby to love, to remember him by."

"I don't want to remember him." Carrie's tone was defiant. "But will I love the baby? Sometimes I wonder." She let her voice trail off into silence.

"You'll love him no matter who his father is." That she could say with all the conviction in the world. She knew from her own experience, her own profound sense of grief and loss.

"I think I will, too." Tears sparkled on Carrie's lashes but she blinked them away. "I suppose I could ask my parents to contact Evan. His wife knows about us. He told her right away." Another blow to her self-esteem, Rachel surmised, another painful lesson learned. "He could have the results of the blood tests sent to them. They could forward them to me and he'd never have to know where I am."

"Is that what you want?" Rachel frowned slightly. Denial was natural but not always the best way of dealing with a situation. Someday, sooner or later, Carrie and her lover would have to come face to face once more.

"Yes."

"Then I think you should do it as soon as possible."

"I will." Carrie looked as if she were regaining her emotional balance. "Right now." She shrugged, hearing the fierce determination in her voice. "At least as soon as I get to a telephone. I'm going to do some shopping for the baby...and myself." She looked down at her stomach and smiled suddenly, a smile that sent a small, envious dart of pain through Rachel's heart. It was a very private smile, happy, wondering, pleased with herself. "Nothing fits comfortably anymore. My body feels as if it belongs to someone else."

"You'll get used to it." Rachel turned away so that Carrie couldn't see the pain she still felt after all these years.

"I hope so. Rachel, would you like to join me for dinner? We could drive back to the compound together after, if you don't have evening hours." Carrie was leaving her an opening to refuse if she wished, Rachel realized. She was grateful. Her first, habitual response was to say no. Then she changed her mind. She'd been here for over three months and no one had bothered her. No reporters had shown up on the doorstep, no patronizing West Coast television producers had insisted she sell them the rights to her life story, no book publishers had discovered her phone number to urge her to write her autobiography as they had when she'd been living with Annie in Chicago. Or perhaps it was because word had gotten around in those circles of how Micah treated those few who were foolish and bold enough to try to reach her. Her brother so seldom allowed himself to lose his temper that when he did the consequences were frightening to behold.

"I'd like to have dinner together." She found that what she was saying was true, not merely polite. She'd come here to escape the media and to make peace with herself, but lately she'd grown tired of her own company. "I know a quiet little place with a view of the lake. I could meet you there about seven."

"Sounds great. I'm starved already." Carrie smiled and it reached her eyes, setting off sparks of warm, golden fire in their brown depths. "But then I'm eating for two now, aren't I?"

"Yes." Rachel didn't smile. *If she had had sufficient food during her pregnancy her child might have survived.* She cut off her train of thought with a ruthlessness born of necessity. That way lay madness. She could not change the past. She could only go forward into the future. For her peace of mind and for her soul's survival, there was no other choice. Carrie was facing some very difficult choices, also. She could have terminated her pregnancy, but she had obviously chosen not to. She was alone and scared and still she could smile and laugh and love. Rachel wanted desperately to be able to do the same. "That's right," she said, forming a smile with a physical effort that was as difficult as anything she'd ever done, "you are eating for two, and tonight I think we should pull out all the stops."

SUNSET CAME LATE IN THE north country at this time of year. It was already well after nine o'clock and the sun was still a sullen red ball balanced above the serrated edges of the pine trees on the western shore of the lake. Micah took a long swallow of beer and leaned back against the wood piling of the dock.

The sound of feminine laughter carried clearly on the evening breeze. Rachel, giggling. Micah heard her plainly, and the quiet happiness in her voice touched him profoundly. He was glad she had found a friend in Carrie Granger, even though he worried about what kind of effect Carrie's pregnancy would have on his sister's fragile serenity and the painful memories it would bring to mind. It might have been better for all their sakes if Carrie had left the morning after the bear incident.

The trouble was he couldn't let her go. He could admit that now, even if he didn't know any more how to deal with Carrie and the feelings she aroused in him than he did with Doug. It seemed the only thing he was certain about these days was his work. It still afforded him the peace and satisfaction he lacked in any other aspect of his existence.

A screen door opened and closed. The compound was quiet once more. Micah took another long swallow of beer.

"Is that Doug and Reuben out in the boat fishing?"

Micah didn't move, but the sound of Carrie's voice wrapped around him like a summer breeze. He hadn't heard her come along the path to the dock. He hadn't felt her footsteps when she stepped out onto the wooden platform.

"Yes. They're trying for a pike or muskie, but they'll probably end up with a stringer of bluegill to feed the osprey."

"Look!" Carrie walked to his side and knelt on the dock to watch the sleek black and white shape of a loon glide out of the reeds where the cove arced back out into the lake. Its eerie, undulating cry filled the twilight and was echoed from a distance by its mate as they sought each other before darkness cloaked the land.

"There's a pair of chicks with the adult bird. Do you see them?" he asked with quiet satisfaction, as the loon turned in profile and a small disturbance ruffled the surface by its side. Two small gray-downed chicks scrambled out of the water to hitch a ride on the warm safety of their parent's back. "Two chicks hatched. That's a good sign the lake's healthy and there's plenty of food."

"I read somewhere that loons won't nest on a lake that's polluted or overrun by humans." He turned his head to watch her. Absorbed in her observation of the loon family, she looked very young and innocent and, to his bemused eyes, very beautiful. The loon called again and was answered as the pair moved closer together.

"Loons are more adaptable than you might think. If they're left alone and their nesting areas aren't disturbed, they can coexist with man."

"The trouble is that people won't leave them alone, isn't it? Jet skis and powerboats, a cottage along the lakeshore with too many people wanting all the comforts of home in their *wilderness* retreat."

"That just about sums it up."

"In the meantime, God's creatures are running out of time and space."

"Just like man himself." Micah rolled the long-necked beer bottle between callused fingers. "I didn't know you were interested in ecology." He couldn't keep the sneer out of his voice, although there had been no such inflection in her words. The statement sounded so Sixties, so much a part of a generation she couldn't identify with. His generation.

"I haven't had much interest in ecology until the past few weeks," Carrie admitted, settling down to sit beside him. She drew her knees up and wrapped her arms around them. She was wearing a baggy pink sweatshirt that hung almost to her knees and soft gray sweats. Micah usually didn't let himself look at her for very long, but now that she was doing nothing to hide it, her pregnancy was plain to see in the soft rounding of her stomach and the full thrust of her breasts against the fleecy fabric. She spoke slowly, obviously giving her words some thought. "But I know as well as anybody that there has to be a balance. That we can't just keep taking from the earth and putting nothing back, using up resources and returning only waste. It can't go on. And when you see something like this—" she made a helpless little gesture that took in the dark, still water and the sweep of coral and gold and midnight-blue sky above them "—you can't just be passive about it. You can't just let someone else worry about what will happen to it, can you?" She made the last words a question and Micah knew he had to answer.

"You can't let it go to the developers and the tour guides." He brushed at a mosquito singing near his left ear. "You have to fight to save it and everything that belongs to it, even if most of the time you're tilting at windmills.'' He hadn't talked like this to a woman in years, to any living soul about how he felt about this land and its creatures, about his work. But with Carrie it was different. She was beginning to understand, to make sense out of the myriad facts and figures she transferred into the computer so competently. She realized they represented far more than numbers on a page and lines on a graph. Each and every one of them was invaluable data on unique and irreplaceable members of a species pushed to the limits of survival.

''I like being able to do something to help. It certainly beats logging in grade point averages, and making course transfers for spoiled kids who didn't really want to have to work to get a college degree.''

''Kids like Doug.'' The fishing boat was heading for the dock, its wake arrowing out behind, disturbing the water, stirring up the last sparkling fragments of a copper and pewter sunset.

''Maybe.'' She tilted her head and watched the small aluminum boat come closer. ''But I don't think so.''

Micah held up his hand to forestall her. ''I know, I know. You think he'd settle down and turn into a straight A student if he only had a second chance.''

Carrie laughed a little self-consciously. ''I'm not that partisan. I do think he needs the guidance to make the right choice for himself.''

Micah set the beer bottle down so hard it rocked when he took his hand away. ''Hell, don't you think I know that? I'm doing my best. Maybe this trip to Idaho will do the trick.''

''Idaho? The peregrine falcon eggs are ready?'' She brushed several dull gold strands of hair behind her ear, and Micah found himself longing to do the same. She folded her hands on top of her knees and rested her chin on the back of the left one. "How many can you have?"

"Six. Hopefully I'll get a good mix of male and female. Next spring I'll release them over by Munising. Along the cliffs at Pictured Rocks." He wondered if Carrie had been to see the beautiful wild cliffs of the National Lakeshore park. It was the perfect place for the high-soaring raptors to be reintroduced to the Michigan wilderness from which they'd been driven a hundred years earlier by settlers, miners and loggers. He'd take her with him when he set up the hacking boxes that would serve as temporary homes for the young birds. Micah pulled himself up short in his reverie. The falcon chicks wouldn't be ready to turn loose until the spring. Carrie would be a mother then and long gone from his life.

"When are you leaving?" She was looking out over the water and her voice gave little away.

"We're booked on the first flight tomorrow. I've decided to take the boy with me." He shook his head as he rose to his feet in one powerful surge of motion. "Maybe I'll find the right words to say to him on the way out. Or the way back." He half turned to watch Doug in the stern of the boat, guiding it closer. Then he swiveled back, holding out his hand to Carrie. She hesitated for a long moment and Micah found himself holding his breath. He hadn't meant to touch her but the gesture to help her rise had been automatic and beyond his will to disobey. Now he couldn't withdraw his hand, but she could certainly refuse to accept it.

She looked up at him, her great brown eyes shadowed by the twilight and her own thoughts. Micah's heart thudded slow and heavy beneath his healing ribs. Carrie was not a beautiful woman, but her face held purpose and character and when she smiled, as she did just then, she touched places so deep in his soul he'd forgotten they existed. "You'll do fine with Doug." She raised her arm, letting him enfold her much smaller hand in his, then pushed herself up off the dock. "I'm going to have to watch where I sit from now on." She was breathing quickly and her expression was a mixture of embarrassment and surprise at the unexpected awkwardness of her movements.

"I've heard," Micah said, surprising both of them with his teasing reply, "that it gets worse before it gets better."

Carrie eyed him sharply for a long moment, then giggled, softly, enchantingly, like tiny chimes ringing in the breeze. "So I've heard, too, and at the moment, I'm inclined to believe it." She rubbed her bottom ruefully and then turned her attention to the triumphant fishermen in the boat.

CARRIE WAS GLAD FOR THE interruption Reuben and Doug's arrival provided. Her tête-à-tête with Micah was stretching her already frazzled nerves to the breaking point. She joined in the playful banter between the two fishermen as they argued over who would clean the two fat, golden walleyes and half-dozen yellow perch on the stringer, but she wasn't really paying attention to what was going on around her. She had too many other things on her mind. And Micah was too near.

She'd been telling herself she was imagining her growing interest in the man, her infatuation, but no matter how many late-night lectures she gave herself on the necessity of remaining heart-whole and fancy-free, it didn't help. Micah McKendrick dominated her waking hours with his physical reality, and haunted her dreams with his fantasy presence. She didn't want him to go to Idaho even if it was only for a few days, even if it meant he might make meaningful contact with Doug. She wanted him nearby, regardless of the fact that they never touched, never shared more than a few private words of conversation, never were alone together. He was haunted by a war she barely remembered and loss far greater than Evan's betrayal of her love. She had problems enough of her own without wanting to deal with his. She didn't listen to her own advice. She wanted Micah whether he was good for her or not . . . whether he wanted her or not. . . .

"It's getting late, Carrie. We'd better go in. The mosquitoes will be out in force as soon as it's full dark."

Carrie whirled around at the sound of his voice. She'd been staring sightlessly out over the water, lost in her thoughts, and hadn't realized Doug and Reuben were gone. She looked over her shoulder. Lights bloomed from the windows of the cabin and the blinded osprey and goshawk called loudly from the big flight cages in anticipation of a meal of fresh fish and red meat. She looked at Micah. He was tightening the last of the ropes that held the rowboat firmly against the dock. His hands were big and darkly tanned, the skin puckered with scars, both old and new, where the talons and beaks of terrified birds had broken the skin.

Too often lately she had imagined those hands on her body, knowing they could be as gentle as they were strong, yet oddly unable to forget the warning he'd given her the night he'd learned she was pregnant. What terrible secret lay buried in his past that he trusted himself so little where women were concerned? She knew instinctively that he would never tell her, and she could never ask.

"It's getting late and you have to be up early in the morning." She took a step and so did Micah, effectively blocking her path on the narrow walkway.

"I left some reports for you to transcribe on your desk."

"I'll see to it in the morning." They were alone. The words sang through Carrie's head, repeating themselves over and over again in a dizzying whirl.

"Don't overtire yourself."

He seemed as reluctant to move away as she did. They were standing very close. She longed to reach up and run her fingers over the silky blackness of his beard, outline the hard, straight line of lips, the angle of his jaw. She clasped her hands in front of her to control the erotic prompting of her heart.

"I can..." Carrie began in a huff, hoping to break the spell of her own sensual musings with the cold shower of irritation.

It didn't work.

"I know. You can do anything any other healthy twenty-eight-year-old woman can do. Within reason. You are healthy, aren't you?" he asked her suddenly, throwing her off guard so that she responded without thinking.

"Perfectly."

"Perfectly," he repeated, raising his hand to touch her cheek. Carrie held her breath. Their gazes clashed and held. "Perfect." He lowered his head as if to kiss her again, as he had that day in the woods. Carrie's heart raced and her breath came in quick short pants. She wanted him to kiss her. She wanted to feel the strength of his arms around her, the taste of his mouth on hers. This time she wouldn't hold back, she wouldn't pull away. It would be a beginning for both of them. And there was no telling how far it might go, what happiness and love they might find together. Micah's hand traced the curve of her cheekbone, tangled briefly in stray wisps of hair near her ear, then dropped to his side, leaving her suddenly chilled and totally bereft.

"And the baby?" He spoke reluctantly, as if the words were hard to form. Carrie felt the pain of the simple statement all the way to the marrow of her bones. The frightening mask of nothingness had slammed into place before her eyes, between one heartbeat and the next.

"The baby is fine. We're both fine." Carrie took a step back and Micah moved aside. She wrapped her arms around herself and walked past him without saying another word. None of what had happened that day, the doctor's appointment, the time she'd spent with Rachel, the unexpected need to contact Evan whether she wanted to or not, not even the tiny pastel-colored baby clothes she'd bought at the mall, brought the reality of her situation home to her as forcefully as Micah's sudden pulling away.

She was going to have a child, Evan's baby, and that would forever set her apart from this battle-scarred and emotionally distant man who stirred her senses so deeply, and left her aching for a love that could never be.

CHAPTER SEVEN

"I'M TELLING YOU FOR THE last time, Officer. If you touch that case again, you're going to lose the use of your hand."

Doug had never really expected to hear anyone say those words to a guy carrying a loaded gun. Not in real life, anyway. But then he'd never seen Micah so mad before. At least not like this where he let his anger show. His words were hard, his face was hard. With his black hair and beard and broad shoulders straining the fabric of his shirt, he looked mean enough to tear a guy's head off, not just break his fingers.

"Back off, fella." The Denver airport security guard evidently agreed with Doug's assessment of Micah's strength and degree of belligerence. He stepped sideways and put his hand on the butt of his revolver. "I said you're not going anywhere until that case goes through the machine."

"Officer." Micah actually ground his teeth. Doug could hear him from where he was standing. Each word he spoke came out clipped and cold. "I've tried to explain...." He shut his mouth with a snap as the security guard waved him silent.

"I heard what you said, buddy. Now do what I say."

Doug tightened his grip on his shoulder bag and braced himself for a fight, but Micah didn't lunge at the guard. He stood still as a stone. In Doug's opinion the smart-ass guard was asking for it. They'd been standing here in front of the X-ray machine or whatever you called it for almost ten minutes. Micah had shown the man his ID. The metal case was plastered with the logo of the World Center for Birds of Prey in Boise, Idaho, where they'd picked up the eggs early that morning. In addition to the logo, there were so many brightly colored stickers attached to the outside that a blind person could probably read them. The largest took up half the front of the case. It was blazing orange and said Fragile: Fertile Peregrine Falcon Eggs. Handle with Extreme Care. Another one was almost as big and bright a blue with Endangered Species in fluorescent yellow letters. What did the guy want?

"If you refuse to cooperate, I'll have to put you under arrest." The people in line behind them began to move restlessly. Doug glanced over his shoulder. Some of the women looked scared. Some of the men looked mad enough to grab the case from Micah and throw it on the conveyer belt themselves. Micah scowled harder and the guard loosened his gun from the holster. "I'm telling you for the last time. Everything goes through the machine. Airport policy. If you don't want it X-rayed you should have checked it through at the baggage counter."

"Don't be any dumber than God made you." Micah's voice was a low, menacing growl that made Doug's skin crawl. "Can't you read? These are fertile eggs. They can't be put in the baggage hold of an airliner.''

"They can't go through unchecked.'' The guard tightened his grip on the handle of his gun. Doug swallowed hard. He hadn't counted on getting shot trying to protect the eggs. He'd figured he'd only have to worry about the plane crashing or maybe worse than that, having to make conversation with Micah all the way to Idaho and back.

"I'll show you the eggs but keep your hands off them.''

"Don't open that.'' The guard's voice rose a couple of notes; his pale blond mustache quivered nervously. Doug bit his tongue to keep from sniggering but his stomach felt all tied up in knots. The gun came all the way out of the holster. The people behind them in line crowded backward, causing even more noise and commotion.

"You can't seriously believe we have a bomb in there, do you?'' Doug was relieved that his voice didn't squeak. He looked at the case again. It *was* kind of suspicious-looking, like one of those attaché cases the bad guys were always carrying around on *Mission: Impossible.* He supposed with all the crazies running loose in the world blowing up airplanes and everything, maybe the guard had a point.

"Let me talk to your supervisor,'' Micah said, and this time his voice was so even and controlled it almost didn't sound human. He didn't look as if he was going to fly off the handle and throttle the guy anymore but he still looked plenty tough and dangerous.

"You betcha, buddy.'' The guard motioned them out of line and unclipped his walkie-talkie from his belt. Micah stood stiff and silent, one hand clenched at his side, the other one wrapped around the handle of the egg carrier so tightly the skin was stretched white across his knuckles.

Doug looked down at his shoes. His stomach was still all knotted up with nerves. He didn't want to look at the shaking guard with his hand on his gun. Guns made him remember things he didn't want to remember sometimes. And he certainly didn't want to look at the other passengers, staring at him like he was some kind of freak. Or worse. He wanted to yell at them that he was helping to do something really important here and to mind their own business.

In the past two days he'd seen all kinds of birds of prey, Philippine eagles and tiny little hawks from South America no bigger than robins and even a pair of California condors, so rare there were only thirty of them left in the whole world, all of them in cages. They were trying to keep the same thing from happening to the peregrine falcon by taking these eggs back to Michigan, but that didn't seem to matter to anyone in this busy place. Except he had to admit, in his old black Iron Maiden T-shirt and grungy jeans, he probably did look like some kind of loony. He couldn't really blame anyone for being leery of a big, tough guy and a scroungy foreign-looking kid carrying a suspicious metal box, being held at gunpoint by a security guard.

A few minutes later, really long minutes in Doug's estimation, a woman in a navy-blue skirt and jacket, with a gun at her waist, walked briskly up to them. They'd gathered quite a crowd and Doug was rapidly getting more embarrassed than scared. Micah didn't pay attention to anyone but the guard and his supervisor.

"This guy won't cooperate, ma'am. The box looks damned suspicious to me."

The woman eyed the egg carrier with sharp blue eyes. "May I see your identification, please?" she asked, politely enough. Her voice was brisk and nononsense. She had red-brown hair and freckles like Doug's mom had, but she was about six feet tall and looked like she could play football for the Broncos. She gave Doug a quick once-over, while Micah fished in his pocket for the rest of his ID. The guard had already taken his driver's license and hadn't given it back.

Micah handed over his wallet. The woman studied the driver's license she'd taken from the guard and the receipt for the eggs they'd gotten from the Birds of Prey Center, as well as the government permits they'd had to have to be allowed to carry the eggs at all. "Everything here seems to be in order." She frowned at the guard and his mustache quivered harder than ever. "Didn't you look at these permits?"

"Yeah, but they could be fakes." The woman was silent for a long moment.

"Indeed, they could. Dr. McKendrick, please allow me to inspect your case." *Dr. McKendrick*. Doug was still having trouble getting used to people addressing Micah by his title. The first time he'd heard it in one of the big flight barns at the center, he'd really got a jolt. Doctor meant Ph.D. and that meant he'd gone to college for years and years. All this time he'd been fooling himself into believing Micah had learned most of everything he knew about birds just from working with them, that he, too, could learn to be an expert bird man just by watching and listening and doing. Now he was beginning to wonder if he'd been wrong.

Micah opened the case. He was still angry, but it was a cold anger now, strictly curbed and held in check. Inside was a smaller, clear-plastic, insulated rectangle where six red-brown spotted eggs were nestled in lamb's wool. Smaller plastic pouches of a special heat-absorbent gel kept the case at just the right temperature. It was kind of a traveling incubator that Micah and Reuben had rigged up, but it only worked for so long. If they missed their plane to Minneapolis, the eggs might get cold and then they wouldn't hatch. Doug didn't want to see that happen.

"Six peregrine falcon eggs, just as the receipt says." Micah didn't look at the guard again; his eyes were fixed steadily on the woman in charge.

"May I see your tickets, please, Doctor?" The lady was tough, Doug had to give her that. If Micah kept glaring at him that way, he'd have been stammering and stuttering and probably couldn't even get his own name right if he asked him. Micah handed over the tickets. "You're changing planes in Minneapolis/St. Paul and then flying through to Marquette, Michigan, correct?"

"Correct." Micah indicated the open case with a flick of his wrist. The woman nodded. He took a moment to check the eggs and read the thermometer attached to the inside of the plastic container and then snapped the case shut.

"I'll call ahead to Minneapolis/St. Paul and let them know you're coming. There will be no further delays, Dr. McKendrick.'' She handed him the papers and his driver's license.

"Thank you." Micah threw his canvas carryall down on the conveyor and indicated Doug should do the same.

No problem there, Doug thought with relief. He was just glad to get out of Denver without getting shot or going to jail. He'd been thinking about what it would be like in jail too much anyway, since he'd gotten involved with Hank Kisabeth and his gang. At first what they were doing had seemed a little like playing Robin Hood, sort of taking from the rich to give to the poor kind of thing. Now he wasn't so sure. Hank Kisabeth was a pretty poor excuse for Robin Hood. The last deer they'd shot hadn't gone to Willie Jenks and his family or anyone else who needed it, as far as Doug knew. It had been sold to a man who bought wild game for fancy restaurants in Detroit and Chicago, who didn't ask too many questions about where it came from. They'd offered Doug fifty dollars as his share of the take but he'd turned it down. He wasn't about to take money for committing a crime. What they were doing was poaching. And if you got caught, you went to jail. Being arrested wasn't something he wanted to experience firsthand.

MICAH LEANED BACK AGAINST the seat and closed his eyes. They were sitting over the wing and the vibrations of the jet's powerful engines were perceptible through the floor of the plane. He touched the metal egg case under the seat ahead of him with the toe of his shoe, found it secure, then settled back to try to get some sleep. The plane had taken off right on schedule, despite their altercation with the overzealous security guard. Still, it would be midnight before they arrived back at the compound and that was cutting it close. The eggs would have been out of their incubator for almost eighteen hours. It was a gamble moving fertile eggs, but the risk was acceptable. Transporting newly hatched chicks involved even greater risk that he wasn't willing to take.

The truth of the matter was Micah didn't like taking chances anymore. He'd taken too many in his lifetime, some more dangerous or foolish than others, but none so foolish and dangerous as letting Carrie Granger into his life and into his heart. He couldn't get her out of his thoughts. Or out of his dreams. Because of that uncomfortable fact, he'd been getting almost no sleep at all. It was starting to get to him.

Maybe that's why he'd gone off the deep end with the security guard back at the airport? Or maybe it was because he'd relaxed the stranglehold he usually kept on his emotions and the rage had come boiling through like acid eating through metal? Whatever the reason, he couldn't let it happen again. For a few godawful minutes he'd wondered if they wouldn't call in the guys in white jackets and have him hauled away, tied down, shot full of the same chemicals that had nearly destroyed his reason all those years ago. The panic attack had lasted only a few seconds but his anger had not dissipated along with the anxiety; its remnants still churned inside him.

He'd been kidding himself if he thought he could control his emotions, even after all this time. Maybe he'd never abuse Doug or Rachel—or Carrie—the way he'd hurt Elaine, but he could never be sure. That was the hell of it. No one wanted to believe what had happened to him had been a classic psychotic manifestation of chemical intolerance to the drugs they'd given him more than he did, but the truth was he couldn't remember a damned thing about those months. What if the doctors were wrong? What if he'd hurt Elaine because there was an animal inside him waiting to explode into a killing rage? What if the anger that sometimes threatened to choke him did come boiling to the surface in maddening fury that swept all reason before it? He could never be certain that wouldn't happen if he allowed himself to start feeling again.

He just couldn't take the chance.

"Would you like something to drink?" the flight attendant asked.

"I'll take a Coke," Doug said.

"Anything for you, sir?"

"Coffee."

"Janeen will be along with the coffeepot in just a wink." He trundled his cart down the aisle.

Janeen arrived right on cue. "Coffee or tea?"

"Coffee. Black." Micah didn't return her smile, but she'd already started pouring his coffee and didn't notice. "We'll be serving lunch in about fifteen minutes."

"Great." Doug had already finished his Coke. Micah suspected he'd inhaled it. "I'm starved."

"Me, too." Micah set his plastic coffee cup on Doug's tray table and reached down to retrieve the case from under the seat. He snapped open the lid, read the thermometer and checked to make sure the eggs hadn't shifted in their insulated nest.

"Worth their weight in gold, aren't they?" Doug sounded just the tiniest bit awed. "Little guys all okay?" He was looking over Micah's shoulder at the eggs with a very interested expression on his face.

"Safe and sound." He shut the lid and slid the container back under his seat. With a muttered "thanks," he retrieved his coffee cup and took a sip. It tasted just about as bad as he'd expected it would. Airline food got its share of bad publicity but in Micah's opinion, airline coffee was worse.

"How long will it take the eggs to hatch once we get them stowed away in the lab?" Doug was poking at the ice in his glass with a swizzle stick the flight attendant had provided with the soft drink. He guided one of the cubes into his mouth with the end of the implement and bit down on the ice. The sound sent a shiver up and down Micah's spine. How could kids do things like that?

"They'll be out of the shells in about three weeks if everything goes as it should." Micah took another swallow of coffee, grimaced at the bitter taste and dropped his half-full cup into the plastic bag the male attendant was filling with refuse as he walked up and down the aisle. Doug bit into another ice cube.

"Do you have to do that?" Micah growled.

"What?" Doug looked at the glass of ice. "Oh, that. Sorry. It bugs the heck out of my mom, too."

"It's bad for your teeth."

Doug sighed. "She says that, too."

"I used to do it," Micah said, surprising himself as much as Doug, "because it drove Rachel crazy."

"You really had ice cubes back then, huh?"

"No, we chipped it off the glacier out in the back-yard."

"Hey, that's pretty good. Glacier. Back in the ice age." Doug chuckled. "You're pretty quick for an old guy."

"I have my good days." Micah reached into the pocket of his gray cotton jacket and pulled out a pair of reading glasses. He hadn't brought anything to read but he began leafing through the magazine he found in the seat pocket in front of him. He couldn't sleep and he certainly wasn't in the mood for any more solitary musings about where he'd been and where he was going with his life. He'd rather be bored to death by an article on the glories of French nouvelle cuisine.

"Simon said you used to be a real hoot when you guys were in high school."

Micah closed the magazine and turned to look at the teenager beside him. He'd probably inherited his height and broad shoulders and the slight curl in his brown hair from his American father. His almond-shaped brown eyes and olive skin were gifts of his Vietnamese ancestry. He was a good-looking kid when he didn't have his face all screwed up in a scowl. Micah couldn't say he liked his long hair, but the boy kept it clean and neatly tied back in a ponytail so he couldn't really complain.

"Simon was a freshman when I was a junior. You've got younger brothers. You know how they tend to exaggerate what the older guys do. But yeah. I did have some good times in high school." Micah's first instinct, as always, had been to shut off, turn away from Doug's questions, but he didn't allow himself to give in to the promptings of habit.

He'd promised his brother and Annie, Rachel, and most of all, Carrie, that he'd try to get through to the boy if he got the chance. This was just about the first conversation he could remember Doug initiating that didn't have something to do with his work or when they were going to eat next.

"He said you played linebacker in college."

"Junior college. And I barely squeaked through on my grade point average or I couldn't even have played for them."

"He said you were a war hero."

"Not much more than anyone else who was over there." Commendations and decorations didn't mean a hell of a lot when you were so strung out you couldn't even remember your own name. He hadn't thought about them in years. The conversation was getting uncomfortable. Micah didn't want to talk about the war at all.

"You flew spotter planes in Laos, didn't you? My dad had a book about the Ravens. You flew Cessnas a lot like Reuben's plane, didn't you? Unarmed, too. Coming in low over the enemy to pinpoint the air strikes." He made a sweeping gesture with his hand imitating a plane in a power dive, but his voice sounded strange. Micah shot him a quick glance. He was staring out the window, his hand still raised above his knee.

"I did what I had to do, Doug. We all did."

"I remember a little bit." Doug leaned his head against the back of the seat. "Planes and bombs and people crying..." He looked over at Micah, his face shadowed with memories of events no small child should have been forced to endure.

"You all right?" Micah didn't know what to say, what to do. Not for the first time in the last months, he realized others had been as affected by the traumas of Vietnam as he'd been. First it was Rachel's return. Then Simon and Annie's stories of the last days of the war. Now the boy. All of them had nightmares to deal with as real as his own.

"Yeah, I'm okay." Doug sat up straighter. The stewardess was already at the front of the cabin with the lunch trays. Micah tightened his jaw in vexation. *Damn, he didn't want to be interrupted now.* "Micah, what happened to you in the war?"

"What do you mean?" How could he tell Doug anything about what had happened to him those lost years after he'd returned from Laos?

"I heard Mom and Simon talking one night when they were trying to decide what to do with me. You know, after I got kicked out of school."

"You mean, after you told them you wouldn't go back?"

Doug had the grace to flush. "Yeah." He was silent a moment. "Simon told Mom you spent almost two years in a VA hospital."

The words hit Micah like a body blow. What else had the boy overheard his brother tell his new wife? That Micah had been within an ace of losing his mind? That his violence and abuse had led to Elaine's death . . . her suicide? That he wasn't certain he could be trusted not to hurt her son?

"I did. In Texas."

"You must've been hurt real bad, but I've never seen any scars."

"There aren't always scars to see." Part of him had been hurt so bad it had died. Hope, heart, joy in the future—he didn't know what to call it—but it was gone. Maybe that was worse than losing your mind. "But I was hurt real bad, only it was here, inside my head, not my body." He wasn't ready yet to talk about those dark months to anyone. He'd evidently jumped to conclusions about Simon and Annie, though. He should have known his brother would stand by him, no matter what. He already had in the past. He would do it again if necessary in the future.

"Is that how you got interested in birds of prey? While you were getting better in the hospital?"

"Not till later."

Doug had no idea how ironic his words were. Micah hadn't gotten better in the hospital. He'd gotten worse. And there was no one to blame. Fifteen years ago doctors didn't know that much about delayed stress syndrome. And they sure as hell hadn't known enough about how certain drugs and combinations of drugs can wreak havoc on a human mind. He decided to tell Doug a version of the truth.

"My Mom inherited the house at Blueberry Lake from her grandfather. I went up there to . . . finish getting well...and started watching the eagles in that big nest across the lake. I got hooked. That winter I enrolled at the University of Michigan down in Ann Arbor. I studied raptor biology. It took me six years to get my degree, going to school in the winter and doing research in the summer. It took me three more to get my doctorate."

"I thought you . . . just learned about eagles from working with them." Doug sounded disappointed.

Micah knew this was his chance to make his point, but if he didn't do it right, he'd lose any hope of getting through to the kid. *Lord, how did parents ever deal with teenagers and their problems on a day-to-day basis? Having custody of Doug was just about the hardest thing he'd ever taken on.*

"It doesn't work that way. I'd have probably done more harm than good if I'd just started climbing around out there with no grounding in the sciences."

"But you're so good with birds. Any birds."

"Maybe. I'm not saying you don't need the touch. But you also need the technical background of a good education when you're working with an endangered species. Mistakes can be fatal. They can also lead to that species' extinction." He watched the boy's face from the corner of his eye but Doug had the irritating ability to hide his feelings behind a mask of surface calm when he wished. Micah sighed and took off his glasses. He rubbed the bridge of his nose between his thumb and forefinger. Had he gotten his message through that thick, stubborn skull?

"I . . . I figured you could just learn about eagles from hands-on experience."

"You can. But I won't need that kind of help in the future." Micah hesitated, then decided to be blunt. "It's just not enough. No matter what it is you want to do with your life eventually, go back to school first. Do it right. Maybe someday, if that's where your interest lies, there'll be a job for you with me."

Doug ignored the bait. Micah hadn't expected him to jump at the offer but it had been worth a shot. Doug turned his head away and stared out the window.

"You sound just like Mom and Simon and all the rest."

"Maybe we all say the same thing because we're right and you're wrong." Micah let the words sink in. Doug turned his head away from the window but he wouldn't meet Micah's eyes. The flight attendant with the meal cart was only two rows away. Micah reached forward to unhook his tray.

"Maybe." Doug didn't sound all that convinced, but Micah figured he'd made his point. At least the kid was listening. It was a start.

CHAPTER EIGHT

THERE WAS A SQUARE PANE of glass, a viewing window of sorts, set in the wall between the lab and the big cement-floored flight cages behind the building. Carrie stood just inside the lab itself, near the glass-sided incubator that held the peregrine eggs, and watched as Micah hosed down the cages. Usually that was Doug's job, but this morning the boy had gone off into town with Reuben and they hadn't returned yet.

The osprey preened and arched her wings, enjoying the rainlike mist. She tilted her head this way and that to locate the sound of Micah's voice. Even though she couldn't hear him from where she stood inside the building, Carrie knew he was talking to the osprey. And his tone of voice would be the one she had imagined countless times that he would use to gentle and caress a lover as he held her in his arms.

With a jerk Carrie turned away from the window and the view of Micah's broad, powerful back as he moved to direct the spray of water into the smaller cages holding the three red-tailed hawks that would act as surrogate parents to the peregrine chicks when they hatched in a week's time. For the first five days of their lives they'd reside in an incubator, designed for premature human babies and donated to the project by the hospital in Marquette. "Just like they was little people," Reuben had joked.

She'd smiled at his humorous attempt but inside she hadn't been laughing. Any mention of babies still gave her heart a nervous flutter. Even though she'd decided to keep her child, love him, raise him to the best of her abilities, she was still frightened of the prospect of being a single parent, of bearing a child alone.

Micah came back into the lab. Carrie pretended to study the egg chart very closely. He acknowledged her presence with a half wave. "I think the goshawk's wing has mended well enough that he can manage these little guys on his own." Micah was looking down at three ordinary field mice he'd taken out of their cage and put in a small shoe box. "Would you carry them out for me? They aren't as smelly as the fish." He paused, looking down at the covered box in his hand. "Or are you afraid of mice?"

Was he testing her as he sometimes did in small ways? Carrie shook her head, laughing. "Of course not." She wasn't too sure about watching the goshawk catch and eat his prey, though. While Micah had been away Reuben had fed the crippled hawk dead mice and an occasional rabbit or squirrel but no live prey.

"Are you squeamish about watching him eat?" Micah looked at her uncertainly but with little of his usual habitual coolness.

"No."

"With the baby and all..." Micah broke off. He wasn't teasing, she realized. Carrie had come to recognize, and longed to see, that rare lightening of expression, the faint gleam of amusement she could sometimes bring to life in his blue-gray eyes. This wasn't one of those times. A man who lived so alone, so apart from women, found nothing amusing about pregnancy.

"I'm not squeamish," Carrie said, scowling in mock irritation. "I can do—" She spread her hands in a wide, encompassing gesture.

Micah held up his free hand to fend off her verbal attack. "I know. You can do anything any other healthy, twenty-eight-year-old—"

"Don't mention my age again, Micah McKendrick, or I'll have a fit of the vapors."

"What the devil are the vapors?" Micah looked intrigued despite himself. He tilted his head, his strong, dark brows pulled together in an inquisitive frown.

"The vapors," Carrie said, lifting the back of her hand, limp-wristed, to her forehead, sighing loudly. "You know, like all the Atlanta ladies in *Gone with the Wind*." Two nights before they'd watched the classic motion picture on videotape. At least she and Rachel, Doug and Reuben had watched. Micah had worked at his desk, present physically in the same room but remote and distant from human contact as always.

"Except for Scarlett O'Hara." He was smiling, almost.

Carrie straightened from her languid, affected pose. "Of course except for Scarlett." So he had been paying attention to the film.

"I take it this means you won't burst into tears or fall down in a dead faint when the hawk makes its kill?"

"Not on your life!" Carrie stuck her nose up in the air. "I've been watching *National Geographic* television specials and Disney wildlife adventure movies since I was a little girl. I can take it."

"All right. All right." Micah shoved the shoe box of mice toward her. "I give up. C'mon, the birds are hungry." This time he did smile, a quick twisting of his lips, over in a heartbeat, but Carrie didn't care. In fact she'd go on babbling like a fool for the next hour if he would only keep on talking with her, laughing with her... *loving her*.

"The red-tails are still a little off their feed from the move but they'll be settled in by the time the chicks hatch."

"When are you expecting that?" Carrie walked through the door into the runway between the flight cages that he held open for her.

"About a week after the Fourth."

Carrie thought of the letter she'd received from her parents in yesterday's mail. They were coming to see her, bringing the results of Evan's blood tests and medical history that Dr. Sauder had requested. They were planning to arrive on the first and stay over the Fourth. The nearest motel was on the highway about twelve miles away. She needed to see about making reservations for them. She also needed to ask Micah for some time off to spend with them.

She waited while he propped open the door and returned to the lab to get the osprey's fish. "Micah, I need to ask a favor."

"Sure, what is it?" She saw his shoulders tense as he tossed a perch carcass onto the osprey's high nest perch. The bird cocked her head, looking at the fish with her undamaged left eye. She spread her beautiful brown and white wings and covered the body, mantling her prey, protecting it from enemies seen and unseen before tearing into the flesh with relish.

Carrie thought of the small, scurrying mice in her box and took a deep breath. She wasn't about to make a liar of herself. She moved on down the aisle toward the goshawk's cage. "I...I'd like to have a day or two free over the Fourth of July weekend."

"I think that can be arranged." He was washing his hands, using water from the hose that he'd been spraying down the cages with earlier. His voice had resumed its even, unemotional tenor. Carrie felt a surge of disappointment that their fragile rapport of just a few moments ago was so easily broken. "Do you have something special planned for the holiday?" His voice wasn't quite as even as before. Or had she only imagined he sounded interested in her plans?

"My parents are coming." She lifted the latch on the small opening at the base of the flight cage and emptied the mice onto the concrete floor. "I'd like to spend some time with them." She congratulated herself that her voice was as even as Micah's, even though her stomach was doing flip-flops. The goshawk spread his good wing and prepared to drop onto one of the mice from his position on the perch at the far corner of the cage. The goshawk's eyes followed the rodent's every move. The big gray bird, its stomach barred with gray, irregular stripes on a white background, half-glided, half-flew from its perch, favoring its injured wing, to pounce on the first of the unwary mice. It was over in the blink of an eye. The hawk, a hunter of woodlands and forests, eyed its small catch disdainfully but hopped to a low perch and began to feed.

"He's fully capable of taking a pigeon or full-grown rabbit down in the wild, but since he's not active here, the mice will be enough." Micah gestured back toward the lab as the goshawk snared a second mouse. Carrie turned away from the cage without reluctance.

The osprey had left a portion of her fish for a later meal, wedging the remains in the fork of the tree limb that served as her perch. Carrie averted her eyes. The osprey was a very messy eater.

"When will your parents be arriving?" Micah asked as they reentered the lab. He appeared to be very busy checking the falcon eggs and making notations on their chart, but Carrie still thought she detected an unusual note of interest in his words.

"Probably sometime Saturday." Carrie glanced at the calendar above the sink. It was hard to believe that in another day or two it would be July. Time had passed so quickly. She'd been at the compound for more than six weeks. That meant, also, that Micah's broken ribs must be healed, although he'd given no sign that they had bothered him for several weeks already.

"Where will they be staying?" He turned around and leaned his hips against the incubator, folding his arms across his chest. The width of the room separated them but Carrie was vitally aware that they were alone, together.

She shrugged, more to give herself a moment to order her thoughts than because she didn't know. "At the motel out on the highway, I suppose. I noticed it has an Automobile Club sign. That usually means it's a nice clean place.''

''Humph.'' Micah stared at his shoes. ''They could stay here.'' He glanced up, meeting her eyes for a moment before looking away again, past her, through the open doorway, as the goshawk gave voice to a raucous cry. The third mouse must have met its fate. ''It won't take much to air out one of the other cabins. They'd be near you. You'd have more time to spend together if they're not staying long.''

''They won't be here long,'' Carrie affirmed. ''My mother still works part-time at the public library in my hometown. She loves her job and in the summer she's head of the preschool reading program. And my dad's on the county fair board. He'll be busy from now till the end of August.'' She smiled, realizing for the first time in weeks how much she'd missed seeing her parents. While she was by no means ready to go home, or to confront her baby's father, now that she'd made some necessary decisions, she could think about picking up the pieces of her life once more. Letting her parents know she was getting her priorities back in order seemed very important all of a sudden.

''Then it's settled. We can get started airing out the cabin when Reuben and Doug get back. It'll keep them busy for a couple of hours. Now that the banding's done, everyone's got too much time on his hands.''

''Everybody but me,'' Carrie said, laughing. She walked ahead of him through the swinging door into the office. On her desk a pile of folders waiting to be transcribed into the computer bore mute testimony to her words.

"You aren't planning to finish all those today, are you?" Micah's brows pulled together into a frown.

"I was."

"No, you're not." Micah surprised her by taking her hand and leading her toward the door. "It's a great day for sunbathing, or swimming, or just plain taking a nap. Tomorrow it's supposed to rain."

"But I want to get these finished."

"Pregnant women are supposed to get a lot of rest. And extra vitamins and . . . fresh air and . . . all that stuff."

"Who told you that?" Carrie couldn't help the smile that tilted the corners of her mouth. He sounded so earnest, so much as if he were reciting facts and figures carefully learned.

"Everyone knows that." It was back again, that faint half smile, that flash of reluctant humor in his eyes. Carrie didn't want to spoil the moment by pushing him too far. Besides, he still held her hand in his and she probably couldn't have said anything witty or humorous if her life depended on it. Her heart was beating too high and fast in her throat to even get the words out.

"Well," she said, tilting her head to catch his eye and hold his gaze with the intensity of her own. "You are the boss. . . ."

"I am." He didn't break the touch of their eyes or his hold on her hand, but leaned past her and opened the door. Bright, warm sunshine flooded the room; bird song and the slap of waves against the narrow sand beach rushed in to fill the sudden silence. Carrie realized she was very tired and the thought of sitting in her hard chair, tapping away at a computer terminal for several more hours, was unappealing. Her fatigue must have showed, at least momentarily, on her face. Micah tightened his grip. His expression resumed its usual implacability but his eyes didn't reflect the hardness of his voice. "Now go, before I change my mind."

"Or you'll be tempted to do what?" Carrie knew she was pushing past the limits she'd set for herself, and surely she was in danger of pushing Micah's new-found lightness of spirit too far. She must move very carefully because neither of them really knew what they wanted from a relationship. She was as uncertain in that respect as he was.

"I might be tempted to pick you up, bodily, and carry you to your cabin, dump you on your bed and see that you take a nap."

"No thanks." Carrie didn't think she'd mind him doing that at all, but she wasn't about to let this teasing conversation get out of hand. Micah was as wary as his birds when it came to human contact. She disengaged her fingers from the strong grasp of his big scarred hand. "I know when to retire gracefully. And as much as I hate to admit it, you're right, it is too nice a day to spend staring at a computer terminal. I'll finish those files first thing in the morning."

"Good." He didn't try to follow her out of the building and Carrie felt a momentary sting of disappointment, but she kept it well hidden and smiled saucily instead.

"But I'm not going to take a nap, either." She set her jaw, her chin jutting out stubbornly as she caught his eye. She had to be so careful what she said to him. He could so easily be scared back into his shell. "I'm going to get into my new bathing suit, get the sunscreen, something cool to drink and a good book, and go lie in the sun. And you know what?'' she called back over her shoulder as she walked away, unable to resist the temptation to have the last word. ''It might not be such a bad idea for you to do the same.''

''I'M SORRY MOM AND DAD couldn't make it up here for the Fourth,'' Rachel said, piling graham crackers, chocolate squares and a bag of marshmallows on a tray to carry out to the beach. ''They'd have liked Mr. and Mrs. Granger very much.'' Carrie's parents had arrived on Saturday. They were quiet and unaffected people, seemingly oblivious to the tensions swirling among the small group in the compound. Once they'd gotten over the initial shock of seeing Carrie, obviously and undeniably pregnant, they'd adjusted admirably to the prospect of a new grandchild in the not too distant future. Rachel was glad for Carrie's sake. And for her adoptive parents.

''Carrie's lucky to have them. Did you take the test results from...the baby's father...into town with you today?''

''Yes.'' Rachel watched her younger brother from the corner of her eye. His expression was carefully controlled, but a small muscle jumped in his cheek just above the dark line of his beard. It bothered him to talk about the father of Carrie's baby, but it bothered him even more, obviously, not to know what was going on with her. *Good,* Rachel thought to herself, *very good.* ''We were swamped today with campers and hikers, the usual this time of year, sprained ankles, stomach flu, you name it, but Doc got a chance to go over the results. The baby's father is a strong, healthy man. No problem there.''

Micah grunted but went on stirring the lemonade as she'd directed. Then Rachel picked up the tray and took two steps toward the kitchen door. ''Is it really so uncomfortable for you to have so many people about?'' She'd pulled her hair back off her face with a pair of pink combs. Now that she was used to the silver threaded through the dark strands, she didn't mind it nearly so much and had let it grow into a soft sweeping curve just above her shoulders. She was wearing a new pink cotton shirt and white drawstring shorts. She felt younger and prettier than she had in years, but worry for her brother's continued isolation was always with her.

''No.'' Micah added a tray of ice cubes to the pitcher of lemonade. His automatic denial didn't convince Rachel.

''Do Mr. Granger's war stories bother you?'' She thought of the heavyset, graying man sitting by the small camp fire on the beach near the dock, talking of days long gone by when he was young and slim and fighting to keep General Patton's tanks in good enough shape to last out the war. He'd been trading anecdotes with Reuben for the past hour and a half.

''Good Lord, Sis.'' Micah swung around with a snort. ''Do you think I'm still that close to going over the edge that stories of a war that was over before we—'' He broke off abruptly.

''I was thinking of Reuben's tales....'' It was Rachel's turn to grow silent.

''Do they bother you?'' Micah ignored her question in favor of one of his own.

Rachel shook her head slowly. "No." She searched her heart and her memories but no dark shadows lurked at the edges of her awareness tonight to spoil her good mood. "No, they don't," she repeated firmly. "It's history. Someday what happened to us will be so long gone that we'll be able to talk about it, too." But what of Micah's memories? Old ones and not so old ones? She shrugged and gave him a sad, crooked little smile. "Maybe."

"Sure." Micah tossed the wooden spoon he'd been using to stir the pitcher of lemonade into the sink. He gave a bottle of vodka a long, considering glance, then set it back onto the high shelf from where he'd taken it without opening it.

"If it isn't Mr. Granger and his World War II stories and it isn't having strangers here, then is it the responsibility you feel for the rest of us that's keeping you awake at night?"

"Hey," Micah barked, holding up a hand to stop her. "We're supposed to be having a party here. An old-fashioned, night before the Fourth of July wiener roast with those god-awful Girl Scout summer camp things—" he waved at the tray "—whatever-you-call-'ems, fireworks and the whole nine yards."

"They're called s'mores," Rachel said without a trace of levity in her voice. "I used to dream about them in the Hlông village. Cinnamon grahams, Hershey bars and all. Tonight I intend to eat my fill."

Micah swung his head around, catching her eyes until she looked away with a hopeless little shrug. He grabbed the stack of plastic glasses by the pitcher. "Let's go then. Tonight we'll make your little dream come true. I don't want to talk about responsibilities. Mine or anyone else's."

Rachel stood her ground. "I do."

Micah set the pitcher of lemonade down with great deliberation. He hooked his thumbs in the waistband of his jeans. His expression and his stance were equally daunting. "Okay, what is it you want to know? But hurry. Doug's going to start setting off the fireworks in about five minutes' time. If he doesn't, the mosquitoes are going to put an end to this party damned fast." He swatted at one of the annoying insects singing past his ear to emphasize his point.

"Annie called last night while you were in town. She's worried about Doug. So is Simon. I had to tell her I don't know how you're making out with him because you won't tell me."

"Did you tell her about him getting drunk?"

"No." Rachel shook her head, looking down at the food on the tray. "I...it hasn't happened again. I don't want them to worry any more than they already are...." She looked at him for reassurance. It was hard to know what was the right thing to do. That's why she wanted Micah to confide in her if he felt the need. Maybe between the two of them, or three, or four of them, if you counted Reuben and Carrie, they could get Doug back on track.

"Good. Like you said, I don't think he's making a habit of it."

"I wish he'd talk to me about what's bothering him, but he won't." She wasn't positive but she thought Doug avoided her because he had unresolved feelings about his Vietnamese ancestry. She hoped it wasn't because he might have sensed she occasionally found herself comparing him to the child she had lost. She didn't mean to do that, it just kept happening, and was perfectly natural for her, but must be uncomfortable for the boy. "Have you made any headway with him?"

Micah poured himself a glass of lemonade. It was growing dark outside. Only the light above the sink was on in the small, pine-paneled kitchen. It threw Micah's face into shadow, making it harder than usual to read anything at all in his expression.

"We talked a little on the plane home from Idaho, after I made a jackass of myself with a security guard." He waved off her inquiring glance. "I'll tell you about it some other time. It's so damn hard to tell if you're getting through to the kid. I laid it on the line, Sis. I told him he needed an education to do much of anything in this world nowadays. Hell, I even half offered him a job here if he wants it. And if he's qualified to take it. He can be pretty inscrutable when he sets his mind to it." His grin was a quick, rueful twist of his lips. "Know what I mean?"

Rachel nodded. "I know."

He swallowed the lemonade in his glass in one long gulp. "I just don't know if he was listening. I'm not sure if I got through to him at all." He crushed the plastic cup in his hand. It splintered with a loud crack. "I'm flying blind on this. I told Simon and Annie that when they asked to send him up here. I'm telling you the same thing." He tossed the ruined cup into the trash basket. "If you think you can do any better, you're welcome to try."

"Hey, you two! What's holding up the grub? The fire's just right for marsh..." Reuben's head poked itself inside the kitchen doorway; the rest of his body was out of sight in the main room. The smell of wood smoke and mosquito repellent clung to him like cheap shaving lotion, and was every bit as potent. He stopped short at the angry scowl on Micah's face, the set, tight look on Rachel's. "Here, give me that stuff," he said, stalking into the kitchen, making it seem even smaller and more crowded that before. He took the tray from Rachel's hands and motioned Micah to add the pitcher and glasses. "Don't be too long arguin' in here, you hear me? We've got a dozen Roman candles ready to go off and a whole passel of them sparkly fountain things with all the pretty Chinese flower names."

"We're not arguing," Micah said, setting the pitcher on the tray with a thump.

"Sure." Reuben didn't sound convinced. "Anything you say, boss. Don't let him browbeat you, Rachel."

"Out," Micah growled.

"And if you're talking about the boy," Reuben called over his shoulder, "he's not doin' bad. Just use the sense God gave a duck when you get him alone. Don't give up on him yet."

CHAPTER NINE

HE SHOULD HAVE SPENT THE DAY back at the compound with everybody else.

Doug sat wedged into the back seat of Hank Kisabeth's Bronco along with Willie Jenks and Hank's brother, Leon. Leon smelled like he hadn't had a bath in days and Willie was hung over from too much beer the night before. He'd been laid off from his job at the garage out on the highway and he was in a real bad mood. His mom depended on him to help out with money for his younger sisters and brothers.

To top it off, Hank was yelling details of last night's date with a girl from one of the summer resorts from the front seat. Doug wished he'd keep his hands on the wheel, instead of using them to emphasize his description of what he'd done to her and what she'd done to him. Hank's language was pretty graphic and while Doug didn't think he was a pansy about stuff like that, he was just as glad he couldn't hear half of what he was saying with the windows open and the wind blowing in his face.

Hank's cousin, Lance, who was sitting next to Hank in the front seat, didn't seem to have any trouble hearing. He'd been laughing himself sick over Hank's sexual exploits for the past ten miles. He was also waving his new rifle around like Rambo, and Doug wasn't altogether certain it wasn't loaded.

"Hey," Doug yelled when they slowed down to take a turn off the highway onto a gravel road. "Why don't you put that gun down someplace and quit waving it in our faces."

"Yeah," Leon sneered. "Even with that fancy high-powered scope you can't hit the broad side of a barn. You're the damn worst shot of the bunch of us. 'Cept for the city boy, here." He punched Doug in the ribs with a rude laugh.

"Don't get smart, cousin," Lance said, swiveling around in his seat. "You forgettin' who runs this little operation?" Lance was the contact for the game buyer in Detroit. He was with them today, Hank had told Doug when they were too far from the compound to walk back, to scout out a spot where they could find a bear to shoot. A restaurant in the city wanted to add mesquite-grilled bear steaks to its menu. The thought made Doug sick to his stomach. "Stop here," Lance ordered. "I'll show your dumb brother what kind of shot I am."

"Not here," Hank replied, waving his arm, "too close to the highway. Kennedy Lake's just up ahead."

Doug pricked up his ears. Kennedy Lake wasn't all that far from Micah's compound. At least as the eagles flew. The road they were on must be the one that led into Micah's road about six miles from the compound. He'd never had a chance to travel it before today but it made sense. And the direction was right.

He did know that on the far side of Kennedy Lake, which really wasn't much of a lake, more of a marshy pond, there was an eagle nest.

"Jeez, guys, it's too hot for this." He tried to sound as tough and bored as Hank usually did. "I didn't mind staking out a bear hollow in the woods but I'm not going to stand out in the sun and watch you two take potshots at frogs on a lily pad or something."

"Yeah, me neither," Willie growled, his chin slumped down on his chest, his voice pained, one hand shading his eyes from the sun.

Lance glared at both of them. "Okay, city boy. I'll show you I can hit somethin' besides a frog, eh. Stop the truck." Hank did as he was told. Too late Doug realized what Lance was up to. There above the shallow reed-choked waters of the lake, a big bird flew in low, slow circles, searching for an updraft of warm air on which to rise higher and higher above the earth. "There's a damn hawk or something. I'll show you who's the lousy shot in this family." He jumped out of the Bronco before it had stopped moving.

"Hey, wait. Don't." Doug couldn't crawl over Willie's slumped form. He couldn't push slow-moving Leon out of the truck fast enough. Hank already had the powerful rifle to his shoulder. He fired and the shot was swallowed up by the vastness of the open, cutover land surrounding the lake. "Stop it, you jackass!" Doug yelled again, shoving Leon out of his way. "That's an eagle!"

"Don't give me that crap, city boy," Lance called over his shoulder. "That's no damn eagle." He fired again and the bird faltered in its graceful upward spiral, then fell from the sky.

"Jesus, you just shot a bald eagle. That's a federal offense." Doug heard his voice rise to a squeak and didn't care. He bounded up to Lance and jerked him around, oblivious to the gun in the older man's hand. "C'mon. Help me find it. Maybe it isn't dead. It looked like it was trying to fly into those trees."

"You're nuts." Lance jerked his hand free of Doug's grip. "That wasn't no eagle."

"It was an immature one, you idiot. They're brown and white. They don't look like the adult ones." Doug tried to get his voice and his temper under control. He'd need these guys' help if he was going to have any chance of finding the wounded bird. "They don't get their white head and tail feathers until they're four or five years old. Any school kid knows that."

Lance looked murderous. He had small, deep-set black eyes and a big nose. His mouth was thin and mean-looking. Doug began to wish he had a gun of his own. "Then I'd be a real damned fool to help you look for it, wouldn't I?"

"We could save it. Take it to McKendrick." Doug stopped talking. He could tell he was wasting his breath.

"And get my butt throwed in jail." Lance gestured his cousins back into the Bronco. "Don't think of tryin' nothin', Simpson," he said warningly as he glanced down at the powerful gun in his hand. "You're in this just as deep as we are. Remember, you was with us the night we shot the two does. You gave your share of the money to Willie. That's the same as takin' it, as far as the law's concerned. You stood right here, now, and watched me shoot a damn bald eagle.

You're just about eighteen. They'd probably try you as an adult, just like the rest of us. Think about it."

Doug didn't have to think about it. He'd been thinking about it for the past couple of weeks. But sometimes a guy had to take a stand, no matter what happened. "I'm going to look for that bird." He planted both feet, let his hands curl into fists.

"I'll help," Willie called out unexpectedly. He was swaying where he stood and looked white as a sheet. He wouldn't be much help to anyone but Doug was grateful for his support.

"How's your mom gonna make it on a waitress's pay if you're in jail?" Lance sneered without taking his eyes off Doug. "You and the half gook here, gonna share a cell? You two pretty boys?" Willie took a swing at Lance but he was too far away and Leon didn't have any trouble holding him back. Doug was so worried about the eagle he didn't even have time to be mad at the names Lance was calling him.

"You leave my mom out of this," Willie hollered back, struggling in Leon's grip.

"I wish I could. You just better convince your city friend here that it's in everyone's best interests to just forget this whole thing ever happened."

"Doug." Willie stood still. His voice held a definite plea. "I can't afford to go to jail. I've been in trouble with the law off and on since I was thirteen. It'd kill my mom."

"Help me find the eagle. I won't say who did it. People bring birds to Micah all the time. Some of them are shot. He says it's almost impossible to prosecute without an eyewitness."

"Go on, hunt all you want." Lance shrugged and motioned Willie and Leon into the Jeep. "It's your word against ours. We've been together all afternoon, haven't we, boys? Without the China-boy, right?"

"Right," Hank said without hesitation.

"Right," Leon echoed his brother.

Willie didn't say anything but climbed into the back seat of the truck. He didn't look at Doug again.

"Get in now and I'll forget the whole thing," Lance said, holding open the door. "Or start walkin'. You ought to make it back to your crazy eagle man's place in three or four hours, if you keep hoofin' it."

"You'll pay for this, Kisabeth." Doug just couldn't stand there any longer without saying something.

"I'm quakin' in my boots, eh," Lance snorted, then laughed out loud. "See you back in town." Hank drove off with a spurt of gravel. Dust sifted down on Doug's head and made him want to sneeze.

The sun was straight overhead. It was hot and still. The sound of the Bronco's engine faded away. Doug felt very much alone. Mosquitoes buzzed all around him. It was hours until dark. Hours until he'd be missed. He set off along the marshy shore of the little lake, hoping against hope he'd find the wounded eagle and it would still be alive. He didn't think he had much chance, though. He'd probably used up his quota of good luck finding the jumper that day a few weeks ago.

He wasn't fooling himself. Everything Lance Kisabeth said was true. His own neck was on the line just like the rest of them. *Jeez, he didn't want to go to jail.* That was a thousand times worse than getting kicked out of school. But he just couldn't let one of Micah's eagles die, either. Especially when he might have prevented the shooting in the first place if he'd just been quick enough.

Maybe, just maybe, he could find it, take it to Micah and get it well, and this whole thing would blow over without anyone finding out who was involved. Maybe, but he didn't think so.

"DO YOU KNOW HOW TO BAKE a pie?" It was Micah's voice. The words were low, softly spoken, for her ears alone, just as she was always fantasizing, except that she'd never once dreamed of him asking her to bake a pie. Carrie opened her eyes and blinked in confusion. In the background she could hear Reuben and her father playing horseshoes on the other side of the lawn; she could just catch the drift of her mother's and Rachel's conversation as they talked amiably on the screened porch of the main cabin, although she hadn't been paying much attention to what they were saying. In reality she'd been sitting in a chair at the water's edge, half-asleep, dozing over the paperback novel in her lap, dreaming of a future where she wasn't alone, where she and her baby were loved and cared for, where she could love and care for someone special in return....

"I'm sorry," she said sleepily. "What did you say?"

Micah dropped to the balls of his feet, kneeling beside her half-reclining lawn chair. She sat up straight. Their eyes were nearly on a level. He wasn't smiling, he never did smile easily, but the frightening emptiness she sometimes glimpsed behind his blue-gray eyes wasn't there. "I didn't mean to wake you." He didn't move closer, didn't touch her, but Carrie felt the warmth of his fingers on her skin just the same. She shivered a little, although the afternoon was still and hot.

"I was just resting my eyes." He nodded, not contradicting her. "Did you ask me if I could bake a pie?"

He nodded again. "There are wild raspberries on that little island in the middle of the lake. Rachel used to love raspberry pie. I'd like to surprise her with one."

"I see." A hint of disbelief in her tone must have given her away.

Micah let the beginning of a smile curl the corners of his mouth. "I'm not such a bad cook. I've just never gotten the hang of piecrust. Living up here alone, for twelve winters, I had to learn to cook for myself or starve, but a pastry chef I'm not. Reuben and Doug are always raving about your pizza. I figured pies weren't so different."

"Well, they are," Carrie said decisively. "But you're in luck. My dad just happens to bake the best pies in Hamler, Ohio—my hometown." She realized as she spoke that she'd told him almost nothing about herself, just as he'd told her nothing about himself. "He'll bake it if we ask him. And I'll help pick the raspberries. That's the hardest part anyway, isn't it?"

"Yes." He looked down at his hands curled around the wooden handle of her chair. "Do you—"

She didn't let him finish the question. "I can do anything..."

Micah cut her short in his turn. The half smile on his lips grew broader, threatened to become a grin. He rubbed his hand across his beard in a characteristic gesture she was learning to know well. "I was going to ask if you knew how to manage in a canoe. Otherwise, we can take the fishing boat."

"Oh." Carrie had the grace to look sheepish. She just hoped she wasn't blushing. He had the power to unsettle her so easily. It wasn't fair. She so seldom ruffled his composure. "I haven't been in a canoe since high school, but yes, I think I can manage."

"And is it something any other normal, healthy, twenty-eight-year-old woman would do?" One straight black brow rose higher than the other.

Carrie sighed. She was never going to live that impassioned statement down, it seemed. "Yes, it is. Just wait a minute while I put on some slacks and a T-shirt. I like raspberries but not well enough to get scratched to ribbons for them." She was wearing her bathing suit and wondered for a moment if Micah liked her in it. It was a becoming shade of turquoise that complemented her tan, with a full, blousy top that hid her pregnancy, at least for the time being.

"Good idea." His eyes followed the neckline of the suit, resting for just a heartbeat on the thrusting curve of her breasts before lifting to meet her gaze. He swallowed hard and Carrie felt a delicious shiver of purely feminine recognition. Micah *was* aware of her as a woman. Just as she was totally aware of him as a man. He cleared his throat as he rose to stand towering above her. "Can you be ready in fifteen minutes?"

"Yes."

He held out his hand. It was Carrie's turn to hesitate. He hadn't touched her in weeks, although she ached for him to do so. She felt his fingers close over hers, strong and hard, as she stood up. The blood rushed in her ears and her heart beat high and fast in her throat. She couldn't hear her father and Reuben good-naturedly grousing over their horseshoe game. She was no longer aware of her mother's and Rachel's soft-voiced conversation and thought it might have stopped altogether, just like her breath. The only thing on her mind as she stood up was Micah; the touch of his hand, the warmth of his skin, the nearness of his body and the answering ache of desire it awakened in her own. "I can be ready in ten minutes. I'll..." She had to swallow against the sudden tightness in her throat. "I'll meet you at the dock."

Micah nodded and released her hand, but slowly, almost reluctantly, as if he no longer controlled his own movements. "Ten minutes." He turned and walked away. Carrie did the same, but she wouldn't have been surprised to find she was floating along about six inches off the ground.

HE'D LET HIS NEED TO BE with Carrie overrule his common sense once more. Micah scowled at the back of her head, watching the muscles of her neck and shoulders tighten as she thrust her paddle deeper into the dark water to compensate for his last two overly aggressive J-strokes. The canoe righted itself with a little wobble and continued on course.

She wasn't wearing her hair in its usual intricate braid this afternoon. It was pulled into a loose knot on top of her head and tied with a length of thick, fluffy yarn that matched her pale green shirt and complemented the soft, golden glow of her skin. Micah found himself wanting to kiss the skin just above the curve of her shoulder. Once again he dug the paddle too deeply into the water, sending them shooting forward in a curving arc. Carrie turned around with a questioning look on her face.

"Sorry," he apologized gruffly. "I'm not used to paddling with a partner."

"I can paddle faster if you like. I'm afraid I wasn't paying attention. I was admiring the view." She colored prettily and he realized that was something else he liked about her. The way her emotions showed so easily on her expressive face, and in her great doe-brown eyes.

"I'd forgotten you've never been on this part of the lake." He laid his paddle across the thwarts of the old-fashioned wooden canoe and let them drift. "Take your time. We've got all day. It's a holiday, after all." He tried to see the land through her eyes. It was beautiful, he knew, although he hadn't really looked at it that way in years. The low hills that protected the lake from the worst of Lake Superior's winter fury were blue-black in the distance, shimmering in the heat haze of a July afternoon.

The island they were headed for was small, no more than a rocky, pine-crested outcropping near the south shore of the lake. It sloped gently uphill from the sandy crescent of beach they were making for on the far shore, rising to thirty-foot granite cliffs whose shadow they were passing through.

An osprey's nest still rested in one of the trees, but the big fishing hawks had abandoned it for reasons of their own two seasons earlier and moved to a spot on the far shore about a mile away. Loons also nested on the predator-free island, but Micah planned to land the canoe well away from their territory. He wished he'd remembered to bring the field glasses. He could have shown Carrie the low shore-edge nest of mud and grasses. She rested her paddle across her lap at his suggestion, content to let him propel them through the water, engrossed in the sights and sounds of his world.

She was a very restful person to be around, he'd discovered, like Rachel. She didn't throw tantrums or cry over nothing, as he remembered Elaine doing. But then she was older than Elaine had been when she died. Perhaps his wife would have matured into just such a woman as Carrie... if she had lived.

"We'll beach the canoe here." It was an order as much as a statement. "The raspberry canes are just over the rise." This time he tried to sound more congenial. *Lord, it was hard to make ordinary small talk after so many years alone, apart.* Especially to Carrie, a woman he desired more than was safe for both of them.

Micah beached the canoe with one long, fluid stroke of his paddle that sent them sliding onto the narrow sand beach. He stood up slowly to avoid rocking the boat and jumped ashore, turning to help Carrie out of the canoe. He could see that she felt awkward and unsure of her balance at times. Her center of gravity was shifting, her body compensating for the growing burden of new life she carried within her. A baby, a love child conceived of her affair with an unknown man, a man she still cared for so much that she could never mention his name.

Micah looked down at the woman in the boat, at the gentle swell of her stomach beneath the cotton shirt, the questions in his mind clamoring for answers. He found her watching him as well, her brown eyes narrowed, her face, as expressive as always, mirroring her sadness. With a jolt that knotted his insides, he realized his own emotions, usually so carefully concealed, were plain to see.

"Carrie," he said helplessly, damning himself for hurting her.

"I can't change the way I am. I can't change what's happened to me in the past any more than you can." There were tears in her whisper but none in her eyes.

"I'd be the last person on earth who deserved to ask that of you." He took her hand and helped her from the boat almost roughly. He let her go just as abruptly and started up the slope without waiting to see if she followed.

WHAT WAS THERE IN THIS man's past that had scarred him so? Why wouldn't he tell her what it was? Carrie picked raspberries absently, dropping them into the plastic bucket Micah had provided for her, without really thinking about the task. Looking down, she was surprised to find it was half-full. Her heart and mind had been so centered on the short, charged exchange with Micah on the beach that she hadn't noticed, until now, how much time had passed. The sun had moved into the western sky. A late afternoon breeze had sprung up to sift through the pine needles with inquisitive fingers.

She glanced at Micah. His bucket was almost full of berries. He was crouched beside a low-growing cane a few yards away. His big scarred fingers were stained dark red with berry juice. So were her own. Could she tell him about Evan? Did he care enough to want to know her story? Surely she wasn't wrong in thinking that someone who had been hurt as badly as Micah in the past would understand at least some of her pain and betrayal?

"Micah?" He looked up slowly. There was no light in his blue-gray eyes, no expression on his hard, angled features.

"Tired?" he asked, as though to forestall what she might say.

"I think we have enough." She straightened from her kneeling position and couldn't hide a gasp of pain as a red-hot streak of fire raced across the knotted muscles of her neck and shoulders. She felt a little dizzy, too, from moving too quickly, but attempted not to let that discomfort show as well. Micah was beside her in an instant, urging her into the shade of a stunted maple a few feet away, taking her pail, settling her with rough, absent courtesy against the trunk.

"I'll get you a drink of water. There's a spring on the island pure enough to drink from." His expression was grave.

"I don't need water." Carrie took a deep breath. "And I don't need you to feel responsible for me." She'd always been a fighter. She wasn't going to back away from a challenge now. She reached out and caught his hand between her own, holding him in a crouch beside her. "I want to talk. I've seen you looking at me," she gestured helplessly down at her stomach.

"I told you before, you don't owe me any explanations." He looked wary, trapped, she realized with a small painful dart of recognition. He didn't want to be shaken out of his comfortable, emotionless void by her revelations.

"I think you do deserve some explanation. I think I've owed you that since... since you kissed me in the woods." She finished the sentence in a rush. Making contact, intimate and personal, with Micah McKendrick was proving the greatest challenge she'd ever faced. To her amazement he smiled slightly.

"Do you think about that kiss as often as I do?"

"Yes." She blurted out the word, then pulled her lower lip between her teeth.

"I thought so." He shook his head, his expression still carefully neutral.

"You must wonder why I've never mentioned the baby's father." She spoke again before she could lose her courage.

"Carrie." His tone was as daunting as his sudden frown. Obviously he regretted his momentary show of feeling and hoped to silence her.

"He's a married man." She lifted her chin and stared straight ahead. Sobs threatened to choke her words. "I fell in love with a married man. He let me love him and never planned on telling me he had lied." *Micah hated tears, she remembered, so she wouldn't cry.* "I hate him for what he did to me. And for weeks because of that I hated my baby, too. That's something I'll never forgive him for as long as I live." She did cry then, though she tried not to. "I hate him. I never want him to have anything to do with my baby." That was the most hurting truth of all. That was what left her feeling cold and bereft. She, who had no family, no blood family of her own, would now be passing the same emptiness that was always there at the center of her spirit on to her child."

"That might not be possible."

"I'll make it possible," she said, and her voice carried a hint of steel beneath the tears. "Evan didn't care about me. He won't care about the baby."

"Are you altogether certain of that?" He didn't want to hurt her but hiding from the truth wouldn't help.

"What do you mean?" She looked down at her hands, unwilling to meet his eyes.

"I know he writes you. I've seen the envelopes forwarded from your parents. What's he asking you for, Carrie?"

"To consider the child's future. He doesn't want him to be raised by a single mother. I won't give him up." She started crying in earnest then.

Micah watched her cry and felt a stabbing, unwelcome pain deep inside. After a few moments he gathered her into his arms, holding her stiffly, reluctantly. He settled himself against the tree trunk, torn between having her in his arms again and the instinctive need he had to protect himself from the emotions she brought to life inside him. Her distress tore at him, ate at his defenses. He knew there was more to her story than she had revealed. If the man who had betrayed her love had been within his reach at that moment, he would have torn him to pieces and never regretted the loss of control.

Her tears were wetting his shirt. Her hair smelled of sunshine and her lips were stained garnet red with berry juice. The scent of pine needles rose around them and the wind murmured in the trees. She felt good in his arms. He pulled her closer, ignoring the frantic prompting of his battered heart.

"I'm sorry," she said after another minute or two of weeping. "I despise crying women." She tried to sit up but Micah held her head against his shoulder.

"Be still," he said gruffly. "Go ahead. Get it out of your system."

"I was a fool." Her hand clenched into a fist against the buttons of his shirt.

He didn't argue with her. "If you were, does that mean you have to spend the rest of your life regretting one mistake of the heart?"

Carrie sniffed, then took a deep breath. "The consequences of my actions will always be with me."

"Yes." There was no denying that.

"You know that because it's happened to you, too, hasn't it—learning to live with something you can't change?"

"Yes." He looked out over the lake. "But you'll have a child to love. That's a blessing denied to many."

She'd been plucking absently at one of his buttons. Her fingers stilled. "Rachel?" she asked very softly.

He nodded.

"I have been thinking about her . . . and her baby. Often." Carrie sat up. He didn't try to hold her any longer. He let his hands drop to his sides. She brushed at her eyes with her fingertips. Tears sparkled like crystal drops on her cheeks. She wiped them away. "My baby will be born strong and healthy. I'll do everything I can to make him happy. I'll come to terms with Evan and what part he'll play in the baby's life . . . someday." She smiled slightly. "I am lucky."

"But it doesn't make the pain stop, does it?"

"No." She was looking at him. He could feel her eyes on his face but he didn't turn his head to meet her gaze.

"Living with regret is sometimes part of life, as you just said."

"Overcoming it is, too, I think," she said softly, consideringly. "I wouldn't want to believe that I'd lost my only chance at love because I once loved unwisely."

There was great strength of spirit within her, Micah realized. For a woman like Carrie, learning to love again would not be hard. But for others, like himself, it was impossible. "Some things are given to us only once." He couldn't keep the bitterness from seeping into his voice. She heard it. Her delicately arched brows drew together in a frown.

"We can all be lucky enough to love a second time."

"Perhaps." He shrugged, regretting the conversation, regretting that he'd allowed himself to be drawn into revealing a part of himself he'd kept hidden for so long. He also regretted that Carrie was no longer nestled in his arms. She sat back on her heels, regarding him from solemn fawn-brown eyes.

"What happened to you, Micah?"

"It doesn't matter." He pulled one knee up as if to rise. She leaned forward and put her hands on his shoulders, stopping him.

"Yes, it does matter. It matters very much. You listened to my sorrows, let me hear yours."

He shook his head. "What matters now is you."

"Tell me."

"The war happened to me," he said gruffly, "just like half a million other guys." She was very close. Her lips were only inches from his. *He would not kiss her.* Micah balled his hands into fists. Already his body was betraying him, making him aware of its demands, the denial of years, the desirability of the woman beside him.

Carrie took the decision out of his hands. With a little sigh she lowered her head and kissed him. Her mouth was awkward at first, as though she wasn't experienced in taking the initiative in lovemaking. But as their lips touched and held and warmed from the contact she grew more assured. She reached out, put her arms around his neck, rested the soft fullness of her breasts against his chest. Micah groaned and the sound came from the very bottom of his lonely soul. He threaded his fingers through the silkiness of her hair. Her mouth flowered open beneath his and he drank deeply of her sweetness.

Later he was never sure which of them moved first, but before he knew it she was beneath him. He rested his weight on his elbows, cradling her head in his hands. Their kiss deepened and blood pounded in his ears. He tasted her lips, the velvet skin of her cheekbones, the creaminess of her throat. He wanted more of her, all of her, and knew it could never be.

"Micah." He stared down into her passion-bright eyes and felt a cold hand grip his heart. He knew what she was going to say. If it cost him what little humanity he still possessed, he could not let her say the words.

"Don't." Her eyes widened in confusion at his gruff command. "Don't say anything, do you hear? It's a classic case of rebound. You'll get over it." He had talked too much already, listened too much, felt too much. It had to end now.

"No." She shook her head. "I know my own mind, Micah McKendrick." She didn't sound completely convinced, however. He took advantage of the slight hesitation and drove home his point.

"We're both alone. We're both lonely." He bit the word off, shut his mouth with a snap.

She reached up to touch the line of his jaw beneath his beard. He knew she felt the tension there, and in the rest of his body, as well. She began, "I think I'm falling..." He jerked his head away from the sweet torture of her stroking fingers.

"No."

"Yes." She smiled and he felt more of his hard-won detachment erode from within. Micah hardened his heart and ignored the wonder shining softly from her eyes.

"You might think you're falling in love with me," he said harshly. "I know I'm not in love with you." He levered himself up, pulling her with him to her feet. He made his voice hard, his attitude uncompromising.

She smiled again but this time it was in confusion. "I can wait—"

He cut her off. "Can you?" He looked pointedly at her stomach. Carrie stiffened.

"I see."

This time she didn't cry. Her pride wouldn't let her. Micah ran his hand through his hair. "You don't see anything, Carrie, but I'm not going to explain it to you."

She shook her head, ignoring his words. "You don't have to. I won't pry anymore. I won't try to learn who you are and what you're feeling ever again." She stooped over and picked up her bucket.

"Carrie..." *God, what did he say now?*

"Look, I made a fool of myself. Again. Do me the favor of forgetting all about it. Please." This time she did sound as if she might cry again. "Let's just blame it on some kind of... hormone surge or something." She laughed but it was thin and shaky. "Sometimes pregnant women do strange things." She didn't smile, just looked straight ahead. "You're right. I'm tired. I want to go home." She started walking toward the stretch of shoreline where he'd beached the canoe.

Micah watched her walk away. His hands curled into fists at his side. He set his jaw against an overwhelming urge to call her back. He'd gotten the reaction he wanted from her but he wasn't proud of his methods. He had let her think that her baby, another man's child, kept them apart. It wasn't true, at least not anymore, but she would never know. He had protected her from the truth about himself, from the demons within him once more. He'd just never thought it would be so hard to do.

CARRIE WAVED GOODBYE as her parents' car disappeared around the first curve in the road. Her mother was still looking back, her face grave, her blue eyes clouded with worry. They hadn't wanted to leave her but she'd insisted they go. There was nothing they could do to make her next decision any easier. There was nothing anyone could do. Carrie looked down at the envelope in her hand. It was addressed to her in Evan's nearly illegible scrawl. He'd sent it to her parents with a covering letter asking them to deliver his message to her.

It was simple and direct, as straightforward as she'd always believed Evan himself to be. He and his wife wanted her baby to raise as their own. He wanted her to think of the advantages a two-parent family would bring to the child. He wanted her to know the child would be loved and cherished by both of them. He'd apologized again for hurting her. He'd also enclosed a money order for a considerable amount to help defray expenses. Carrie resisted the urge to rip it into pieces and scatter the remains to the four winds. Instead, she'd calmly put the check in an envelope and asked her parents to mail it back to Evan when they returned home. She didn't want his money. She didn't want his apologies.

She didn't want him to have her baby.

The door of the main cabin opened and Micah emerged, buttoning his shirt. He looked up and saw her standing in the driveway. His step faltered, but then he came steadily forward, his expression carefully guarded.

"Have your parents gone?" he asked, turning the cuff of his shirt above his wrist with great deliberation. His hair was still damp from his shower and drops of water sparkled among the dark waves in the first uncertain rays of morning sun.

"Yes. It's a long drive. They want to stay ahead of the traffic." Carrie looked down at the letter in her hands, unwilling to meet his eyes. Instead she watched his blunt, strong fingers and the muscles and tendons of his wrist as he began folding back the other sleeve.

"I'm sorry I missed saying goodbye." His words were stiff, formal.

"They enjoyed their visit very much." She was equally polite. "Thank you for letting them stay here."

"It was a pleasure."

Carrie twisted the letter between her hands. It was so awkward meeting him like this. It hurt so badly to feel his resistance to being near her. He was in pain and to protect himself, he'd pushed her away. She'd agonized over what had happened between them yesterday afternoon for most of the night. She thought she'd understood her own feelings and she'd been determined not to let him retreat once again into his armoring shell. At least she'd been determined on that course until an hour ago, until she'd read Evan's letter.

"I want to talk about yesterday, Micah."

"I don't think there's anything more to say."

"Yes, there is. I don't want you to feel you have to avoid me, or anything like that." She took a deep breath and hurried on. "You were right. I don't know my own mind anymore. Maybe I never did." She smoothed one hand protectively over her stomach, noticed the unconscious gesture and stopped. She laughed in confusion. It sounded troubled and uncertain, even to her own ears. Micah looked at her sharply.

"What's wrong?" he demanded. For a moment he looked anything but detached and unconcerned. Carrie blinked, but the sudden darkening of his hard, angular features was gone as quickly as it had come.

"I've been doing a lot of thinking."

"What's in the letter?"

She wanted to say, nothing at all, but she was still twisting it between her hands. It was impossible to deny its importance. "It's from Evan Walsham...my baby's father." She stumbled over the words, was silent a moment, gathering her thoughts. "He wants to adopt the baby. He...and his wife. They'd give him a good home. Love him and make him happy."

"And you're considering taking the man up on his offer?" Micah spoke so harshly Carrie took a step backward.

"No!" The word exploded from her lips. "But it's made me see something about myself."

"What's that?" Micah was staring at a point just past her shoulder. Carrie didn't notice. She wasn't looking directly at him, either.

"My feelings for my baby are the only emotions I can trust at the moment. I didn't see that clearly yesterday but I think you did." She'd been so certain twenty-four hours ago that she was falling in love with him, not because it was convenient, not because he would make a wonderful father, even if he didn't realize that himself, but because he was a man she could love and honor and care for, for the rest of her life. It had seemed so simple then, a challenge, considering her condition and Micah's resistance, but not an impossible dream. Now she wasn't sure at all, of anyone or anything. She couldn't trust her feelings. She felt bereft and alone. "I hope we can still be friends."

"Friends?" His voice was gruff, the word barely audible over the sound of bird song and morning wind in the pines. Carrie wasn't certain if he was confirming or denying her request. She stared down at Evan's crumpled letter, not willing to risk his gaze. He reached out and lifted her chin with his fingers. "We're here for you. All of us."

Tears stung behind her eyelids. She blinked them back but their residue left her eyes diamond bright. "Thank you." He turned to walk away just as the sun broke free of the serrated tops of the pines. Carrie shut her eyes, dazzled by the sudden brightness. When she opened them he was gone.

She was alone. By her own choice but also by necessity. *As Micah was.* It was a frightening prospect for the future, endless days and nights of solitude, no one to share her happiness and her heartaches... except her baby. At least when he was born they'd be alone together.

CHAPTER TEN

FROM THE WINDOW OF DOC'S office where she was finishing her charting, Rachel had an unobstructed view of the mall parking lot. There were always several carloads of teenagers driving around, no matter what the weather, just as she and her friends had done twenty-five years before. It was comforting to think that some things never changed.

"What are you looking at over there, Rachel?" Doc asked, coming into the office with the latest copy of his favorite fishing magazine in his hand.

"Nothing really. Just that it's nice some things never change. Like kids and cars and trying to squeeze all the rest of the summer into Labor Day weekend."

Doc ambled over to the window and surveyed the parking lot for himself. "Looks like the Kisabeth brothers' Bronco. Wonder what kind of trouble they're stirring up."

Rachel tried to look past him without getting up from the desk. "Is Doug with them?"

"Not that I can see. But there's some guy I don't recognize. Older, scruffy-looking." Doc lost interest in the scene and turned away from the window. "Glad to hear that nephew of Micah's has better things to do than pick up on that crew's bad habits."

"He's been spending most of his time with Micah," Rachel explained, as she bent her head over the charts. "Between the chicks hatching and the eagle to take care of, he hasn't had a lot of free time." Doc was one of the few outsiders to know of the peregrine chicks' arrival. He'd also been by to have a look at the young bald eagle, almost dead from a gunshot wound, that Micah and Doug had been caring for for the past few weeks after it had been found by a couple of backpackers. Everyone had been drafted for duty, taking turns feeding the voracious new chicks, helping Micah change the poulticelike dressing on the infected wound beneath the eagle's wing and coaxing her to eat slivers of meat impregnated with antibiotics. The summer had gone by very quickly.

"Says here in this article that the fall coho run is going to be big this year. Think I'll take a couple of days off week after next and go fishing."

Rachel punched up the appointment schedule on the computer screen. "Tuesday is just about full that week but Wednesday morning and Thursday we could rearrange, if you like."

"Why don't you do that. I'll ask Dr. Feeney to cover for me at the hospital. I could use a break." Doc grabbed his sweater off a hook on the wall, rolled his magazine into a cylinder and stuffed it into his medical bag. "I'm out of here. Don't stay too late."

"Fifteen minutes, no more," Rachel promised with a smile.

When Doc left she found herself looking out the window again at the group of young men gathered around the Bronco. Perhaps it was her own unsettled mood that made the Kisabeth brothers' companion

seem so sinister. The man seemed to be in charge of
their discussion. He looked tough and unscrupulous,
the kind of man that always sent her pulses racing in
remembered fear. A sheriff's deputy cruised through
the parking lot on a routine patrol and paid them no
attention at all, so maybe it was only her own uncer-
tainties that made the gathering suspicious.

Coming here last winter had seemed the right thing
to do. She'd been healed in body and partially in spirit
by the quiet serenity of Micah's wilderness home. But
now the restless, aching emptiness inside her was back.
She was torn between wanting to see Carrie and Micah together and the cowardly desire to have the
younger woman gone from her life.

If Carrie stayed, if her baby was born here, in Marquette, how could she bear to see it, touch it, hold it
and not give in to the dark grief for her own dead child
that lay buried in her heart? How could she ever lay
the past to rest?

CARRIE STOOD IN THE DOORWAY leading to the big
flight cages and watched the activity going on outside. The peregrine chicks and their red-tail surrogate
parents were being moved from smaller inside cages to
the roomy open ones. They would stay there, Micah
explained to her, until the first hard snows of winter.
Then they would come back inside until spring when
they would be released into their cliff-side homes in the
wild.

"The young'uns'll keep you company, boss," Reuben had chuckled one day, "when I migrate down to
Ann Arbor for the winter quarter. You ought to have
some real interesting conversations with 'em come the

last of February or thereabouts.'' His little joke hadn't struck Carrie as very funny. She didn't want to think of Micah alone again. Of course Rachel would be with him, but that knowledge didn't make Carrie feel any better.

By the end of February she would be long gone from his life. Or she ought to be. It was September. By rights, her work here should be done. In eight weeks' time...or less...her baby would be born. Her parents were expecting her back in Ohio. It had never been her plan to stay in the UP this long. She had no future here. Not even if she yearned for one more than anything else in the world.

"Hold still, boy. Hold still." Doug maneuvered one of the half-grown chicks into its new cage. The young falcon's white baby down was almost gone. In its place the beautiful slate-blue adult feathers, as yet more brown than gray-toned, were beginning to appear. Doug's movements were deliberate and precise. He had a way with birds, Carrie had come to realize. He was good with them. He was oblivious to her presence in the doorway, or seemingly, to Micah, who stood a few feet behind him with another one of the chicks. The teenager chewed on his lower lip, his expression intent as he worked to transfer the bird with as little human contact as possible.

"Take your time," Micah cautioned, moving inside the cage with his own hooded chick. As always when working with his birds, Micah showed the softness and caring he kept so well hidden at other times. "Handle them slow and easy. Talk to them. It helps."

Doug nodded in wordless reply as he knelt to remove the cloth hood from the chick's eyes. Immediately the youngster flapped its way across the cage, blinking in the bright sunlight, regal and proud, the falcon of kings. Until it tried to hop up onto a low perch and overshot its mark, landing on the other side with an indignant and surprised squawk. Micah's chick took up the raucous cry. The blinded osprey screamed in annoyance. Doug laughed out loud, as did Micah.

The sound went straight to Carrie's heart and lodged there like a small, warm ember. This is how she knew he could be, how she wanted him to be. The pleasure was bittersweet. To be so near him physically and yet so distant emotionally was proving to be very difficult. He had been her friend, as he'd promised that morning almost two months before, but that was all. It was she who had set the boundaries for their relationship in the first confused moments after she'd read Evan's letter detailing his wishes for their child's future, so she couldn't complain.

Evan. His image had taken on nightmare proportions in her dreams. Thoughts of him shadowed her days and ruined her sleep. He...and his wife...could offer the child so much more than she. At least material things. She could offer him love and constancy, that was all. Was it enough?

"That's all of them. Safe and sound." Doug shut the cage door and surveyed the three cages, each holding two healthy chicks and their red-tail parent. He looked proud and satisfied. "Time to feed Igor," he announced.

"Igor is a ridiculous name for a bald eagle." Carrie stepped into the covered walkway between the cages.

Arguing over the injured eagle's name was a running joke between the two of them.

"Hey—" Doug spread his hands wide "—what can I say? The bird looks like an Igor. And the cold war's over, right? You know, Gorbachev and *glasnost* and all that stuff." He reached up onto a shelf attached to the outside of the eagle's cage, recently vacated by the goshawk, who'd been released back into the wild a week or two before, and pulled down a long leather falconer's glove. "Time for supper, pretty lady."

"It's sexist," Carrie insisted, laughing. "Micah says the bird's a female."

"So? Maybe you're being sexist. Maybe eagles think Igor *is* a girl's name." He shot Carrie a quick, teasing look, then opened the cage and walked slowly, deliberately inside. Because the young eagle had been so ill for so many days, it had lost its fear of humans. It sat quietly on its perch, leather jesses dangling from its talons, while Doug coaxed it onto his gloved forearm. "Time to eat, gorgeous."

Carrie smiled and shook her head, acknowledging his point. Something had changed the boy. She couldn't pinpoint the exact day or time it had happened. Doug hadn't confided in her, but his whole attitude had undergone a transformation. He'd spent hours working with Micah, feeding and caring for the peregrine chicks. He'd spent even more time with the wounded eagle. It was almost as if he felt personally responsible for the bird's recovery.

"The baby books all say giving a child an unsuitable name may cause gender confusion later on." Carrie patted her stomach. She still wasn't so big she couldn't tie her own shoelaces, but she could no longer see her toes without bending forward. "I've been reading about this kind of thing a lot lately." She tried very hard to sound serious. She'd come to the conclusion that while the baby guides were interesting reading, common sense was going to be the best tool she could use in raising a baby.

Doug shot her a scathing look.

"No problem there." Micah added his two cents' worth. "The bird's already madly in love with him." He glanced at Doug to gauge his reaction to the taunt as he secured the cage door on the last set of peregrine chicks.

"Yeah," Doug said proudly, ignoring the gibe. He held the young eagle at arm's length. "She's my best girl." The bird cocked her head and regarded him fixedly from brilliant yellow eyes.

"She has been very ill," Carrie reminded him facetiously. "She's probably fallen in love with her nurse. It happens a lot, I understand." She was surprised when Doug answered seriously.

"I know."

Carrie couldn't stop herself from glancing at Micah. He was watching the boy but lifted his eyes to meet hers. There was concern and puzzlement in his gaze.

"Time for some exercise, beautiful," Doug crooned, oblivious to Micah's and Carrie's wordless exchange.

"We got to get that boy a real gal of his own," Reuben called laughingly from the doorway of the lab building. Micah looked past Carrie's beautiful, concerned face toward his friend. "I wondered where everyone was at. Got the little'uns squared away in their new digs?'' He surveyed the flight cages with an expert's eye.

''All present and accounted for.'' Micah gestured Doug to lead the way, with the eagle riding easily on his arm. Doug had rarely left the bird's side while fever from the gunshot wound had raged through its body. Later, he'd worked diligently at its rehabilitation. They'd tag her before she was returned to the wild. Doug had already started a file on her. He knew it wasn't a good idea, not sound practice, to let the boy get so attached. But he'd ignored his years of experience to let his heart rule his head. He hoped he wouldn't regret it.

Sometime before the weather turned cold and winter set in, the eagle would be freed, its familiarity with humans forgotten, erased by careful retraining. But long before that time Doug would have returned to his family and his interrupted education. Annie and Simon would be arriving in a few days to take Doug back to Chicago to enroll him in a private school that promised to catch him up on his studies so that he could graduate with his class in the spring.

Micah wasn't sure why or how the change in Doug's attitude had come about. He certainly wasn't about to take any of the credit for himself. There was nothing specific, no one conversation that seemed to have been the turning point, but they had found common ground in their commitment to the eagle's recovery. And Doug had listened when he talked. Then one day when his mother called, Doug had simply announced he was ready to go home.

''Just got off the phone with the governor's office.'' Reuben stepped back out of the doorway so that

Carrie could pass. He smiled down at her and she smiled back. Micah felt a familiar stinging ache in his heart that the smile wasn't meant for him.

"Dammit, not this soon." He took his frustration out on the only thing he could—publicity-hungry bureaucrats in far-off Lansing.

Reuben continued talking, unperturbed by his outburst. "They want to know how long before you're gonna let them start ballyhooin' the chicks."

"The last thing we need out here is a batch of reporters and TV people. For Rachel's sake, as well as the chicks."

"That's what I figured you'd say." Reuben chuckled, hooking his thumbs in the belt loops of his jeans. "I put 'em off. Told 'em you were off in the boonies for a few days. Wouldn't be back till Monday at the earliest."

"Good." Micah pushed his hips back against the stainless-steel counter. Carrie was looking at one of the observation charts on the chicks. It was almost complete, ready for her to transfer onto the computer. He wondered how much longer she would stay with them. Her time was getting closer. The scowl on his face, put there by Reuben's report on the governor's phone call, deepened. *Lord, he didn't want her to go.* Yet he didn't know how much longer he could stand having her so close, and yet so distant. He folded his arms across his chest.

"What you got in mind, boss?" Reuben ran his hand through his ginger hair.

"Nothing, yet. But I am going out in the field." He looked down, rubbed his hand across his chin, then looked up again. "Doug." He hesitated a fraction of a second too long to sound natural. "Carrie. I've been wondering if you two would like to go with us tomorrow, check out a nest we spotted from the air a couple of days ago and get the hacking box ready for Igor, here." He avoided Reuben's interested gaze. "It's a two-day job, but if we split up, two of us scout the nest and two of us set the box, we can be there and back in a day's time."

"I thought you'd already checked all the nests." Carrie sounded wary, unsure of his motives in asking her along on the expedition. He couldn't blame her; he wasn't sure himself what he wanted from her.

"This one's been deserted for the last three seasons. Now there seems to be a pair of eagles in residence. No chick hatched that we could see." He glanced at Reuben for confirmation, watched him nod briefly in agreement. "I think it's worth checking out."

"The trees that close to the big lake are startin' to turn color. If you take the canoe up the Little Fawn River it ought to be a real pretty trip." Reuben was still watching him. Micah stared past him. His heart was beating like a drum in his chest. One last day with her, that was all he asked.

"Where will you release the eagle?"

Reuben answered Carrie's question before Micah could. "Up along the Pictured Rocks. Way past where the tourists' boats go. It's a tough march, uphill half the way. Best I take Doug and the Jeep for that job."

"Oh." She looked at him once more, still unsure. Micah held his breath. She'd been getting letters from the baby's father, forwarded by her parents. She was upset and confused by them, he knew that without her telling him. She was going soon. He couldn't stop her. He wouldn't stop her. But he wasn't strong enough to deny himself the need to have her close while he could.

"A canoe trip. I'd like that," she said, turning back to the chart.

"Me, too." Doug's response was more enthusiastic. The eagle seemed to have caught the excitement in his voice. She rose up, beating her wings, anxious to be outside exercising cramped muscles, eager to fly. "How early will we be leaving tomorrow? I . . . I have to go into town for a while tonight. Carrie said I could borrow her car." He smiled at her. She looked up from the chart once again and smiled back.

"Jeep leaves at six."

Doug groaned. "I'll be home early then. There's someone . . . someone I have to say goodbye to."

DOUG DROVE CARRIE'S small hatchback into the gas station where Willie Jenks worked. The sun was low on the horizon. It tinted the plate-glass windows of the building blood red. Doug had noticed it was getting dark earlier now that it was September. Summer had ended quickly this far north. The tourists were gone. The "color tours" hadn't really gotten started yet. It made the town seem kind of sad and lonely.

The self-serve pumps were empty. Willie was inside the garage by himself, as far as Doug could tell. He was glad to see the Kisabeth brothers' Bronco was nowhere in sight. He figured Willie had already guessed he had decided to go back home, finish school. He figured Willie probably knew he'd made up his mind after Lance shot the eagle. He thought Willie wanted out, too, but he wasn't sure.

Doug swiveled his shoulders and pulled the collar of his jacket up around his ears. He shoved his hands in his pockets and pushed open the door with his hip. A buzzer sounded somewhere in the back. Willie looked up from under the hood of an old Chevy that he was working on.

"Hey man, long time no see." Willie wiped his hand on a rag he pulled from the back pocket of his dirty blue coverall and stuck it out.

Doug grabbed it between both of his. "Yeah. Long time, man. How've you been?"

"Okay." Willie didn't meet his eyes directly but looked just past his ear.

"Looks like a real good place to work." Doug couldn't think of anything else to say. It was dark and dirty and smelled like old tires and motor oil.

"It's okay." Willie shrugged. "My mom's glad to see me working again." He gestured toward the Chevy. "I have to get this heap out of here by nine."

"Sure thing." Doug looked down at the floor. He scuffed the toe of his high top in a pile of sawdust someone had dumped on some spilled oil.

"You haven't been around much lately." Willie's voice was muffled as he bent over the hood.

"I've been busy."

"Yeah." Willie didn't ask for any more details. "Hand me that wrench on the workbench, will you, eh?"

"Sure." Doug slapped the wrench into his outstretched hand.

"I came to say goodbye." He hadn't meant to blurt it out like that, but he did.

Willie straightened up, turned around and stared at him. "You goin' back to school, eh?"

Doug nodded. "My mom and Simon are coming up to get me next week."

"Hank and Leon'll be back by then," Willie said cryptically.

"Where are they?" Doug felt his guts begin to knot up. Hank and Leon knew that the eagle had been found near Kennedy Lake. The game warden had filed a report with the sheriff's office when it was brought in by the backpackers. The guys had heard about it on the TV news one night, Doug guessed, just like the rest of the UP. The reporter hadn't mentioned Micah by name but everyone around Marquette knew the "eagle man." Even a couple of dorks like Hank and Leon would guess where the bird had been taken.

"They're in Milwaukee. Lance went with them. They took a load of venison down to one of their clients. Rush order, I guess."

"You been going out with them?" He couldn't call what they did hunting. It was poaching and it was a crime.

"No more'n I have to." Willie rested his hand on the hood of the car and peered into the engine. Doug didn't think he saw anything but his own thoughts.

"Why you telling me this, Willie?" They'd talked three or four times since the Fourth of July but never about the gang's illegal activities. Doug liked Willie. He'd hoped he'd break off with the Kisabeths once he got another job, but he hadn't. He was still making only minimum wage, still working only part-time. He needed the meat and the extra cash he got from poaching deer to help his family.

"Lance. He's gettin' big ideas." Willie turned the wrench over and over in his hands. He kept his back to Doug, bending over the innards of the Chevy once more.

"What kind of big ideas, Willie?" Doug grabbed his friend's arm, made him straighten up, made him look him in the eye.

"There's this guy in Detroit he knows. This guy's got connections."

"Get to the point." Doug was surprised by the menace in his voice.

"He knows a real rich dude. A collector."

"A collector?" Doug had an idea he knew what Willie was going to say next and he didn't want to hear it. "What kind of collector?"

"The dude's a bird collector. Lance says he'll pay big money for an eagle. Dead or alive."

"Dead or alive?" Doug shut his mouth. He was beginning to sound like a parrot repeating everything Willie said. He'd kept quiet so far about the wounded eagle because he thought it was an accident. Now he wasn't so sure.

"I ain't saying nothing else." Willie looked stubborn, sullen and scared. "I told you more'n I should have already."

"Yeah, man. I know." Doug turned, his thoughts in a whirl. "I gotta go, man." He stopped, and walked back to where Willie was leaning against the fender of the Chevy. A car pulled up to the full-service pump.

"Yeah." Willie smiled, but it never got as far as his eyes. For a moment Doug saw what he would look like in twenty years, old and tired and defeated. "I know you gotta go."

"I won't rat on you, Willie."

"I know you won't. I can't do nothing to stop them. Hank and Leon won't take the fall alone. The law's catchin' on to us. The only one smart enough to get away with it much longer is Lance. Get out of here while the gettin's good."

"Thanks." Doug stuck out his hand. "Thanks for warning me about the eagle."

Willie waved off the handshake. The driver at the gas pump honked impatiently. Willie started toward the door. "What eagle, eh?" he said over his shoulder. He didn't look back again.

Doug got into Carrie's car and drove out of town. He couldn't decide what to do. It was too late to back out of the trip tomorrow. If he had any hope of saving the eagle he needed a safe place to take her. He'd have to go with Reuben so he'd know where that safe place was. But from then on until she was strong enough to survive on her own, he wasn't going to leave the bird out of his sight.

He wasn't sure when Hank and Leon would try to get her, or even if they would. But he couldn't take the chance of relaxing his guard. *God, how was he going to tell his mom and Simon that he wasn't going back home with them?* That he wasn't going back to school. If he told them the truth he wouldn't be going home anyway. He'd be going to jail. This was the worst mess he'd ever been in. He didn't know what to do next.

The only thing he did know for sure was that he couldn't leave this place until Igor was safely gone. It didn't matter about Willie, or that his own hide was on the line. What mattered was the eagle. And even more than the eagle, the peregrine chicks. If some crazy collector in Detroit or Milwaukee or wherever was willing to pay big bucks for an eagle, just what would he consider six peregrine falcons to be worth?

CHAPTER ELEVEN

THE LITTLE FAWN RIVER was as beautiful as its name, the waters stained the same blue-brown as the waters of Blueberry Lake. The banks were steep, covered with yellow-green and brown ferns, already dead from the first hard frost two nights before. The growing season was short this far north. These were the same ferns that had sheltered the tiny fawn not so many weeks ago when they were soft and newly green. Summer was over. Carrie had no reason to stay and many to go. Her time with Micah could be measured in hours and days. Her time alone would be measured in years and decades.

The current was swift. Carrie's neck and shoulders ached from working to keep the lightweight aluminum canoe on course. Most of the effort was Micah's, but the twisting course of the river and the number of snags and submerged rocks made teamwork essential and for the most part were a welcome diversion from her unhappy thoughts.

It was the middle of the afternoon before the river widened out and began to flow more smoothly. The sun had disappeared beneath a bank of low-lying clouds and taken most of the beauty of the early fall day with it. Rain seemed inevitable. She could smell it on the wind. Micah had been silent for the past hour, ever since he'd climbed down from the newly reoccupied nest he'd inspected to report two unhatched eggs and no sighting of the parent birds.

"The shells were too thin to support the weight of the adult," he'd explained, his voice still ragged and breathless from the climb.

"What causes the condition?" Carrie couldn't bear to look as he carefully packed the pitifully small remains away in his pack for further study.

"Pesticides."

"I . . . I thought that problem was corrected." She sounded naive and knew it, but she wanted information.

"Not by a long shot." Micah shoved his climbing irons, belt and ropes into a canvas tote that had seen better days and started walking. "Sure, it's better than it was in the sixties. DDT and the other hard pesticides are gone. At least in the States and Canada. But there are plenty of compounds out there that can still cause problems and countries all over the Third World that are still using the banned ones."

"Do you believe this pair of birds wintered someplace where their food supply was contaminated?" Her voice was breathless from hurrying to keep pace with his long stride. Luckily it was only a short hike back to the boat. They'd been talking as they walked. Carrie watched now as Micah shoved the canvas tote under the back seat of the canoe, then realigned two other waterproof packs amidships. One held food, the remains of lunch they'd shared on a sun-warmed sandbar in the middle of the river, the other, emergency supplies. Even though they expected Reuben and Doug to meet them at the rendezvous point in less than two hours, Micah had come prepared for any eventuality.

"That's my best guess," he said, standing to help her into the boat. "At least until we can analyze the remains of the embryos and the shells themselves."

"Even if the parent birds are two of yours." She lifted her hand in a helpless little gesture. "I mean two birds that you've tagged. There's no way you'll ever know for sure what caused this, is there?" Carrie sat down while Micah steadied the canoe.

"And there never will be unless they die in their wintering grounds and the tags are returned to me. The odds of that are about one in a million. Provided, of course, they are tagged birds in the first place." He settled himself in the back seat and pushed off from the bank with the end of his paddle. "And maybe I'm guessing wrong. Maybe it was an infection in the mother bird, or some new problem we haven't identified as yet. It's a damned frustrating job sometimes."

"And very rewarding at others." She was thinking of Igor and the six healthy peregrine chicks. She looked at him over her shoulder, challenging, caring, refusing to let him wallow in self-pity. *Who would do that for him, take him out of himself, when she was gone?* she thought with a sudden painful clenching of her heart. Could Rachel, who had very real problems and concerns of her own, also be responsible for her brother's happiness?

He smiled back, although reluctantly. "Now and then."

"I thought so." Carrie turned back to her paddling, satisfaction smooth as honey in her voice. In the past, he might even have ignored her questions altogether. He would certainly never have allowed her to see his frustration and disappointment, never admitted that her opinions mattered to him and made a difference in what he thought and felt. Small victories, perhaps, but every one was precious to her.

By the time they reached the pickup point, a small public campground where the river forked just before it emptied into Lake Superior, it had begun to rain, a slow, steady drizzle that was cold and wetting, and Carrie's mood had turned as somber as the sky.

Micah unloaded the canoe, pulled two waterproof ponchos out of the emergency pack and gave her one. "Put it on," he advised gruffly. "I don't know how long we'll have to wait for Doug and Reuben. They're late."

She sat huddled under a pine tree and shivered each time a stray raindrop found its way through the dense needles to drop on the hood of her poncho. She pulled her knees up, braced her elbows on them and rested her chin on her hands. She listened to the silence around her. Most of the songbirds had headed south for the winter. Only the rain and the wind in the trees competed with the low, murmuring roar of Superior's waves from beyond the narrow barrier beach that separated the river from the lake. She wanted to remember every minute of this day and carry its bittersweet memories in her heart all the rest of her life. Because memories of Micah were all she'd ever have of him.

"Carrie?" His voice was soft and very close. She looked up to find him kneeling by her side. It had grown darker while she was lost in her thoughts. She could barely see his face. "They're not coming. We're going to have to make plans for sheltering here to-night."

"Not coming?" Carrie's brain felt like a chunk of wood in her head. She tried to focus on his first words. "How do you know they're not coming?"

"Because that's my rule. It has been since our second season up here when Reuben and I and that damned Jeep nearly got swept away in a washout one night trying to make it home. From then on, separate or together, we stay put if we're caught on unfamiliar ground at full dark."

"Do you think they've had an accident?"

"More likely the Jeep broke down on them. She's way past due for an overhaul." Carrie searched his dark face for any sign he wasn't being entirely truthful with her. He endured her scrutiny with patience. She nodded, satisfied.

"The Jeep has been running pretty rough lately. I heard Reuben complaining about her just the other day."

Micah raked his hand through his hair, glistening with raindrops because he'd pushed his hood back out of his way some time before. "Hell, she's not only past due for an overhaul, she's past due for the junk-yard." His eyes were hidden by the shifting shadows under the pine but his voice was warm and bracing, with none of its usual habitual flatness of tone. "Reuben knows what he's doing."

"But Doug isn't an experienced hiker, or climber...." Carrie couldn't shake the anxious feeling that was snaking around inside her. She wanted reassurance.

"Reuben doesn't take stupid chances. They're fine. Probably in better shape than we are." He was thinner than he'd been in the spring, Carrie noticed when he frowned. He looked tired, tightly drawn. Micah didn't take stupid chances either, but he'd been hurt once already this season. Briefly she closed her eyes, seeing him again as he worked his way up the dead tree to the eagle's nest. Today had been the first time she'd seen him climb...and it would be the last, she realized with another painful jolt. His movements had been unhurried, graceful, but she'd seen the strain of muscles and tendons beneath the thin cotton of his shirt and knew that the amount of strength and agility it took to make the climb were formidable. "Trust me," he said, laying his hand on hers for the space of a heartbeat. "I know what I'm talking about."

There was no arguing with the certainty in his tone. She accepted his assurance that the others were well with a smile and a nod. "What about us?" she asked, looking around at the small campground. The trash cans were empty but she didn't think that would stop a hungry bear from checking them out. "Are we staying here? What if a bear comes?" She sounded like a lost child, even to her own ears, but she couldn't seem to help herself.

"We're not going to stay here. It looks like this drizzle is going to keep up most of the night. Even if it stops raining the fog will most likely set in." He tilted his head to watch her more closely. "Are you afraid of ghosts?"

"Ghosts?" Carrie felt a little trickle of superstitious fear run down her spine. "A little," she admitted.

Micah smiled at her honest response. "This ghost is harmless. There's only one place anywhere near here with a roof on it. At least, the last time I was up here it still had a roof." He frowned, looking past her, across the narrow fork of the river that snaked off into the trees. "About a mile down the beach is an old lifesaving station. It's been deserted for over sixty years. Most of the campers and backpackers never see it because the river is too wide and deep for a casual hiker to ford. We'll cross here, in the canoe, leave it on the other side and hike in. Can you make it?"

"I can make it. But whose ghost is it?" He held out his hands and she let him help her to her feet. She tried to keep the subject on the supernatural because she didn't want to tell him she was almost too tired to make the trek over the rough, rock-strewn sand to the dubious shelter he described.

"Supposedly it's one of the keepers of the light-house I pointed out up on the bluff. He committed suicide." His voice tightened and Carrie glanced quickly in his direction. His face was bleak, the mask of non-emotion firmly in place. "Years later people started claiming to have seen him walking along the beach when they were out here fishing or looking for agates. Now it's sort of a local legend that he walks the beach below the lighthouse as far as the old station and back again when the weather's unsettled."

"Is it going to storm tonight?" She looked up at the darkening sky. It wasn't quite as dark away from the shade of the big pines that dotted the campground. On the beach it would be lighter still.

"No."

"Then I guess I won't be any more frightened of him than he will be of me. I imagine it might be a real shock for a hundred-year-old ghost to run into a very pregnant woman crashing around in the dark, looking for a convenient . . . bush." She felt the color rush to her cheeks and laughed to hide her sudden embarrassment, but she also heard the ragged edge of fatigue in her voice and so did Micah.

"I'm sorry to—" he began, but she cut him off.

"I admit, I'm partial to electricity, central heating and indoor plumbing but I can live without them. For one night, anyway."

Micah reloaded the boat. They pushed off and angled across the river, finding a place to beach the canoe where the trees thinned out along the high edge of the beach. Carrie took the pack with the remains of their lunch and the boat cushions that doubled as life preservers. Micah took the heavier emergency pack and the flashlight. They walked side by side, not touching but close. Carrie tried to concentrate on her footing and not Micah's nearness. She still felt vaguely uneasy, unsettled, not because she might meet with the harmless ghost of some poor lost soul, but because she would be spending a long, dark night with the flesh-and-blood man by her side.

CARRIE LEANED BACK AGAINST the wall of the small, windowless outbuilding where they were sheltering. Her face appeared pale and drawn in the fitful glow of the small fire he'd kindled in a pit in the sand floor. Micah felt like kicking himself for subjecting her to the discomforts of a night in the open. It had occurred to him that something might go wrong with his plans for the day—he'd lived in the wilderness too long not to be always aware of its dangers—but he'd dismissed the possibility in his eagerness to be with Carrie alone. Now she was paying the price for his selfishness.

What if some harm came to her child? It would be his fault, as Elaine's death was his fault, because Carrie's safety and well-being were his responsibility.

"You know," she said, stretching her feet to the fire, "that freeze-dried vegetable stew was pretty good." Her tone was content, tired but satisfied. Micah looked at her again. She was arranging her rolled-up poncho as a pillow behind her back.

"The soda crackers you provided were a welcome addition to the menu." He felt some of his guilt fade away. He took a last bite of the apple, left from lunch, that he'd been eating and threw the core into the fire. It hissed and popped among the coals before darkening slowly to ash. Carrie was a strong, healthy woman. As long as he watched over her, she would be safe. He picked up the pot that had held the stew and began to scour it with sand from the floor.

"It's a carryover from three months of morning sickness. I take packets of crackers wherever I go." She tilted her head back, watching the thin line of smoke from the fire disappear through a hole in the ceiling where a stovepipe had once poked through.

"I'm glad the roof doesn't leak...much," she added, folding her hands across her stomach. She wasn't wearing her jacket and the baby moved at her touch, as though aware of the caressing gesture of her hands.

"I shouldn't have brought you along today." Micah gave the pot a last swipe with a piece of paper toweling from the lunch pack and set it aside.

"Micah, please don't spoil my adventure." There was just a hint of teasing in her voice, and something else, an emotion he didn't want to identify.

He didn't look her way again. Instead, he rummaged unnecessarily through the emergency pack. He knew its contents by heart. There were two or three more packets of freeze-dried foods, collapsible cups, instant coffee, a first-aid kit and matches and flares in a waterproof container, as well as one of those space-age blankets that folded up into the size of a paperback book. They'd need that covering tonight. It wouldn't be particularly cold, not with the cloud cover, but in the still hours before dawn, the dampness would chill to the bone.

It was a fitting penance, he supposed, as he watched Carrie idly drawing squiggly lines in the sand with the tip of her finger, spending the night so close to her, alone and undisturbed and never allowing himself to touch her, kiss her...make love to her. And all the while knowing that their first night together would be their last.

Carrie yawned. "What time is it? I forgot my watch this morning."

He glanced at his wrist. "Almost eight-thirty."

"I'm so sleepy I can barely keep my eyes open." She stifled another yawn.

"It's been a long day. If you want to make...one last comfort stop...outside, I'll fix your bed." He gestured to the flashlight and the pile of pine boughs he'd cut with the short-handled camping ax that was also part of the emergency gear.

"If I meet up with the ghost of the poor old lighthouse keeper, I'll tell him you said hello."

"I...I could go with you." Sometimes he still couldn't tell if she was joking or not. For so many years his conversation had been limited to giving and receiving information. He'd lost any skills at small talk, if he ever had them, a long time ago. "I mean..." He shut his mouth before he could make a bigger fool of himself.

Carrie laughed merrily at his discomfiture but her eyes held no malice. "Never mind. I'm perfectly capable of making the trip on my own. I'm not one of those women who's going to go around blaming men all her life because they're born with better... equipment...to handle this kind of situation."

He smiled then, too, seeing the humor in her words. She was good for him, making him laugh at himself, making him realize the weight of the world didn't rest on his shoulders alone.

She left the door of the shed open to help her find her way back in the darkness. The sudden draft of air sent the flames of the fire leaping high in its wake. His shadow danced and capered across the walls as he arranged the pine boughs to his satisfaction. He covered them with his poncho, fleece lining uppermost, and stuck one of the boat cushions underneath for Carrie's pillow. He shook out the silvery blanket and spread it over the top.

"Looks cozy," Carrie observed from the doorway. She turned to push it closed. The wood was wet and warped. He stood up quickly, ducking his head to keep from hitting the low ceiling, and moved to help her.

"Let me do that." His voice came out hoarse and sharp. Her cheeks were red from the cold. So was the tip of her nose. Her eyes sparkled in the firelight. It was all he could do not to sweep her into his arms and carry her over to the bed he'd prepared for her, following her down onto its softness, holding her in his arms as he loved her with all his heart and soul.

"Thanks." She took off her poncho and sat down on the mattress of pine boughs. She spread her hands and leaned back experimentally. "This is very comfortable." Her tone conveyed her surprise. Micah looked up from where he'd settled himself on the other boat cushion. His back was to the wall, the fire in its shallow stone-lined pit between them.

"Do you think you'll be able to get a good night's sleep?"

"Yes." She looked around the small room. "Where are you going to sleep?"

He was glad he'd taken his notebook and pencil out of his pocket moments before. It gave him something to do, something to focus on, besides how pretty and appealing she looked, sitting there with her feet curled under her, raindrops shining in her hair, damp curls escaping around her cheeks and across her forehead. "Don't worry about me. I want to get my observations on that nest down on paper while they're still fresh in my mind."

She looked at him consideringly for a long moment. "Micah, I know you might not want to share this bed with me, but at least tell me there's another one of these blanket things in that pack." A piece of half-burned driftwood collapsed in the middle of the fire as she spoke. The flames dipped low and her face was lost in shadow. Her voice was low and sad.

"There's another blanket in the pack. I'll get it for myself later," he lied. Sharing her bed was not the last thing in the world he wanted. It was the only thing. For years he'd believed if he only kept other people, other women, at bay, he could control his emotions and the darkness in himself that had so harmed Elaine. Living apart, separate, would hurt no one but himself. Now he'd met a woman that had breached all his defenses with an ease that was frightening. He knew now he could feel again, perhaps love again, but he was afraid to try. Because nothing had really changed, except his needs.

"All right." She didn't sound as if she believed him but was too tired to argue.

She turned on her side, curled into a ball. He sat quietly watching her for a long time. He knew when her breathing changed, grew lighter, more even, that she was asleep. The night lengthened and turned colder. He watched as she moved restlessly under the silvery covering. She turned on her back, her left hand outside the cover, folded protectively over her protruding stomach. Micah let the fire die, not wanting to disturb her by getting up to put another driftwood log on it. He heard her sigh and knew her dreams were troubling.

He wanted to go to her, hold her in his arms, comfort her and stop the nightmare, but he did not. He couldn't understand or categorize his own feelings. Was he in love with her? If he was, then God help them both.

He was still too afraid of the hidden, shadowy parts of himself to attempt sharing the risk of madness with a grown and caring woman like Carrie. How in the name of heaven would he ever be able to trust himself with an infant? Because he knew beyond any doubt that the man who offered his name and his heart to Carrie Granger would have to be prepared to give of himself just as freely and completely to her child.

CHAPTER TWELVE

CARRIE SAT UP AND LOOKED around her. The wetness of tears streaked her face; her heart beat slow and heavy with nameless dread. The scent of crushed pine needles, wood smoke and rain filled the darkness, anchoring her to reality with tenuous fingers. She wasn't alone, another presence shared the night, but neither was he the cause of her fear. It was the dream, not the man, that terrified her. It was the man who could comfort her.

Micah dropped a piece of driftwood on the dying fire. It was dry and seasoned and flared into brilliance almost at once. Carrie looked up to see him standing over her, looking down, watching her as she wiped tears from her cheeks. He went down on one knee beside her. "You were crying in your sleep. Was it a bad dream?"

She couldn't speak yet. Her throat was still filled with sadness. She nodded.

"Want to tell me about it?" She had never heard his voice so low and warm when he spoke to another human being, only to his birds. But now his words and his caring were for her alone. "Tell me about your dream."

"No!" She resisted the sweet urge to obey him. Her hands shook as she raised them to smooth back wisps of hair that had escaped from her braid to curl around her face. "It was too real," she whispered, trying to make him understand. "It's still too real."

Micah had reached out his hand as if to touch her. Now he drew it back, let it drop to his side. "All right. Try to go back to sleep. It's a long time until morning." The rough warmth was gone, his voice was level, controlled, giving nothing of himself away.

"Don't leave me." Carrie was beyond caring for her pride, or her heart's safety. She only knew she wanted him near, to hear him go on speaking to her in that warm, rough voice, to have him hold her close and chase away the last of the nightmare from her mind and her soul. "I don't want to be alone." She reached out to grab his hand, keep him from standing, moving away.

His hand was cold as ice. She swiveled her head, looking across the shed to the far wall where he'd been sitting when she fell asleep. There was no shiny, lightweight blanket in sight, only her poncho, lying in a heap as though it had been thrown aside in haste. He was wearing the brown windbreaker that matched the blue one she'd confiscated for her own. "You told me you had a blanket, too," she accused, her mind still dulled by the haunting emotions of her dream. "You lied to me. Your hands are cold."

"I've been colder in my life," he said, and a wry smile twisted across his lips. "But not much."

"Stay with me, please."

"I don't think that's a good idea."

"I won't be able to go back to sleep. The dream's still there, waiting. Besides—" she bit her lower lip "—I'll keep thinking about you sitting over there, alone, freezing, maybe getting sick. Rachel will think it's my fault."

"We don't want that."

"No," she said thoughtfully. "Rachel has too many things to worry about." She frowned. "It worries her that I'm going to have a baby. It saddens her, keeps us from being friends." She kept on talking, trying to hold back the dream and releasing other small dark fears and hurts as she did so.

"Rachel's been through so much. It takes time to get over so much pain, so much loss." Micah's voice was low, rough but soothing nonetheless.

"Perhaps someday we can be friends." She trailed off into silence.

"Go back to sleep. Morning's a long way off."

Cold and loneliness swirled around her, around both of them. "Please." She lifted the edge of the blanket. "Stay with me."

She watched him closely and for a brief moment she saw fear, as stark and real as her own, cloud his blue-gray eyes. Then the familiar mask of non-emotion clamped down and there was nothing more of his thoughts to be read in the stark planes and angles of his face. He slid in beside her.

Instinctively Carrie turned on her side, fitting her body into the curve of his. She felt good lying there despite the discomfort of the hard bed and the damp cold that seeped in around the ill-fitting door of the shed. She was still too disoriented, too groggy, to be completely aware of the intimacy they shared. She only knew she had to be as close to him as possible.

Micah lay stiffly beside her on their narrow bed. Carrie laid her head on his arm, curled her hands around his forearm where it rested just above the rise of her breasts. Gingerly he laid his other hand on her rib cage, inches away from the swell of her stomach.

They lay without speaking for a long while, staring into the darkness. Carrie closed her eyes, willing herself back to sleep. She was so tired. Her back ached with the same dull intensity it had earlier in the day. Perhaps that pain had triggered her nightmare? She didn't know but she was certain the dream would return if she went back to sleep. A tiny sob escaped her lips.

"The dream is gone, Carrie," Micah said quietly. "Nothing can hurt you." His breath was warm on her cheek. His body surrounded her with its comforting male warmth. It wasn't enough.

"Every time I close my eyes I see it all happening again."

"I know." There was acceptance in his voice. "If you let them get control, your nightmares can destroy you." He shifted slightly, drawing her closer. Carrie snuggled into the warmth of his body, savoring his nearness. Already his hands felt warmer on her skin. She was very aware of his touch, although several layers of clothing separated them. "Was it my damned ghost story that frightened you?"

"No." She looked up into his face. She could see nothing but stark planes and angles in the flickering flames of the dying fire. "It wasn't your poor lost soul of a lighthouse keeper that frightened me. It was Evan." The baby had been moving slightly within her as though waking from sleep himself. Almost as she said his father's name, a small foot scraped imperiously across her stomach, grazing the heel of Micah's hand. He pulled back as if burned.

"Is . . . he . . . always that insistent?" he asked after a long moment while Carrie held her breath, afraid he would retreat so completely from that small intimacy that he would leave her side.

"He's really being very sedate." She smiled into the darkness, not able to help herself. "I think he's going to be a football player. Maybe a placekicker."

"What if 'he's' a girl?" His hand moved back to her rib cage, gingerly, but this time he placed it slightly lower, splaying his big fingers over the roundness of her stomach. She could feel him holding his breath, waiting for the baby to move again. Carrie swallowed against the sting of bittersweet tears.

"A gymnast." She blinked and swallowed again. Micah didn't like tears of any sort, happy or sad. "In the dream I had a little girl."

"Not a boy?" Carrie thought she detected a slight smile in his words. "When you're speaking you always refer to the baby as a boy." Right on cue a tiny foot aimed a kick outward. Micah sucked in his breath as he felt the faint movement beneath his hand.

"No, a girl." The fear was back, beating like dark wings in her mind. "I was holding her and . . ." Her voice caught on a sob.

"The nightmare won't go away unless you bring it out in the open, face it, defuse its power."

"You sound like you know what you're talking about."

He was quiet a long time. "I do."

She blinked, holding back more tears. She was grateful for what Micah was trying to do. "Rachel was there with me but she couldn't help. The doctors and nurses were all faceless, just eyes behind their masks. I hurt so bad. I was so tired I couldn't move, couldn't make them understand me. Evan came...with a woman I never saw before...she was his wife. They took the baby. I cried and cried. A man in a suit came out of nowhere. He said he was in charge of babies with no names, no families. He said my daughter had to go with the parent who was part of a family—the one of us who knew who they were and where they came from."

"Are you an orphan, Carrie?" he asked quietly, barely disturbing the silence of the rainy night.

"Yes." She tightened her hands on his arms. He moved his arm, capturing her writhing fingers in his strong grasp, stilling them with his touch. "I was adopted when I was fourteen."

"I wasn't sure but once in a while...there were signs."

"Do the scars show? You never asked." The drift wood Micah had added to the fire fell into the coals. The flames died but the embers glowed with luminous fire of their own.

"I never asked and you never mentioned it," he countered. He turned his head very slightly, just so his chin rested against her hair. "You're very like your parents," he observed, as though comparing her to them in his mind's eye.

"Thank you. I take that as very high praise." He was right. The terror of her nightmare was fading away. She grew calmer talking of her parents and the love they shared. "I couldn't love them any more if they were my biological parents."

"They love you. It shows a lot."

"Yes," she agreed, comforted by the knowledge.

"Is Evan's proximity the reason you don't feel you can return to your home?"

She nodded, not trusting her voice again. "If I go home, he'll know. My parents' home is only twenty miles from the university where I work, where Evan teaches. He's already contacted me several times. My mother forwards his letters. He's convinced them it's in my best interest for them to do so even if they won't tell him where I am. He's a very persuasive man." She couldn't keep the bitterness out of her voice.

Micah's arms tightened around her. "Does he threaten you in his letters?" There was no change of inflection in his voice, but she shivered at the barest hint of steely anger that did manage to find its way into his words.

"No. He's not that kind of man, not deliberately cruel. Only thoughtless and selfish." She hadn't noticed those traits in their short time together. She had been too much in love, or what she thought was love, to see his faults. "He's very intelligent." She felt compelled to list his good points as well. "My baby will probably be very intelligent also." The possibility was daunting. She'd always been only an average student herself. How would she ever help him with his homework? She hated math, and science had never been her strong suit.

"Intelligence doesn't guarantee a well-rounded, principled human being. He'll need you and your loving, caring spirit, your priceless common sense, to accomplish that."

"I'll try." She bit her lower lip. "I'm still afraid to go home." There. She'd said it, brought it out into the open. But would Micah hear the deeper meaning in her words? She was afraid to go back and face Evan, that was true. But that wasn't the real reason she didn't want to leave this place.

That reason was Micah himself. She was falling in love with him. She *was* in love with him and nothing could make her believe otherwise. She was no longer unsure of herself in that respect, if no other. She'd thought long and hard on the matter since their encounter on the island on the Fourth of July, lying awake through the summer nights. She hadn't known her own mind then. But now she did.

"I told you before, you can stay with us as long as you like." Micah lowered his head and kissed her temple. The caress was as gentle, as fleeting as the touch of a feather. She turned her head and his lips brushed hers in the briefest of kisses. She wanted more, but he lifted his head and she felt the intensity of his control.

"I want to stay." She still couldn't read his thoughts. It was too dark. He was too well-schooled in concealing his emotions, yet she knew he wanted her as much as she wanted him. The warmth of his body enveloped her. The touch of his mouth on hers set off small, dizzying explosions of longing deep inside her. She raised her hand, unable to help herself, and let her fingers trail through the silky darkness of his beard. "I..." He didn't pull away but lifted his fingers to her lips, silencing her. She wanted to help him as he had helped her, listened to her, but tonight she was too tired and distressed by her dream to fight his past, to help build a future for them both.

"Shh. No more talk." He kissed her again, but this time the liquid heat of desire was absent from his touch. Carrie sighed in disappointment. She wanted him but she was also very sleepy.

"Where can I stay? Snow..." She stifled a yawn. The pain in her back had faded away as Micah lay beside her, supporting her weight, making her feel safe and loved and warm.

"I'll move into Doug's room in the lab building when he goes home. You can have my room in the big cabin."

"Uh-uh." She set her jaw in a stubborn line. "I won't take your room away from you."

He chuckled, surrendering for the moment. "Okay. We'll think of something else. Tomorrow."

"We could put some heaters in my cabin and some more insulation. It would be cozy and warm, then."

"I'll take care of it," he promised.

"I want to pay my share, of course." It was no use, she could not keep her eyes open even if she wanted to savor the intimacy of being held in his arms.

"Obstinate woman. We'll split the expenses fifty-fifty. Now go to sleep." This time his voice held a note of amused sternness. *He was a good man.* She'd learned that from watching him at his work, seeing him struggle with the private demons that drove him so mercilessly, growing to love the softer side he could not completely suppress. No matter how little he valued himself, no matter what nightmares haunted his past, he was a good man.

"I..."

"Sleep."

Carrie obeyed the command in the single word, but just before she drifted off she felt his lips brush her hair in another fleeting kiss. She fell asleep with a smile on her lips and didn't dream again.

DAYLIGHT SEEPED THROUGH the cracks in the walls, slipped around the edges of the ill-fitting door, announcing its arrival hesitantly, like an uninvited guest. It was time to wake Carrie. Her hands were still curled around his arm, holding him hostage against the warmth of her body. He was a willing prisoner; he could have left her side at any time during the long, cold hours before dawn but he had not. Even now he hesitated to wake her. Dark shadows smudged the hollows beneath her eyes, tiny lines at the corners of her mouth testified to her need for additional rest, but it was already after 7:00 a.m. If Reuben and Doug weren't seriously delayed, they'd be at the campground in less than two hours.

Micah raised himself on his elbow. Carrie shifted in the crook of his arm but didn't awaken. He allowed himself the luxury of watching her for a few moments more. His free hand still rested lightly, possessively, on the swell of her stomach. He knew a little now of what other men felt as their child moved within the nurturing body of the woman they loved. *He didn't love Carrie.* He couldn't allow himself to love her. And her child was not his, would never be his, but the echoes of the miracle of life, of continuance, were strong enough for even his resistant emotions to feel their power.

The baby moved strongly within her, as though anxious for his mother to be up and about. Micah savored the moment as a parting gift of what he'd shared with Carrie through the night, then pulled back from her gently, reluctantly, knowing the needs and urges of her body would push her into wakefulness very soon.

Quickly but silently he built up the fire with the last of the driftwood he'd gathered the night before. He heated water, going about the action automatically while his mind wrestled with weightier problems. He'd deflected Carrie's questions in the intimate darkness of the night, but she wasn't the kind of woman to give up on what she wanted without a fight. She wanted him physically, and more dangerously, she wanted to be part of him, his thoughts and words and hopes and fears. He wasn't so blind that he couldn't see she was falling in love with him. And he wasn't so confident in his own inner strength of purpose that he could keep on resisting her love forever. His invitation for her to remain in the compound until the baby was born was proof enough of his weakness where Carrie was concerned.

Enough of his pride as a man had survived his bout with near madness and unending guilt to make him determined to spare her the sordid details of his past. If he could. She was vulnerable now. He'd used that vulnerability and uncertainty to good advantage that day on the island. She had backed away from her feelings for him then because he'd made her unsure of what she felt. He would not hesitate to do so again. And if the only way he could keep that distance between them was telling her about Elaine...and why she had died...then he would.

He looked up from watching the pan of water come to a boil as it sat balanced on two sticks above the fire. Carrie was awake, watching him in her turn, her eyes still sleep-shadowed, her smile tremulous and uncertain.

"Good morning? It is morning, isn't it?"

"It's about a quarter to eight," he said without glancing at his watch. "I'm heating water for coffee and there's a couple of packets of instant oatmeal in the pack. Are you hungry?"

She shook her head. "I'm never hungry in the mornings anymore but I'll eat."

"It's ready whenever you are." He had to work very hard to keep his tone even and uninvolved. She was watching him closely. He felt her eyes on him as he poured water into cups for coffee and emptied the packets of oatmeal into the bowls they'd eaten stew from the night before. "If you add a packet of coffee whitener to the oatmeal it isn't half-bad."

"Okay." She sighed and he felt her look away. The sad little sound lodged in his heart like a thorn, sending a myriad of cobwebby cracks radiating through the icy shell he maintained with so much zeal. He glanced across the dark space that separated them. She was staring down at her lap, sitting cross-legged on the bed of pine boughs. She pushed at straying wisps of hair with her hand. "I'd better make a trip outside before we eat." She raised her chin and in the velvety-brown depths of her eyes he saw pain at his withdrawal, and determination not to give in to that pain. He hardened his resolve against the power of their softness.

"Wear the poncho."

"Is it raining?" She glanced at the closed door as if she could see through its warped planks.

"Not right now but the fog's so heavy it might as well be rain."

"Will that delay Reuben and Doug still more?"

"I doubt it." He hoped he was telling the truth.

"I'll hurry." She stood up and pulled the poncho over her head.

"Be careful out there. The footing will be treacherous." He stood up and pulled open the stubborn door before she could try to do it herself.

"I'll be fine." He was relieved to hear the spirit back in her voice.

"I know you will," he said very quietly after she was gone.

They ate in silence. As Micah scoured the utensils with sand and water from the lake, Carrie scooped up their pine-bough bed and pushed it into a pile in one corner of the shed. It would stay dry there and do no harm. Micah didn't intend to remain here another night but he wasn't taking anything for granted. She packed up the gear while he put the fire out. They left the small building without exchanging more than a dozen words. They stepped into a world white with fog. Only the sound of the waves rolling monotonously onto the shore and the dark bulk of the tree line above the beach gave definition to their steps. Otherwise they might as well have been walking through a cloud.

He carried the packs, Carrie the boat cushions. Water dripped from the tree branches, splattering them with cold crystal drops that seemed to be able to find their way past the ponchos' hoods and down the backs of their necks. The path was faint. Micah led the way. Occasionally he felt the touch of Carrie's eyes on his back. He wondered what she was thinking, if she was thinking about him, about them, until he caught himself and banished the errant speculation with ruthless intent.

Soon they reached the canoe. They paddled the short distance to the campground without even attempting to break the silence that had grown and strengthened between them with each passing minute. When they arrived they found the campground deserted as it had been the day before.

"We'll wait an hour," he said, his voice sounding loud and harsh in their mist-blurred surroundings. "If Reuben doesn't show up by then we'll start working our way back upriver to the highway bridge where we put in. We'll hitch a ride into town from there."

"That sounds reasonable." She didn't let any dismay shade her voice, but her shoulders sagged tiredly before she straightened and walked over to sit on a guardrail near the swinging bridge that spanned the river. "How long will it take us if that becomes necessary?"

"Five or six hours against the current."

"All right." She was silent again for a long time. He fiddled with the packs, checked the canoe, inspected the paddles. He looked at his watch. Twenty minutes had passed.

"Micah."

He turned slowly, warily, as if the word had been a blow aimed at his head . . . or his heart . . . by an unseen foe. "We have to talk." He couldn't see much of her face under her hood but her voice held a note of stubborn challenge he'd heard many times before. He braced himself for battle.

"Do you want to discuss the renovations to the cabin?"

"I want to discuss last night . . . us." She wrapped one hand around the post that supported the suspended bridge. Her fingers looked small and fragile against the darkly oiled wood, the knuckles gleaming white beneath the skin.

"You were half-asleep." She tied him up in knots inside. All of his carefully planned arguments flew out of his head like one of his eagles soaring free high above.

"No." She stood up and pushed back the hood of her poncho. The fog was beginning to lift very slowly; tatters of gray mist swirled and eddied around her as she moved toward him. "There are things I have to say."

"What if I told you I don't want to hear them?" It was hard to deny her anything when she looked at him like that, serious, concerned, determined to have her own way.

"I'm going to say them anyway." She reached up on tiptoe, lifted her hands to push the concealing hood away from his face as well. "You made me doubt myself that day on the island, doubt what I was feeling for you. You can't do that to me again."

"Nothing has changed since that day." The words fell like stones between them. His voice was harsh, grating even to his own ears.

"Last night changed things."

"It didn't change enough." That was as close as he intended to come to telling her how he felt. He was beginning to feel trapped by the strength of her need to be close to him. She was going to make him tell her the truth about himself. Then it would be over. It would end. She wouldn't shun him; she was too caring and softhearted to do that. Perhaps she might even be able to hide her fear of him from the others. But he would know it was there, deep inside her, and he would always be able to see it in her eyes.

Carrie took a deep breath, looked down at the wet ground, then up into his eyes. "I love you, Micah. I have loved you for weeks, even though you made me doubt my love. I think it's only fair to warn you that if I stay here I'll do everything in my power to make you love me too."

"And your baby? Can you make me love another man's child?" He struck first, in desperation, at the point where he knew she was most vulnerable.

She flinched and he saw her eyes momentarily dull with pain. "We aren't discussing the baby, Micah. If you love me, you'll learn to love my son."

"I don't love you, Carrie," he said very softly.

"I don't believe you," she said equally softly. She was such an odd mixture of kindness and steel, of caring and obstinacy. He almost smiled. He could love her so very easily. . . and so very hurtfully.

"I was married once. I failed miserably as a husband." Perhaps she'd take pity on him and leave him alone. He waited for her response.

"I loved unwisely, as well." She lifted her hand, touching his cheek with the tip of her finger. "Loving and failing at it isn't a crime."

He reached out, caught her wrist and pulled her hand away from his face. "It is if the person you loved is so miserable she feels she can't go on living."

"How did Elaine die, Micah?"

"It's not how she died, Carrie. It's why she died. I killed her."

"No!"

"Yes." He didn't think she heard the approaching Jeep. He was so familiar with the sound of its engine he could hear it miles away. He had to end this . . . and in the manner he most wanted to avoid.

"Maybe if it was just you and me I'd take a chance on loving again. But it isn't just the two of us. You have the baby to consider."

"Micah, what are you talking about?" She twisted her hand, still manacled in his grasp. "Please," she said, biting her lip, "you're hurting me." He released her so quickly she took an involuntary step backward.

"I can't trust myself to love anyone. Ever."

Carrie rubbed her wrist. "Stop talking in riddles. Of course you didn't kill anyone. You wouldn't be standing here if you had."

"She's dead and I was responsible." He clenched his jaw so tightly his teeth ached.

"Tell me . . . or I'll ask Rachel." Carrie's chin trembled, tears filled her eyes, but she stood her ground and refused to relinquish his reluctant gaze.

"If I ask you, no, if I beg you to, will you let this drop?"

She was quiet a long moment. Her eyes held his, searching for something, echoes of the past, memories he couldn't completely hide, or ever forget.

"Tell me, Micah." He stared past her, looking down into the abyss. "If you let them get control of your life, your nightmares will destroy you," she quoted softly.

God, she was going to crucify him with his own words. "All right, I'll tell you." He was too tired to fight her any longer. "When I got back from Nam I couldn't settle in, forget what I'd seen... what I'd done. The doctors at the VA hospital started prescribing tranquilizers and antidepressants, all kinds of drugs." He raked his hand through his hair, splattering drops of water over the shoulders of his poncho. Sometimes those memories were the worst: not being able to control his thoughts, control his body. "The trouble was I was allergic, or something, to all of them. The more they gave me, the crazier I got. I took that violence and frustration out on Elaine. The night I woke from a dream and tried to strangle her, she had me committed."

"It wasn't your fault." Carrie's voice was only a whisper. He could hear the Jeep plainly now. They couldn't be more than a mile away through the woods. She heard it, too. She reached out and grabbed his hand, held on tight. "It wasn't your fault."

"Yeah, that's what they all said—" he gave a short, harsh bark of bitter laughter "—eighteen months later when I finally got some of my memory and most of my mind back."

"Elaine should have known that, too."

"She was young and terrified. Of me. Her husband."

"She loved you. She should have stood by you."

Micah shook his head in wonder at her strength of will. "She wasn't like you, Carrie. She didn't know where to turn, how to deal with a man so withdrawn and angry he couldn't string five words together to make a sentence."

She shook her head, denying his words. She opened her mouth to speak. He pulled his hands from her comforting grasp. He took her by the shoulders and shook her, too hard; her head snapped back on her neck, her eyes widened in shock. "Carrie, she was afraid of me . . . of the violence the drugs unleashed in me. You should be, too."

"I'm not," she insisted, obstinate loving tears filling her eyes.

"She swallowed a whole bottle of sleeping pills rather than spend another night of life alone with me. That's what you'd have to look forward to if I admitted I love you, asked you to be my wife."

"I don't believe there's any violence left inside you that you can't control."

"Maybe you're right," he said wonderingly, because her faith and conviction were contagious, soul-healing. He closed his mind to the hope and promise in her words. They were illusions. He lived with reality. "Maybe we could risk the violence for ourselves . . . alone. But not for the baby. I won't take the chance of hurting him, too."

CHAPTER THIRTEEN

"COME ON, DOUG. Get a move on, boy." Reuben banged on the door to his room so hard the calendar on the wall danced around on its nail. October, it said in big black letters, and the month was almost half gone already. In the picture a couple of little kids were sitting on two big pumpkins. The grins on their faces reminded him of the twins. He missed his little brothers, which showed how bad off he was: homesick for those two brats. "Hey, son. We're waitin' on y'all out here."

"Coming!" He pushed himself up off the pillows where he'd been lying with his hands behind his head, staring at the cobwebs in the corners of the ceiling. He'd hoped once September was over things would get better. No such luck. He sat on the edge of the bed and buried his head in his hands. What a mess he'd made of his life.

His folks had been to the compound for a visit over Labor Day weekend. Maybe if he'd told his mom and Simon the truth about the poaching and the danger to the eagle and the peregrine chicks, things would have been different. They could have helped him work something out and then he wouldn't have to watch out for Hank and the others on his own. Instead, he'd tried to bluff his way out of it, griping about how he hated school anyway and what good would it do him to go back. He'd told himself he was doing it so he didn't have to rat on Willie. Deep down, he knew it was so he didn't have to rat on himself.

Even then his mom and Simon had given him a way out. If that's how he felt about returning to school, they would try to understand. He had until Thanksgiving to change his mind. He could still make up enough credits to graduate with his class if he came back by then. He didn't deserve a mom and stepdad who cared that much.

"How long does it take you to change your shirt?" Reuben hollered through the door. "Open up. Hidin' in your room ain't gonna get us out of this documentary thing." He sounded just about as fed up with everything as Doug felt.

He opened the door and Reuben stalked inside, breathing hard. "I tell you, I've about had it with the whole bunch. I got half a notion to head on down to Ann Arbor and leave y'all to fend for yourselves. See how far you get then." He folded his arms across his chest. "Rachel workin' herself half to death for Doc Sauder. Micah and Carrie moonin' around here like a pair of lovesick calves—most of the time not speakin' to each other from one day to the next. Them birds eatin' us out of house and home. And now this." He glared at the brown and black plaid shirt Doug pulled out of the closet. "I thought that she-cat told you to wear somethin' colorful."

"Take it or leave it."

"Don't blame me if that woman bites your head off, then. She scares hell out of me," Reuben admitted with an exaggerated shudder.

Doug grinned as he pushed his hands into the sleeves of his shirt. He couldn't help it. "Me, too. She looks like something off MTV. Or Vampira," he added after a moment's thought. The film crew from Detroit had shown up three days ago to make a video about the peregrine chicks, and the lady director was something else. She wore her hair all spiked up on her head, her nails were as long as daggers and bright red. She had earrings as big as saucers hanging from her ears and she didn't know all that much about raptors.

"There's not much we can do about it," Reuben said for at least the tenth time. "Orders to cooperate came straight from the governor's office. We'll just have to grit our teeth and do it her way. There ain't much money in this business, anyway. If we get cut off from our state funding..."

"I know." Doug finished buttoning his shirt and turned the sleeves back over his wrists. "We'll starve to death next winter." And the way things were going, he'd still be here bird-sitting and starve along with them. At least he'd gotten word to Willie that the film crew was hanging around. He'd pass it on to the others, warn them off, and the birds should be safe for another day or two. After that, well, he'd think of something.

They walked through the office into the lab. Igor greeted him with a scream, lifting up to her full height, spreading her wings. Doug smiled in spite of his heavy heart, proud of how strong and healthy the bird looked. It was lonely doing what you had to do. He wasn't even sure what he was doing *was* the right thing. Maybe he was keeping Willie out of jail and maybe he was only doing it to save his own neck. If anyone found out he'd been breaking the law he'd probably never get back to school, never get an education and a decent job. He'd end up like Hank and Lance, and Willie, too. He'd learned his lesson, but it wasn't going to do him any good in the long run. He just couldn't win. He reached out to open the door of Igor's cage. But at least this way he had a chance to save the birds.

"OKAY. IF WE COULD JUST GET one more shot of you with the eagle, Doug, it would be great. Make her fly!"

The director of the video crew was a royal pain. Carrie had decided that the moment she first saw the woman. Six feet tall, slender as a reed and drop-dead gorgeous, she made her feel more than ever like a pregnant . . . elephant. Carrie looked ruefully down at her stomach, made even larger by the bulky coat she wore. It wasn't that she was jealous, she told herself for the tenth time that day alone. Micah paid less attention to the woman than he did . . . to herself. It was just that she was so tired, and everything was so mixed-up in her life that she didn't feel as if she could deal with any more complications, no matter how minor. And Erika Mannheim and her crew's invasion of their isolated compound was far from a minor inconvenience. It was a major upheaval.

"Okay, sweetie, give me a good profile shot this time," Erika demanded, managing, somehow, to sound wistful and imperious all at once. She motioned to her cameraman to start taping as Doug, seemingly innocent, turned his back on the shot. "Young man," she called, making a slashing gesture with a carmine-tipped hand. The cameraman took his eye from the shoulder-held camera and waited. "The sooner we get this shot, the sooner we'll be out of here."

"Doug." There was no cajoling in Micah's voice. He was standing in the doorway of the lab, his arms folded across his chest. The scowl on his face matched the angry gray clouds racing by overhead. "Do as she says."

"Thank you, Dr. McKendrick." Erika's brilliant smile was for Micah alone. Carrie felt her hands curl into claws inside the pockets of her coat. She felt like slapping the woman's beautiful face. Jealousy was not a pretty emotion. "Now, Doug, please." Once more Erika gestured for the camera to start taping.

"If that she-devil says 'please' like that one more time," Rachel said through her teeth, "I'm not going to be responsible for my actions. Doesn't she know the boy is a child?"

Carrie bit her lip. She might give Erika the benefit of the doubt about Doug's age but Erika certainly knew what she was doing where Micah was concerned.

"I suspect she'd use that same tone of voice to a seven-year-old," Carrie replied.

"As long as that seven-year-old was a male." Carrie smiled, even though she didn't want to. Rachel's tone bore an uncanny and unflattering resemblance to that of their unwelcome visitor from Detroit.

"Meow," Carrie said, and giggled.

Rachel pulled her pink knit cap down over her ears as a strong gust of cold wind swirled across the lake and up onto the porch of Carrie's recently winterized cabin where they were standing. She blushed slightly, then giggled, too.

"We do sound catty," she agreed, unrepentant.

They continued to watch the director in her designer jeans, knee-high leather moccasins and down vest as she ordered her two-man crew around like a marine drill sergeant. Doug did as she asked, or Micah ordered, but his expression remained sullen and uncooperative. Carrie still had no idea what had happened to make him refuse to return home with his mother and stepfather. He'd made no effort to confide in her, although she'd given him every opportunity to do so. Doug's unfathomable behavior was just one more unresolved conflict affecting the already tense atmosphere of the compound.

At least Igor was doing well. Carrie watched with satisfaction as the young eagle preened and postured on Doug's forearm, aloof and uninterested in the filming, as long as the strange humans kept their distance. She was gaining strength with each passing day, relearning her hunting skills, and soon, when she was recovered enough to return to the wild, to "hack out," she'd relearn her healthy fear of man and once more be free to soar with her own kind.

"Why do you suppose the governor's office sent her out here to film in the first place?" Carrie asked, voicing her thoughts. It didn't make sense that Lansing should send someone so lacking in experience where wildlife was concerned, to document the peregrines' progress.

"Bureaucrats," Rachel said, putting a great deal of meaning into the single word. "When have any of the rest of us ordinary mortals been able to fathom the workings of their devious little minds?''

"She's probably sleeping with one of the governor's aides," Carrie said before she could stop herself.

Rachel shot her a quick, assessing glance. "Meow," she said in her turn.

It was Carrie's turn to blush. "Well, she obviously knows next to nothing about wildlife photography."

"Agreed." Rachel turned back to the action. Igor was beginning to take exception to the unfamiliar voices, the confusion and movement and the strange-looking human with the big videotape camera perched on his shoulder, a menacing, unhandsome twin to herself.

"How much longer is she going to be here?" Carrie put her hands on the small of her back and stretched. The movement set off a series of small, stinging cramps. She stood still. Her back ached, had been aching on and off for the last day or two. Today it was worse, the ache tightening now and then, as it just had, into a cramp, moving around to her side and across her middle. *Almost like a contraction.* Except that she was three weeks away from her due date, so it couldn't be that.

"I'm hoping they're leaving today," Rachel said, looking guilty but with a mischievous twinkle in her eyes. "I think the weather reports have them worried." An early winter storm was roaring down out of Canada, and even if the snow and sleet accompanying it missed this section of the UP, gale-force winds and record cold temperatures were predicted for Marquette and vicinity.

"Let's hope you're right," Carrie said with real feeling. Left unspoken between them was the knowledge that Erika Mannheim was aware of Rachel's identity, although to give her credit, the woman had done nothing to capitalize on that knowledge. Yet. Carrie didn't trust her any farther than she could throw her. And in her present condition, that wasn't very far at all. Rachel's relative happiness and contentment was too new and too fragile to risk exposure to any more of the kind of media hysteria that had swirled around her after her return from Vietnam. Carrie hadn't known her then, of course, but she didn't have to have been involved to want to save her from a repeat of the media circus she remembered at the time.

"What in heaven's name is she up to now?" Rachel put her hands on the porch rail, leaning forward as if to better see and hear what was happening in the yard. Doug, with Igor on his arm, was standing in approximately the same place where he and Carrie had had their encounter with the she-bear and her cubs all those weeks ago. Erika was striding forward, one hand waving above her head. Igor, already nervous, screamed and mantled, showing her distress. Doug held tightly to the long flying lead attached to her jesses. He stepped backward, trying to put distance between himself and the woman Igor now clearly perceived as her enemy, tripped over an upthrust root and fell. Creeing in distress, Igor launched herself into the sky.

"Oh, no," Rachel said on a sharp, indrawn breath.

"Damn it, she's not ready to fly!" Micah's voice was a roll of thunder in the stormy afternoon. Carrie turned her head in his direction as though drawn by a magnet. He was halfway across the compound, his angry strides eating up the distance in only seconds. His face was twisted with rage. Carrie shuddered. She'd never seen him this way. He skidded to a halt in front of Erika. "What the hell do you think you're doing? I told you not to frighten my birds!"

"Stop him," Rachel said, starting forward. Carrie was already halfway down the steps despite the handicap of her awkward bulk. She couldn't let Micah do anything that he would regret later.

Carrie halted at the edge of the gravel drive and looked up. Igor had managed to gain enough altitude to make it to the tree line at the edge of the clearing. The dangling lead and long leather jesses attached to her talons were entangled in the topmost branches of a dead sycamore about thirty feet inside the woods. The young eagle, already frightened, was struggling frantically to free herself. It was only a matter of time until she did herself great harm.

"Jake, are you getting this?" Erika crowed. "Don't miss a shot. Damn, I wish the sun could come out from behind that cloud." She talked on, oblivious to Micah's towering rage.

"Don't count on it," the man called Jake answered, frowning at a light meter attached to his camera. "I'll do my best."

"Barney, get in closer to the bird." The second man, nondescript to the point of being invisible, scurried forward. He didn't get more than a few feet. Micah sent him and his video camera flying with one sweep of his arm. "I told you to get the hell out of my way."

"All right. All right." Erika held up a placating arm and backed off a step or two. "Use the long lens and keep shooting, Jake. Barney, are you all right?" He nodded, grumbling, as he scurried on hands and knees to retrieve his camera.

"Get off my property." Micah ground his teeth; his hands were balled into fists at his side.

"I don't think so." Erika stood her ground. As Carrie watched, Rachel's restraining hand on her arm, she stood nose to nose with Micah. "We'll discuss the possibility of a lawsuit for assault later, McKendrick. Right now I suggest you let me finish what I came to do. If not, I might be tempted to go to the networks with an even bigger story."

"I don't know what the hell you're talking about." Micah's voice was as cold and hard-edged as the north wind blowing down the back of Carrie's neck.

"I think you do." Erika held his gaze with deliberate malice. Carrie held her breath.

"You're bluffing."

"No. I'm doing this piece on your damned birds because I need the money. I can make a hell of a lot more money doing a piece on you. The mysterious recluse eagle man and his back-from-the-dead sister." She nodded over her shoulder. "A lot of people still wonder where she got to. Think about it, Captain McKendrick." She caught and held Micah's gaze. Carrie could see nothing of what he felt, of what he was thinking, but a muscle jumped in his cheek at the sound of his military title. "I've done my homework . . . on both of you."

"Get what tape you need and get out." Micah turned on his heel, dismissing her rudely and completely. "Reuben," he shouted into the wind, "bring my gloves and irons."

"Way ahead of you, boss," Reuben hollered back from the doorway of the lab building. "The boy's all ready to go." He gestured toward the edge of the woods. Doug was barely visible through the screen of leafless branches as he strapped on the climbing irons. Carrie had been so intent on the confrontation between Micah and Erika Mannheim she hadn't noticed he was missing. Now he was back and ready to climb.

"Doug!" Micah swerved, headed for the woods. Erika motioned for Jake to start taping, Carrie brushed rudely past her, Rachel at her heels, without a second glance. It was too windy for her to be anything but apprehensive about Doug's climb. Micah shared her fear.

"That tree's not safe. You don't have enough experience to climb in this weather," he yelled.

"She's my bird," Doug insisted stubbornly as he pulled on his gloves. His face looked tighter, older than before. He might still be a boy, but the problems he carried around inside him were man-sized. "Besides, if this is such a bad tree, how will you make it up? You outweigh me by seventy-five, eighty pounds." Igor was creeing helplessly, hanging upside down as she struggled to free herself from the imprisoning leather jesses. "She knows me. She'll let me help her."

Micah had moved into the woods as he talked. Now he stood face to face with the teenager. He studied Doug's ashen face for a long time. Carrie stood just inside the tree line, out of the wind, and waited along with the others. Doug stared back at Micah, his gaze steady and unflinching. "I can get her down."

"Okay." Micah dropped down on one knee. He hoisted Doug up to the lowest branches of the big old sycamore. "Check her out. If she's hurt, wrap her up and we'll lower her with the rope." Doug had a coil of lightweight nylon rope draped over his shoulder, a large canvas drawstring bag secured to the end.

"Right." Doug started to climb. Micah reached out and wrapped a restraining hand around his ankle.

"If she's not hurt, let her fly."

"She's not ready." Doug looked down. He was already six feet up the trunk.

"She's not ready to go back to the wild, but she's ready to fly. She'll stay with you." He let go of Doug's ankle. The boy didn't move. His brown eyes searched Micah's face for the truth of his statement.

"Okay," he said finally. "If she's not hurt I'll let her fly."

Carrie watched with her heart in her throat. Everything was quiet except for the wind in the branches. She could hear Rachel breathing beside her. Even Erika Mannheim seemed to know enough to keep her mouth shut. Micah stood, as immobile as the trees around them, until Doug reached the top. Carrie could hear the boy talking, soothing nothings that seemed to calm the frightened bird, at least long enough for him to reach out and free the tangled jesses. Igor flapped her way upright onto a branch. Doug curled one arm around the trunk, secured the jesses and with the other examined Igor on her perch.

"She's all right, as far as I can tell," he called down.

"Then let her fly." Micah didn't raise his voice.

Doug hesitated. Carrie crossed her fingers inside her pockets. It was a childish talisman, but comforting.

The tree swayed slightly with each gust of wind. It was stronger now, colder, tugging at the wisps of hair around her cheeks, rustling through the dry leaves underfoot. Beside Carrie, Rachel was holding her breath.

"Don't miss this, Jake," Erika said, her voice a harsh, triumphant whisper.

Doug released the leather jesses and Igor flew, catching the wind, spiraling upward as though searching for heaven. She made a long sweep out over the lake and Carrie thought she was gone. Doug hollered her name and started down the tree at a dangerous pace. "Slow down," Micah ordered, and Doug did as he was told.

Igor continued to soar upward, then, with a nerve-tingling cry of triumph at finding her wings again after so long, she came to a flapping, unglamorous landing on top of her flight cage. By the time Doug was safely on the ground she was willing to be coaxed back to hand with the fresh carcass of a bluegill.

"Great stuff," Erika said, striding toward Doug, with Jake and the nondescript Barney following in her wake. "Let's get back inside and get some more stuff to finish up." Micah swung around, blocking her entry to the lab.

"You're finished here." His voice was as cold and hard as a January day. He reached out and took her by the arm, as if to shake her or push her away.

"Don't threaten me, McKendrick." Her tone was shrill. "I won't stand being manhandled." She was suddenly far less beautiful than she had seemed to Carrie only an hour ago.

Micah let go of her arm so quickly she stumbled back a step. "I'm not threatening you. I'm stating facts." Carrie wished the anger was back in Micah's voice. That he would holler and rant and rave, anything but the steely control, the total lack of feeling he displayed now. Emotion, however violent, didn't frighten her nearly as much as the awful emptiness she saw in his face, heard in his voice. "Pack up and get off my property or I'll call the sheriff."

"The man who hired me has a lot to say about who gets state funding and who doesn't. He isn't going to be happy about this."

"I managed for a long time without state grants. I can do it again. Don't try to bring me to heel with that line."

"You aren't going to give up and play the game, are you, McKendrick?" Even Erika, as brash as she appeared to be, didn't have the nerve to threaten Rachel's privacy again, it seemed. Carrie stood just outside the lab and felt as useless, and as big, as a tree stump, but she couldn't just walk away from what was happening.

"I am playing the game," Micah said, not budging an inch. "My way."

"My boss answers directly to the governor."

"That's what I figured." Reuben appeared behind Micah in the lab doorway. He shouldered his employer aside, breaking the standoff and focusing attention on himself. "Comin' through, boss. Got a long-distance call here for Miz Erika Mannheim." He flourished the portable telephone under her nose. "This here's the governor of this great state of Michigan on the line."

"The hell it isn't." Erika backed away from the ginger-haired Texan.

"The hell it is," Reuben corrected her with great satisfaction. "You've got some explainin' to do. These here birds are the governor's pet project, sorta. If I were you I wouldn't keep the gent waitin'. I called collect."

MICAH STARED DOWN AT THE half-full glass of whiskey in his hand. It had been one hell of a day. It was turning into one hell of a night. He didn't often allow himself the luxury of getting stinking drunk. He probably wouldn't again tonight, but it was good to know he had the option.

"Listen to that wind. Sounds like a banshee wailing. Or maybe our lady director when she lost her temper." Reuben chuckled, pleased with himself. "I sure enjoyed seein' her squirm when she got on the line with the governor."

"You saved my butt," Micah said, offering him the whiskey bottle. "I nearly lost it today."

Reuben walked away from the window where he'd been standing, rested his hip on the edge of Micah's desk and took a swallow of whiskey straight from the bottle. "Woulda took a saint to keep from wantin' to belt that hussy." He rubbed the mouth of the bottle with his sleeve and handed it back to Micah.

"We both know I'm no saint." Erika Mannheim had meant nothing to him, less than nothing, but she'd gotten to him, just the same. He'd felt the sensual vibration she gave off the moment she stepped into his office, and he blamed Carrie for that awareness. He blamed her because she was the woman who made him feel and touched his heart as no other. She'd changed him and left him vulnerable to the rage still buried deep inside him. Today it had nearly broken free. "I acted like a goddamn fool."

"Let's both get drunk and drown our sorrows. That'd be more productive than sittin' here, beatin' your breast cause you lost your temper a might, same as any sane man woulda done."

"Sane. That's the operative word, isn't it."

Reuben's response was short and to the point.

"But you're right, sitting here and getting drunk will only get us hung over in the morning." Micah capped the whiskey bottle and returned it to the desk drawer. "I'm going to check on the birds and go to bed."

"I'll do that." Reuben stood up and stretched his arms over his head. "No need for both of us to be up any longer. It's been one hell of a day."

"Let me know if Igor needs anything. She got banged up pretty good." Micah decided to take Reuben's offer to make a final check on the birds. "Looks like she'll need another two or three weeks to get over the setback. After that, I think it's best we start hacking her out. Doug's getting too attached. If we wait any longer than that, it'll be cutting it close to get her rehabilitated before winter sets in."

"Damned woman caused a sight more trouble than she's worth," Reuben said under his breath. "Good night, boss."

The whiskey was working its magic. He felt calmer, more at ease. Or was it something other than the whiskey? Maybe it was his work that soothed him—the satisfaction he felt, knowing they were bringing a species back from the brink of extinction. Even the blinded osprey had recently found a new home in an

Illinois university's aviary that covered several acres and reproduced the habitats of scores of North American birds.

Yet, when Igor and the peregrines were gone, he'd be alone again, and for the first time in years, he dreaded the prospect. He turned up the collar of his coat and walked out into the storm, automatically glancing toward Carrie's small, recently winterized cabin. The lights were on, shining softly through the curtains.

If she was having a restless night, it was none of his business. She wouldn't appreciate him butting in. He started walking, but before he'd gone ten feet, he turned and headed for her cabin. The nagging feeling that something was wrong wouldn't go away. In Viet nam he'd trusted his hunches to keep him and his men alive. He couldn't ignore this one. If he had any hope of getting to sleep before dawn, he had to make sure she was all right.

Micah walked up the steps, stood listening before the door for a long moment, then lifted his hand to knock. She didn't answer. He twisted the knob. The door wouldn't budge. *Something was definitely wrong, he could feel it*. Micah put his shoulder to the warped wood and shoved. The door flew back on its hinges and he stepped over the threshold. Carrie was sitting in her rocker, doubled over, her hands wrapped around her swollen middle.

"Micah, I'm so glad you're here." She tried to smile but couldn't. "I . . . I don't feel well at all. I think . . ." She stopped, gasped, then continued talking through clenched teeth. "I think the baby's coming." She held out her hand. "Help me, please."

CHAPTER FOURTEEN

"MICAH, SOMETHING'S WRONG," Carrie whispered, leaning back in the rocking chair she'd bought for the cabin several weeks before—when she'd decided to stay. Her voice sounded thin and scared, even to her own ears. She took a deep breath; blessedly, the pain was gone, at least for the moment. The red haze around the edges of her vision receded. Her brain felt marginally functional once more. "It's too soon for the baby. It's not due for three weeks." She felt like crying, but from relief at his appearance, not fear or discomfort.

He dropped to his knee beside her. "It's all right." Carrie grasped his hand between her own, just to make sure he was real, not a dream. *He was here.* He was with her. She had needed him and he'd come. "How long have you been awake?" he asked. His hands were cold but it didn't matter. She could smell whiskey on his breath, but only faintly. *She could use a drink herself.* His hair was ruffled from the wind. He pushed his hand through it, distracted. Carrie smiled to herself. She loved to see him do that. His hands were so big and strong, yet oddly gentle when he touched her. "Have you been in labor very long?" he asked. He reached up with his free hand, smoothing her hair back off her face. She needed his touch, the strength of his nearness. "Carrie?" She blinked, trying to focus on what he was saying.

"I don't know." She smiled, wanting to reach out and touch him also, but another contraction rippled across her stomach. She braced herself for the pain. "What time is it?" she managed to ask. She must think of her baby now, not herself. She tried to remember how to breathe properly, how to relax, what time it had been when the last contraction started. It was hard. But not as hard as before, when she was alone, because now she had Micah's strong, callused hand to hold on to.

"It's after three," he said, his voice rough around the edges, but gentle, so wonderfully gentle.

"Almost two hours." She gasped. She couldn't help it. The contraction was stronger than the one before. "The pains weren't bad at first. But now they are. Uneven. I can't...time them...I lose track." She panted, trying to recall the breathing exercises from the childbirth classes she'd attended only two weeks before.

One of the delivery-room nurses at the hospital was going to be her coach. She had wished for someone she knew better but didn't dare ask Rachel. It was hard having a baby alone. She felt like crying again. She was dizzy and her head felt like a block of wood. Her only reality now was the increasing strength of the contractions and the solid warmth of Micah's hand.

"I'm not ready for this, Micah. I don't have all the things I need for the baby. I don't even have a place for him to sleep." It suddenly seemed very important— that one small detail out of so many.

"I'll get Rachel for you." Micah's voice was as even and controlled as ever, but Carrie felt the fine tremor in his fingers even through her pain. He looked tired and discouraged. His confrontation with the film crew, his momentary loss of control that afternoon, had taken its toll. Carrie wished she'd never heard of Erika Mannheim, or the governor, or peregrine falcons. "She'll know what to do."

He tried to stand up. Carrie clutched his hand so hard he winced. "Don't leave me." The contraction was easing, but only a little. The books she'd read had all mentioned long, pain-free intervals. That wasn't happening. "I . . . I thought first babies always took a long time." She clenched her fist over the distended mound of her stomach. "At least that's what all the books say."

"To hell with the books." Micah tugged his hand from her grasp, picked her coat up off the floor and held it for her to slide her arms into the sleeves. "Put this on," he ordered. "It's cold outside."

Carrie did as she was told. It was good to have someone else make the decisions, someone she trusted, someone she loved, even if he couldn't love her back. "I . . . I don't think I can walk."

Even standing seemed more effort than she could manage at the moment. It brought on another rippling contraction that faded away almost as quickly as it had come, unlike the others. What did that mean? One more thing the books hadn't told her about. Was it a good sign? Or a bad one?

"You're not going to walk. I'll carry you." Micah pulled the door open and then turned back to scoop her up into his arms. Carrie didn't protest. It was where she wanted to be. She didn't try to resist the feeling of security, of comfort his strong arms gave. Here was a man who would love her, take care of her, protect her and her child, if he would only allow himself to be so vulnerable again. "I'll take you in to Rachel while I warm up the car. It's colder than a witch's ... never mind," he amended when he realized what he was going to say.

"You'll have to wake her up. Oh, dear." Carrie didn't know why she was apologizing but she was. "Everyone's going to be awake now. I wanted to wait ..."

"Wait," Micah barked, starting off across the frozen grass at a swift pace. "Good Lord, wait? For what?"

"It was such a difficult day...."

"It was one helluva day," Micah corrected.

"It's turning out to be one helluva night."

Micah chuckled. The sound went straight to Carrie's heart and lodged there like a small, sustaining kernel of warmth.

"Maybe Reuben won't hear the car," she suggested hopefully.

"He can miss an hour or two of sleep—it won't hurt him. And Doug sleeps through anything. I'll bet you he won't even know we're gone until breakfast."

A gust of sharp wind took Carrie's breath away. She didn't try to talk anymore, just wrapped her arms tighter around Micah's neck and let her mind drift, trying not to think beyond the moment, trying not to imagine that Micah was her baby's true father so that she wouldn't have to face this scary, unknown ordeal alone, trying not to brace herself for the next contraction and waste her energy and strength.

The wind ceased battering them as they approached the house. Micah reached down, opened the door and flicked on the overhead light, still holding Carrie in his arms. He kicked the door shut with his heel. "Rachel." He didn't yell and Carrie was grateful. Rachel would be scared to death if he bellowed her name at the top of his lungs.

"Micah?" Rachel's voice from the bedroom didn't sound sleepy at all. "What's wrong?"

"It's Carrie. The baby's on its way."

"I'm coming."

Micah laid Carrie on the couch. She propped herself against the arm and pulled her knees up. It was more comfortable that way. She wrapped her coat around her. She was shivering uncontrollably although the cabin was warm, the embers of a fire still glowing faintly in the fireplace.

Rachel walked into the room, tying the belt of a fleecy pink robe around her waist. Her hair was tousled around her shoulders, her eyes sleep-shadowed but alert.

"How far apart?" she asked Micah, getting her first good look at Carrie.

"They're close."

"It's too soon," Carrie whispered, unable to hold back two big tears that rolled down her cheeks when she tried to blink them back. "I don't know what's happening."

"Babies often pick their own time to be born, no matter how inconvenient for the rest of us." Her words were lightly spoken, but a mask, almost as frightening as the one Micah employed to hide his true feelings, slipped across her features. Carrie felt her heart contract in sympathy for the other woman's pain. Rachel didn't want to see her baby born. She couldn't forget her own dead child and Carrie's labor was bringing back all the old memories of terror and loss.

"I'm sorry, Rachel," she fumbled for the right words. "I know..." The contraction strengthened. Carrie lost her train of thought.

"Don't be sorry for anything. Get the car started," she ordered her brother sharply. "Use mine. The Jeep's out of the question in her condition and Carrie's car is too small to buck this wind all the way to the hospital. I have no intention of being blown into Lake Superior on the way."

Micah was gone before she'd finished speaking.

"Relax," Rachel said, sitting down on the edge of the couch, smoothing Carrie's hair back from her forehead. "It won't be long. We'll have you safe and sound in the hospital in no time."

"I hope so." Carrie sniffed back another tear. "I don't care how right and natural this whole thing is. I'm scared. And I don't want my baby to be born in the back seat of a car."

"I CALLED THE EMS and Doc Sauder," Micah said forty minutes later. He kept his voice low. Neither of them wanted Carrie to hear. "It'll take them at least half an hour to get the ambulance out here from the township building and another forty minutes back into town."

"It won't be that long," Rachel said, picking her coat up from the back of the couch where she'd tossed it when they reentered the house. She hung it on a peg by the back door, then rubbed her hand over the tense muscles at the back of her neck.

"What do you mean, it won't be that long?"

Rachel stared at her brother long and hard. Beneath the stoic calm he maintained with such diligence beat the heart of a concerned and frightened man. He cared for Carrie Granger far more than he would admit to another living human being, possibly more than he could admit to himself. "Her labor is progressing very quickly. Being bounced around in the back seat of a car, over unpaved roads, didn't help." She changed the subject slightly. "What did Doc say?"

"He'll be standing by at the hospital, but he trusts your judgment."

Rachel nodded. "Carrie's baby is going to be born tonight. Here. In this cabin."

"Damn the luck!" Micah swore, running his hand through his hair. "What a night for a blasted tree to blow down across the road. That hasn't happened in years."

"I'd say it's just about the perfect night for something like that to happen," Rachel responded wryly. They were both quiet a moment, listening to the wind, remembering the shock of finding the way blocked, of having to turn the car on the dark, narrow road and return to the compound. Outside it was blowing harder than ever, shrieking down the chimney and rattling the storm windows in their wooden frames.

"I'll get Reuben and Doug up. We'll get the chain saw, get that tree off the road. Won't take more than fifteen, twenty minutes."

"Micah," Rachel spoke quietly. She laid her hand on his arm. The muscles and tendons beneath her fingers were corded with strain. "It's not your fault. None of this is your fault. Not Carrie's labor, not the storm, or the fallen tree. You can't stop nature. Carrie will be all right. I promise you."

But could she keep that promise? Rachel felt new anxiety bubble up inside her. She didn't want to be responsible for bringing this baby into the world. Why couldn't that dead tree have fallen at a different angle so that Micah could have driven the car past it on the narrow dirt road? Why couldn't Carrie's baby have waited one more day to be born?

Why had God let everything terrible that had happened to her happen at all? Why had he let her baby die when so many others lived?

A low groan from Carrie brought Rachel out of her thoughts and back into reality with a jolt. Micah twisted his head in the direction of his bedroom. His face was white as chalk.

"I'll get Doug and Reuben up and at it."

Rachel nodded. "Go ahead, but come back, Micah." She didn't try to hide the fear she knew lurked deep in her eyes. "I might need you."

"Okay, Sis." He stalked out of the room, leaving Rachel alone with the laboring woman.

"Were you talking to Micah?" Carrie asked when Rachel stepped into the bedroom a few moments later. She looked pale but composed. The pains were strong, but steady now, coming every three minutes. She was well into the second stage of labor, but everything seemed to be all right.

"I'm so sorry," Carrie said, twisting the sheet Rachel had covered her with to counteract the October predawn chill.

"Shh," Rachel hushed her. "I'm going to have to leave you for a few minutes. I need to get things ready for your delivery."

Carrie tried to smile. "I said I didn't want my baby to be born in the back seat of a car. I should have qualified that." She gestured around the sparsely furnished bedroom. "I didn't want him born in Micah's bedroom, either."

"Then you should have gone over the drill with the baby, made arrangements for him to make his appearance at a more convenient time." Rachel forced herself to smile, too. She hoped it was sincere enough to fool Carrie. "Now rest if you can. The hard part's just beginning, I'm afraid."

Rachel turned to the doorway. Micah was standing just beyond, snowflakes dusting his thick, dark hair. Carrie didn't know he was there.

"I guess this isn't so scary for you. You must have helped deliver lots of babies," said Carrie.

"Yes, I have."

That was part of the nightmare. There was no reason to tell Carrie that the Hlông, being superstitious, only called on her experience and expertise for difficult deliveries, when their fear and anxiety for the mother and child outweighed their fear of the *phi* spirits that ruled every aspect of their lives. Rachel was an outsider, a foreign woman, a nonbeliever, tolerated, not mistreated, but never welcomed into the life of the village. More often than not the tiny scraps of humanity died in her arms, as her son had died, and she could only weep silently, inside, because the tears would never come.

"Then I'm not going to worry," Carrie said. "I know you won't let anything bad happen to my baby."

"No," Rachel whispered, looking at Micah once again. "I won't. I promise."

"RACHEL..." MICAH DIDN'T know what else to say. He understood the hesitancy in her voice, even if Carrie could not. He was familiar with the Hlông, with their way of life. He'd flown with them in Laos, fought alongside them until the day the United States pulled out of the war, leaving them virtually defenseless against the Vietnamese. He'd brought as many out of Laos as he could—until they'd grounded him and taken his plane. He knew something of what Rachel's life had been like living among them in a primitive society where women were little valued. He was aware of her pain, though they never spoke of it. He knew also what it would cost her emotionally to deliver Carrie's baby.

"Micah's here," Rachel said brightly, too brightly, forestalling any clumsy attempt he might have made to comfort her. He wasn't their brother, Simon. He didn't have the words, know the right things to say. "He can sit with you while I get things arranged." She looked up and met his gaze; for a moment, only a heartbeat, everything she'd suffered was there for him to see in her blue-gray eyes. Then she blinked and the illusion was gone. She was all business once again.

"Micah?"

Carrie's voice sounded tired, weaker than when he'd left to get Reuben and Doug started on clearing the road. He dragged his eyes from Rachel's face. Looking through the open door, all he could see was the foot of his bed. "How is she?" he asked, making no attempt to move into the room. It was alien territory now. He knew nothing about childbirth. He was pretty sure he didn't want to learn. At least not if it meant he had to see Carrie in more pain. His brain knew what she was going through was natural and necessary. In his heart, so newly reawakened from its frosty sleep, he had no such assurance. He was scared, for Carrie, for her baby, for himself.

He squared his shoulders as if bracing to fight an unseen enemy and stepped into the room. Carrie was propped up against pillows in his narrow bed. She was wearing her own nightgown, pale peach with little sprigs of flowers, taken from the small suitcase that he'd last seen on top of her bed and that now was sitting behind the door.

"Is it snowing?" she asked, indicating the melting snowflakes in his hair and on the shoulders of his old blue wool coat. There was genuine dismay in her voice. Micah realized she'd been hoping against hope there was still time for her to get to the hospital. He sat down, gingerly, on the side of the bed. Her hair was damp, her face shiny from the exertion of each new contraction. Another one rippled across her swollen stomach as he watched. She grabbed his hand and held on for dear life. "Talk to me," she gasped, pulling her lip between her teeth. "It helps . . ."

"Just flurries," he said, answering her question about the weather because he didn't know what else to say or to do. *Where the hell was Rachel? Wasn't there something she could do to ease the pain?* "The storm missed us, just like the weatherman said. According to the radio it moved north across the Keweenaw and out over the lake to Canada. South of here there's lots of rain and thunderstorms, even a few tornadoes." He shouldn't have said that, he realized almost at once.

"Mom and Dad...they won't be..." She stopped trying to talk, just rolled her head from side to side on the pillows and squeezed his hands so tightly he almost yelled, himself.

The contraction seemed to go on forever. He wanted to take her pain into himself, make it easier for her. He didn't want to see her suffer because... *he loved her?* Micah dismissed the notion as quickly as it came into his thoughts.

"Should I call Rachel?" He leaned forward, wanting to smooth back the damp strands of hair that lay against her cheek, but unable to remove his hand from her clutching fingers.

"It's okay. It's passing. How long?" She was quieter. Her death grip on his hands relaxed. Hesitantly, Micah reached out to tuck a stray curl behind her ear.

"How long?" He was entranced, as always, by the silky feel of her hair, by the softness of her skin beneath his roughened fingertips.

"The contraction. How long did it last?"

"I...I forgot to time it."

"It doesn't matter," Carrie said, moving restlessly among the pillows. "It was a long one. Have you called my parents?" she asked suddenly. Her fingers tightened around his once more.

"Not yet. I will, if you want me to."

"No," she shook her head. Her hair was the dull gold of autumn leaves against the white pillowcase. "It's the middle of the night. They'll worry. I'll call them ... later." She started breathing more quickly. Micah's insides churned. "I don't want them...to call Evan ... they might think they should—" She bit off a cry of pain. "Oh, Micah. Get Rachel, please. I think it's time. I mean ... really time.... Hurry!"

He turned his head, hollered at the top of his lungs. "Rachel, get in here. Now."

"You didn't have to yell." Carrie tried to laugh and ended up sobbing breathlessly instead. "Oh, Micah...it hurts...so much." Her nails bit into the palm of his hand but he didn't make a sound. "Promise me ... if ... anything ... happens ..."

"Nothing is going to happen except that this baby is ready to be born," Rachel said forcefully, walking into the room, her arms full of towels and sheets. "Micah, get out of here. Carrie's trying to be too damned brave because you're here."

"I'm staying as long as she wants me," he said so fiercely Rachel blinked.

"So that's the way it is?"

"No," he said just as fiercely, but she was right and they both knew it. Rachel looked as if she wanted to say more. Another low, animal-like moan from Carrie stopped her and drove every other thought out of Micah's head. "Do something," he growled, helpless as any male in the same situation.

"I am." Rachel tugged on his coat sleeve. "Get out of here. Go see that Reuben and Doug stay out of this cabin, too. We don't need any of you underfoot."

"There must be some way I can help." He looked down at Carrie, unaware that his true feelings showed plainly on his face.

"There is," Rachel said softly, still maddeningly in control. "But it's not in this room." She laid the clean linen she'd been holding on the top of the dresser. "Find me a pair of sharp scissors and some nylon fishing line." He looked blank. "To cut and tie the cord after the baby's born," she explained gently.

He nodded, tight-lipped. "Anything else?"

"Don't tell me you don't know your next line?" Rachel teased, but still gently, tenderly. She made a clicking sound with her tongue against her teeth. "I'll give you a hint. Water."

"Water?"

"Boil some water. Lots of it."

"OKAY, CARRIE, YOU'RE doing fine, just fine." Rachel's voice came from a long way off through a fog of pain that affected her ears as well as her eyes.

"I'm tired, Rachel." She couldn't seem to get a good, deep breath. The contractions were almost continuous, the pain constant. She felt dizzy and weak, disoriented by her strange surroundings. She'd been so adamant about not taking Micah's room for any reason. Now her child was being born in it. Strange. Very strange. She drifted off into the haze.

"Push." It was Rachel's voice, a drill sergeant's voice, unrelenting, merciless. "Push, Carrie."

"I am." She wanted to scream and cry out in pain but she didn't dare. Micah might hear her. He had looked so scared before. She didn't want him to be scared of anything, not babies being born, not of the violence inside him, not of living and loving with all your heart.

"It won't be long now." Rachel's voice held a note of soft excitement. Carrie sensed the change in her own body. The pain was just as fierce, but more focused, more purposeful. "The head's almost ready to be born."

Another contraction built in strength and intensity. Carrie couldn't even find the breath to scream. All she could do was pant and groan. *Like an animal,* she thought, hearing herself. And push. She pushed with all her might. Rachel's voice came from far away. Rest. Push. Rest. One more push. The shoulders were through at last and then she felt the child slip from her body and the pain lost its grip on her soul.

"Is it a boy or a girl?" she managed to gasp, struggling to sit up so that she could see what Rachel was doing at the far end of the bed. "Rachel, what's wrong? The baby isn't crying. Babies are supposed to cry right away. All the books say so. Rachel?"

"Shh, Carrie." Her voice held not the least hint of fear, only wonder... and memories of her own? Carrie couldn't be certain. "The baby's tired, too, from all that work, and just a little lazy." Rachel kept talking in a singsong croon that soothed and comforted Carrie as much as the child. She wiped the tiny body with a clean, white towel. She used a cotton swab to clean his nose and mouth. She laid him on the bed, flicked the soles of his feet with the tip of her finger.

Tiny hands flailed the air, small fists waved in anger and surprise. A healthy wail shattered the quiet, and blue-tinged skin turned pink and healthy before Carrie's tear-misted eyes. Rachel held the baby up for her to see. "Congratulations. You have a fine, healthy son."

A son. She had known all along her child was a boy.

"I knew. I knew." Carrie watched, fascinated, as Rachel tied and cut the umbilical cord as quickly and efficiently as Doc Sauder would have done. She wrapped the baby in a clean, soft towel to keep him warm and laid him in Carrie's arms.

Carrie unwrapped him almost at once. She counted his fingers and his toes, giggled with relief over the tiny penis and scrotum. "He's perfect, just as he should be."

"Anatomically correct," Rachel said, and giggled too.

"He's beautiful," Carrie said as she smoothed a damp, downy wisp of hair off his forehead. "I wish he would open his eyes."

"It's not easy being born." Rachel sat down on the side of the bed, reached out tentatively, almost against her will it seemed, and touched one small, tightly curled fist as Carrie wrapped the towel around him once again. For the first time she noticed that Rachel's hands were shaking. The baby opened his eyes. They were as dark blue as a night sky. His hair was reddish-brown like his father's, growing lighter and silkier as it dried in the warm air. Tiny fingers opened, curled around the tip of Rachel's index finger, closed tight again.

"Welcome, little one," Rachel said so softly Carrie barely heard the words. "May heaven bless you."

"Thank you," Carrie said, tears and fatigue blurring her speech. Suddenly she was so tired she could barely stay awake. "Thank you for helping me bring him safely into the world."

"It was my pleasure." Rachel leaned forward and gave Carrie a quick hug, but not before Carrie saw the tears sliding silently down her cheeks. "It was my pleasure."

DARKNESS WAS COMING EARLY. The clouds were still thick and heavy with moisture, but there was little snow on the ground and the wind held less of a sting than it had that morning. Micah stood looking out of the window of his bedroom. The house was quiet. Rachel was taking a much needed nap. Helping Carrie through her labor had been a traumatic, but also, he thought, a healing ordeal. Reuben and Doug were in the lab. Behind him he could hear Carrie's quiet breathing and if he listened very closely, the quick, shallow breaths of her newborn son.

He had never seen such a tiny baby. Although Rachel had assured him, more than once, that he wasn't so small, close to six pounds, she would guess, and not so far ahead of schedule as Carrie had feared. It was always hard to tell when a first baby would arrive, she'd explained patiently and gently, especially when the date of conception was uncertain. He couldn't hide the quick, dark frown that had followed her words. She had hinted then that he should leave the subject alone. Carrie didn't want to think about her short, unhappy love affair, or the baby's father. Micah didn't think that was wise, but then it was also none of his business. He was the last person on earth to give advice to anyone where matters of the heart were concerned.

Carrie stirred, came awake with a small sigh. He could feel her watching him. He turned away from the window. She gave him a welcoming, sleepy smile. She looked down at her child, cradled in her arms, and the smile softened.

"Did I wake you? I promised Rachel I'd check in on you two."

"No. I was just catnapping. What time is it?"

"About five-thirty. Are you hungry?"

She shook her head. Only the small lamp on his dresser was turned on. Her hair glowed softly, loose around her shoulders in the dim light.

"Are you sure you don't want us to take you into the hospital, get you and the baby checked out?" He knew Rachel had already discussed the matter with Carrie. He just wanted to hear her say it himself.

"I'm fine. We're fine." This time her Madonna-like smile included him. "We'll go see Doc in a few days. Right now I'm so tired I just want to stay here, warm and cozy." She looked around her, then back at him. "Oh dear. I forgot. This is your bedroom...."

"Never mind." He turned fully away from the window and crossed the small room in two quick strides. "Stay as long as you need, as long as you want."

"Tomorrow I'll go back to my own cabin," she said stubbornly.

"We'll see," he replied, not wanting to argue with her. She looked so tired, so delicate, unlike her usual self. There were blue shadows under his eyes and lines of strain on either side of her mouth. He didn't want to think about what she'd gone through. He couldn't imagine why people thought childbirth was such a marvelous thing. At least he couldn't until he looked closely at Carrie's son. She shifted position in his hard, narrow bed.

"Is something wrong?"

"No," she smiled at the nervousness in his voice. "I think my arm has gone to sleep." She pulled the sleeping baby closer to her heart. "He's heavier than he looks."

"Rachel says he weighs about six pounds. We can bring a scale over from the lab to weigh him officially, if you like."

"Thank you."

Micah was quiet for a moment. Carrie patted the side of the bed with her free hand. "Sit down." He hesitated, then did what she asked, gingerly, as though he might do her or the baby some harm if he sat down too abruptly.

Small fists jerked into movement as he settled his weight on the bed; dark blue eyes blinked open and seemed to look straight at him. "He's awake," Micah said, surprised. "I thought they slept all the time when they're that small."

"Not all the time."

"Maybe he wants his diaper changed."

Reuben and Doug had headed into town for baby supplies as soon as the fallen tree had been cleared off the road. They'd come back two hours later, laden down with disposable diapers, tiny shirts and fuzzy socks and receiving blankets, just as they'd been instructed. They'd also brought presents of their own, a miniature baseball bat and glove, a football the size of an orange, and the latest edition of the *Sports Illustrated* swimsuit calendar, which Reuben selflessly offered to keep in trust in his room until the baby was old enough to appreciate it.

"He might need changing," Carrie agreed.

"Should I call Rachel to help?"

"No," Carrie said, checking his diaper. "He can wait a minute or two."

"Have you picked a name?" He'd deliberately stayed away from the house all afternoon, working on reports and a grant proposal that he'd been putting off for weeks. Now he couldn't seem to keep his eyes off the baby. He watched, fascinated, as the tiny, perfect mouth opened and closed in reflexive sucking motions. One surprisingly long leg kicked free of the blanket, a foot popped into view. Micah had the greatest urge to reach out and touch it. The littlest toe was no bigger than a match head. He couldn't help himself. He reached out. The baby's skin was warm and velvet soft. The heel of his hand brushed the full curve of Carrie's breast. Their eyes met and held for a fraction of a second, for the space of a missed heartbeat.

"A name?" she asked, drawing in a deep breath. "Didn't Rachel tell you?" Micah shook his head, unable to trust his voice. His insides were all knotted up. He wanted her and needed her and the realization hit him like a blow to the stomach. He'd never wanted to feel this strongly again and now he had no choice. He felt trapped and scared, for Carrie and the baby more than himself. "His name is Robert Douglas. Robert is for my father, of course. And Douglas is for Doug," she said simply.

"It's a good, strong name." Carrie had made far more progress with Annie's son than he had. He couldn't let the boy go on drifting aimlessly, but he'd had too many other things on his mind the past few weeks to prod the teenager into making any kind of decision about his future.

Carrie saw the frown on his face, guessed his thoughts. "It will all work out. Doug's just mixed-up. He'll come to his senses and make the right choices."

"I hope so. I'm running out of ideas to get him moving. Maybe he isn't going to amount to anything." He said it more to hear her deny it than from any conviction that the boy was bad. He wanted to think her indomitable will could change anyone or anything...even hopeless cases like himself.

"Give him time."

"Time is running out." He didn't want to continue the argument. Carrie was looking very tired again. More than once, when he'd heard her cries in those long hours before dawn, he'd been afraid she would die, and that fear had shaken him to the very foundations of his being. He changed the subject.

"The baby's asleep again."

"I think I'll take a short nap, too." Carrie leaned back against the pillow. She was wearing a pale blue nightgown and her hair was tied back with a blue ribbon. The room was growing darker by the minute. The wind had picked up again and hard pellets of snow rattled against the windowpane. "It's nice and cozy in here." She settled the baby more comfortably against her side.

"I have something for him," Micah said, suddenly remembering what he'd brought with him. He gestured to the maple cradle his mother had stored in the loft above his bedroom.

Carrie twisted around in the bed, frowning a little in momentary discomfort when she moved. "Oh, Micah," she said, quick tears shining in her great brown eyes. "Thank you. Is it an heirloom? It looks very old."

He stood up, moved the hooded cradle closer to the bed so that she could feel the rich texture of the wood. It was hard-rock maple, solid and sturdy, even after four generations of use. "You're welcome to use it as long as you need it." He had no other words to ask her to stay.

"Thank you, Micah." Carrie looked up at him, shyly, hesitantly. "Would you like to lay him in it for me?" Rachel had put a quilted pad and blankets in the cradle. It was all ready for use. Micah felt his stomach lurch. He didn't want to hold Carrie's son, not now, not yet, while memories of his anger, his near loss of control with Erika Mannheim, were too damn fresh in his mind.

"I'm not used to holding babies."

"Of course you are." Carrie lifted her son, offering him. "You hold far smaller babies than Robbie D all the time."

"Robbie D?" Micah kept his hands at his sides, willed them not to ball into fists.

"That's Doug's name for him," she said with a smile that grew stiffer as he watched. "He said with his lungs he'll be a rock star. I kind of like it. Take him," she said with just a hint of challenge in her soft voice.

"I can't." The words came out harsh and rough-edged.

"All right." She sounded defeated. Her arms were trembling, he noticed, as she lowered the baby to cuddle him against her breast. The room was nearly dark. If he didn't look closely, he wouldn't see her tears.

"I...I have to go." His feet remained rooted to the floor.

"I won't keep you." She didn't look at him again. "I don't understand why I'm so sleepy." She laid her head wearily on his pillow. Her words were slurred with fatigue—and sadness? They also dismissed him. "Will you ask Rachel to come in, please?"

"Yes," he said, taking a step toward the bed, not away from it. "Carrie?" She didn't answer. He bent forward. She was asleep, her son cradled in the crook of her arm, his face nestled against the soft fullness of her breast. A tear glistened on her cheek. Micah reached down, unable to stop himself, and wiped it away. She didn't move.

"I love you," he said very softly. "God help us, I love you both."

CHAPTER FIFTEEN

SNOW LAY HEAVY ON THE GROUND. It glittered in the light of a half-moon riding high in a velvet sky as though sprinkled with diamond dust. The night was still and quiet, achingly cold. Carrie pulled the folds of her heavy wool robe more tightly around her. Inside her small cabin it was snug and warm. She turned away from the window for a moment to watch her son, asleep in his cradle. A wondering smile curved her lips as it always did when she looked at him. He was already five weeks old. Where had the time gone?

He was a good baby. He'd been sleeping through the night for almost two weeks, since she'd given up trying to breast-feed and switched him over to formula and the bottle. She still felt guilty, but the fact of the matter was she didn't have enough milk to satisfy him. He was growing so quickly she sometimes thought she could see him change from one hour to the next and bottle-feeding was the only solution to the problem.

She had never seen her father. She remembered her mother as small and pretty and fair. It was obvious already that Robbie would be tall. A basketball player perhaps? Were there athletes in her family? In Evan's? If they were all like him, studious and intellectual, probably not. He was only an inch or so taller than she was. Robbie definitely had his father's impressive nose, but he had her chin, thank heaven. Evan's was nothing to brag about and made his nose look much too big for his face. He did have a full head of hair, she recalled with a grudging smile. That would be nice for Robbie to know when he was old enough to worry about such things as losing his hair.

Carrie reached down and smoothed a downy wisp of red-brown hair off his forehead. Her son frowned in his sleep and searched blindly for something to suckle. He found his fist and started sucking noisily but didn't waken. If she was lucky he'd sleep for at least two more hours. Carrie knew she really ought to try to go back to sleep herself. Instead, she walked across the cold floor, back to the window, and looked out into the November night once again.

Her parents were anxious to see the baby. They thought she should come home. They thought she should tell Evan about Robbie. They were right. The problem was she didn't want to make any kind of decision about her future now because they all involved leaving this place. Leaving Micah.

And in the end, when she'd exhausted all her solitary arguments, she knew that was what she would have to do. If only because she owed it to her son to make a life, the best life she could, for both of them. She loved Micah McKendrick as she had never loved before, would never love again. But she couldn't break through to the man trapped inside the impenetrable shell of solitude he'd built around his heart. She was running out of time to make the attempt. And the knowledge of that fact came close to breaking her heart.

Soon. Very soon she must go.

Moonlight glinted on metal. Carrie blinked back the tears that came so easily these days and looked again. Three figures moved at the edge of the woods. For a moment Carrie could only think of the she-bear and her cubs that she and Doug had stumbled onto that spring night so many months ago. But these figures were not bears out for a last stroll before settling into their winter dens. There were standing upright, walking on two legs. Men. On skis—no, on snowshoes.

As she watched they skirted the empty flight cages at the rear of the building and disappeared, but not before Carrie had glimpsed the rifle slung across the second man's back.

Carrie walked to the table beside her bed. She hit the button on the cordless intercom that both Rachel and Micah had insisted she install when she moved back to the cabin after Robbie was born, grateful for the first time for its presence in her home. It beeped three times before Micah answered.

"Carrie? What's wrong?" He didn't sound sleepy and she wondered if he'd been awake reading as he did so many nights. As always, a wave of longing washed over her when he spoke her name. She pushed the longing aside ruthlessly.

"I saw three men." Her voice came out breathless and strained. "They're trying to break into the lab."

"Are you sure?"

"Yes." She didn't waste words explaining. "Doug's there alone." Reuben had left for Ann Arbor six days before, promising to be back for Thanksgiving dinner.

"I'm on my way."

"Micah." She spoke before he could disconnect her. "I'm almost positive one of them was armed."

"I figured as much." He was silent a moment. "Carrie, don't leave your cabin." She didn't answer. "Do you hear me?" It was an order, not a question.

"Yes," she lied. "I'll stay put."

"Do that." The intercom beeped off. Carrie was already reaching for her clothes.

She literally threw on her jeans and a shirt and pulled on her boots. She gave the baby one last, quick look and headed for the door. She was all he had, but Micah had no one, either. She didn't bother with her coat. It was too heavy and cumbersome. The cold hit her like a blow. Her face stiffened, her hands burned. She kept running, stopping just outside the lab door, her breath coming in quick, painful gasps that hung in the frosty air like smoke. She opened the door just a crack. A hand reached out, snatched her inside and covered her mouth all in one blindingly quick motion. Micah, it seemed, had been waiting for her inside the door. He clamped his hand across her mouth so she couldn't make a sound, could barely breathe.

"Dammit, I told you to stay put." Micah removed his hand from Carrie's mouth.

"What do they want?"

He shrugged, evidently understanding her mumbled whisper. "I'll find out. You get out of here. Go back to the baby."

Carrie twisted her head violently. It was pitch black in the office. Through the glass window in the steel door leading into the lab itself, she could see the beam of a flashlight playing across the walls. She was scared to death of what was happening, and still very much aware of the man holding her, his scent, his touch, the feel of his long, hard legs pushed up against her own.

"Okay." Micah's voice was a dark whisper. She felt his words as much as heard them. "Go along to Doug's room. Wake him up. Keep him quiet. Both of you stay put!"

She nodded to show him she understood. The hand on her mouth loosened, slid away to rest briefly on her shoulder. She thought she felt his lips brush her hair before he pushed her toward the short hall leading to Doug's room, but she couldn't be sure.

"Go."

She shut her eyes tight for a moment, a heartbeat, no more, then started walking, carefully, so she didn't bump into anything and let the men in the lab know they were there. She reached out, touched the doorknob and felt it turn. The door opened. Doug was standing on the other side. A very faint light came from under his bedroom door. They stared at each other in the dark. Carrie reached up, touched her fingers to his lips.

"Someone's in the lab," she whispered as quietly as she could. He nodded.

"Micah?" Doug wasn't wearing a shirt. He was barefoot and shivered in the cold.

"In there." Carrie jerked her head backward. "They have guns."

"I know." He didn't sound like a boy. He sounded like an angry man. This time Carrie shivered. She couldn't help it.

"Micah has the shotgun."

His next words made her go stiff with fear. "He won't use it. They might. Stay here."

Carrie pushed her hair behind her ears to get it out of her face. "No."

Doug didn't argue. "Stay behind me." He lifted a baseball bat that Carrie hadn't seen him carrying. "It's Reuben's. C'mon." She followed him into the dark.

They caught up with Micah at the door. "Keep out of the light. Keep out of the doorway—it'll be in his line of fire," he ordered, still so quietly Carrie could barely hear the words.

The shotgun was resting on his hip, the barrel pointing toward the ceiling. He reached down with his free hand and twisted the latch. It seemed to Carrie, then, as if everything happened at once. Micah swung open the door to the lab and snapped on the lights. Carrie didn't look away quickly enough and found herself blinded by the strong fluorescent overheads. Doug leaped forward, dragging her with him, and crouched behind the big stainless steel worktable just inside the door.

For a moment nobody moved. It seemed Micah had caught the intruders completely off guard, just as he'd intended to do. From below the table edge, Carrie couldn't see anything but the men's legs, covered with camouflage-patterned snowsuits and boots. There were only two pairs of legs. She had seen three. On that thought she turned to warn Micah.

Still crouched on the floor, she looked up to find herself staring directly into the third man's ski-mask-covered face as he walked out of the shadows behind the cages that housed Igor and the peregrines. *Behind Micah, where he couldn't see him.*

It was the man with the rifle. He raised the weapon. Doug yelled. So did Carrie. Micah swiveled on his heel but he didn't raise the shotgun to his shoulder. He never got the chance. The masked man reversed his rifle and brought it down, butt end first, with vicious intent. The stock caught Micah a glancing blow on the shoulder. He dropped to his knee and the shotgun clattered to the floor.

Doug jumped forward, brandishing the baseball bat before Carrie could stop him.

"Hold it, gook," the man with the gun said. "Stay put."

"What the hell you going to do now? Shoot us all?" Doug yelled back but he stayed where he was, sheltering Carrie, still crouched behind the table.

"Don't tempt me." The man glanced down at Doug's bare feet, at Micah struggling to rise from the floor, at Carrie, now standing white-faced and silent behind them both. Igor and the peregrines had been awakened by the intruders and began voicing their dissatisfaction with loud, raucous cries of anger. "Let's get out of here."

With his free hand, the masked man grabbed a freestanding metal shelf full of bottles and glassware and pulled it over. Glass shattered, liquids poured out over the floor. The choking odor of spilled chemicals filled the air. Carrie's eyes watered. She started to cough. She wiped her hand across her eyes and when she looked up again, the three men were gone, the door to the flight cages standing open to the cold.

Doug started after them. Carrie took one long step, grabbed him by the waistband of his jeans and held him back.

"Don't! Your feet will be cut to ribbons. Help Micah up. We can't stay here . . . the smell . . ."

Micah was already struggling to his feet, using the shotgun and the table edge as a prop. Blood stained the collar of his shirt. "Get the birds out of here."

"You're hurt," Carrie protested.

"I'm okay. Do it. Those bottles were full of chemicals. Damn their souls to hell." He staggered toward Igor's cage.

"Doug," Rachel's voice came from the doorway, alert and calm. "Help Micah to a chair. Then get some shoes on. Carrie, help me with these cages." She moved into the big, cold room. Her face was pale, her eyes big and scared, but she never faltered. "I've already phoned the sheriff. What happened?"

"Thieves," Carrie said. "I...I couldn't sleep. I saw them trying to get into the flight cages. What did they want?"

"The birds," Doug said darkly. He reached out to give Micah a hand. Their eyes locked and held a long moment before Doug looked away. "They were after the birds."

DOUG LOOKED DOWN AT THE grilled cheese sandwich on his plate. He couldn't swallow a bite. There was a lump in his throat the size of a gum ball and it wouldn't go away. But if he just sat there, staring at the thing until the cheese got hard and gummy, Carrie would know something was up. He took a bite. It wasn't as hard to swallow as he'd thought. He took another and then a swig of Pepsi. He started to feel just a little bit better. He realized he hadn't had anything to eat since the night before. Breakfast had been forgotten in the scramble to clean up the lab, hunt up some old padlocks to replace the locks on the jimmied door, and assess the damage to the flight cages. Finding someplace for the peregrines and Igor to spend the rest of the night had been the easy part. They'd put them in Reuben's room. He and Carrie and Rachel were so tired by then they'd started giggling like kids over it. Micah hadn't thought it was funny at all. He'd walked into the room holding an ice bag to the back of his neck, and the hard, angry look in his eyes had been enough to sober up anyone, no matter how punch-drunk they were.

The sheriff and his deputy had been thorough in their investigation of the lab and the tracks leading off into the woods. The thieves had been wearing snowshoes, as Carrie had thought, and he said plainly that he wasn't optimistic about catching them. Doug had been torn between anger and relief. Anger that Hank and the others were going to get away with it, and relief that Willie hadn't been one of them. It was a miracle no one knew he had once been part of the gang. *Jeez, his life was a mess.* But he was going to do something about it. Starting right now. He just couldn't sit on the sidelines, keeping an eye on Igor and the peregrines, hoping his problems would go away. It wasn't going to happen like that.

"Micah's still asleep," Carrie said, stepping into the kitchen, catching him lost in his thoughts. He nearly jumped straight up out of the chair. She'd been checking on Micah about every fifteen minutes since Rachel had left for work, after talking him into taking a nap to get rid of his headache.

"Good," he said, not knowing what else to add. He looked down at his plate. The sandwich was gone and so where the chips piled beside it. He took another swallow of Pepsi and held out his hands for Robbie D, resting bright-eyed and interested in his mother's arms. Carrie handed him over without a moment's hesitation. That made Doug feel good, that she trusted him with the baby, but he didn't let on. She walked over to the stove and set about fixing a sandwich for herself.

"Carrie," he said, not giving himself any time to think about what he was going to ask. She would help him. They were friends. She knew what he felt about a lot of things...not knowing who he really was... what he felt about his family. She liked him. Hadn't she proved that by naming her baby after him? Robert Douglas. It sounded good.

"Yes?" She turned away from the stove. The kitchen in the main cabin was so small he could almost have reached out and touched her from where he sat jiggling Robbie D in his lap. The baby started to fuss. Carrie took a blue pacifier out of her pocket and handed it to him. Doug stuck it in Robbie's mouth. He started sucking noisily, content for the moment.

"I need your help." He looked at her without flinching. "I know the guys that broke into the lab last night. It was Hank Kisabeth and his brother, Leon, and their cousin. I know what they wanted and why."

She hesitated before flipping the sandwich on the griddle. "Have you told Micah this?"

"No!" The word exploded out of his mouth. Robbie stiffened and let out a wail. Doug cuddled him to his chest and in a moment he stopped crying. "Micah's hurt. And...I want to make everything right that I can...before I do tell him."

"The men last night. They were the guys you ran around with last summer, weren't they?" She didn't say hoods or punks, and he was grateful.

"Yeah." He didn't look at her but down at the baby in his arms. Robbie D looked a lot like Carrie, except for his nose, which was big for a baby, and his hair, which was darker, more red than blond.

"What exactly did they want?"

"They wanted the birds. At least they wanted Igor. For some rich collector. Dead and stuffed," he added because he had to, not because he wanted to. He chanced looking directly at Carrie's face. She looked shocked and angry but not disgusted with him as he'd feared.

"I see," was all she said. She took a bite of her sandwich, but Doug didn't think she tasted anything.

"I can't do anything but keep on watching over the peregrine chicks. But I can get Igor safely out of their way."

"How long have you known about this?" she said softly, in case Micah was awake, he told himself, not because she felt sorry for him. If she let on she felt sorry for him being such a fool, he'd probably start bawling louder than Robbie D.

"Too long." He shut his mouth with a snap. "I want to let Igor go. Today. Now. Micah said she's ready anytime. She won't even let me handle her anymore, you've seen that." Carrie nodded. He sat back, took a deep breath, looked down. Robbie D was watching him from dark brown eyes. He'd never seen a baby's eyes turn color before, but one day when

Robbie was about three weeks old he'd looked at him and seen the blue in his eyes was all gone. They were just as brown as Carrie's now. Babies were a hoot.

"Is that all?" Carrie asked when he'd finished.

"Yeah." He wasn't ready yet to tell her about Willie, or the poaching. Later. When Igor was safe and gone.

"I'm going with you." She pushed herself away from the table.

"That's probably not such a good idea. What about Robbie D?" He really shouldn't let her go with him. It was a cold, miserable day. He tried to sound stern and discourage her, but he couldn't keep the quaver out of his voice. "This is something I have to do on my own. I don't want Micah involved." At the mention of Micah's name, Carrie's face tightened.

"He'll sleep for a couple more hours. Where do you want to release Igor?"

"Remember when we went up to Lake Superior and the Jeep broke down?"

Carrie's words came out kind of strangled and hoarse. "I remember."

"Reuben and I fixed a place for Igor there, on a cliff. One of the Pictured Rocks."

"We'll take my car and leave Robbie with Rachel. Doc only has office hours until two this afternoon."

"Thanks, Carrie. I won't forget this. I promise."

SNOW WAS PILED UP TO THE door handles on either side of the car. Doug stared at the closed trail at the end of the parking lot at the base of the cliff near Miner's Castle, a popular spot in the Pictured Rocks National Lakeshore, even in winter.

"God, I never thought about the place being snowed in. What'll we do?" His tone was full of disappointment, and anxiety. "I'll never be able to hike in carrying Igor's cage in snow that high. I'm not too good on snowshoes." He looked over his shoulder at the pair he'd thrown into the back seat of Carrie's car next to Igor's traveling cage before they left the compound two hours ago.

"We'll have to go back," Carrie said reasonably. She wasn't certain she was doing the right thing letting Doug take Igor out to the wild this way. The snowed-in trail seemed to be making the decision for her. And she missed her son. This was their first separation. The first time she'd tested her growing friendship with Rachel by asking her to care for him.

"No." This time he sounded desperate. "We can't take her back. I know those guys. They'll be back. This time they'll kill her first, then worry about how to get her out of the lab."

"Okay." She rested her gloved hands on the steering wheel. "Is there anyplace else we can take Igor before it gets dark?" She looked up at pink-tinted clouds. The sun was already well down in the western sky.

Doug was silent a long moment. "Kennedy Lake," he said finally. "It's a hell of a long drive...sorry—" he apologized automatically "—but it's the place she came from. She'll be able to get her bearings there." He rubbed his hands in front of his face. "I should have thought of it first."

"Doug," Carrie asked gently, "how do you know that's where Igor came from?"

He looked at her, and his dark, almond-shaped eyes were bleak and shadowed. "Because I was there when she was shot."

"Okay." She didn't press him further, not now when he looked as if he might burst into tears and was trying so manfully not to. "Point me in the right direction. We've still got three hours until it gets dark."

They almost made it.

Carrie had slowed automatically at the last intersection of the highway and a major county road before the turnoff to Kennedy Lake when a Bronco turned onto the highway behind them.

Doug swung around in the seat, startling Igor, who'd been dozing in her cage. "Cripes. I can't catch a break. That's them. Hank Kisabeth and the others. Step on it, Carrie. Maybe we can get far enough ahead of them they won't see us make the turnoff to Kennedy Lake."

"Maybe we should just head back to the compound," Carrie suggested nervously, but she accelerated past the speed limit just the same.

"No. I don't trust them. We've got to set Igor free."

The Bronco fell behind.

"They aren't trying to catch up with us," Carrie said, looking into the rearview mirror. "It's possible they didn't recognize my car. After all, you only drove it once or twice last summer."

"Yeah," Doug said, but he didn't sound convinced. "Slow down. This is the turn. God, I hope this road is plowed."

It was, but barely. Carrie threaded her way down the slippery, narrow lane toward the access sight Doug had told her lay ahead. The highway and any signs of human habitation were soon left behind. The road wound among the trees for a mile and a half before opening into a small, windswept parking area that hadn't been plowed. There was only a space big enough to turn the car around where the snowplow had done the same.

"I'll use the snowshoes and take her out onto the lake a way so she can get airborne more easily." Carrie didn't say anything to deter him. The lake looked small and shallow. It would have been frozen for a couple of weeks. The ice should be safe. Igor would no longer come to hand. She was almost as wild as the day she'd been brought to the compound.

"Don't go too far." Carrie pulled her scarf tighter around her neck as she stepped out of the car. Twilight shadows were already thick on the snow. The wind was sharp, the sun just above the treetops and devoid of warmth. It was over a week until Thanksgiving. Back in Ohio the leaves would still be on the trees. But here it might as well have been the middle of January.

It was so quiet she could hear the engines of the big trucks on the highway two miles away. She could also hear the whine of a four-wheel-drive engine as Hank Kisabeth's Bronco turned off the main road. Doug jerked the strap on his snowshoe tight.

"Turn the car around. Get ready to get out of here," he ordered, and he didn't sound like a boy anymore at all.

"Doug, wait. We'll do this later. Get back in the car. We'll lock the doors. They can't hurt us." Her hands were trembling, her voice was shaky—and not from the cold.

"They all carry guns. They'll hurt us if they think they have to. They already hurt Micah," he reminded her unnecessarily. He picked up Igor's cage and started walking, clumsily, on the snowshoes. "Do what I say."

He wasn't wearing a hat, Carrie thought absurdly. She should have told him to put his hat on. "Wait," she called.

He turned impatiently, his breath like frosty mist in the air. "I've screwed up this whole damn year, probably the rest of my life. Let me do the right thing this time. Let me do it my way."

"Hurry," she said, and got back in the car. Carrie turned the car as quickly as she could, too quickly. She accelerated too abruptly and slipped off the gravel roadway into the soft, deep snow bordering the single lane. She tried backing up, seesawing from forward to reverse. Nothing worked. The harder she tried, the worse it got. Finally with a sickening lurch the front wheels dropped into a hole and the whole car tilted to the right. Carrie turned off the engine and crawled out. The Bronco was close. She could hear it coming, see flashes of its headlights through the trees. Her own headlights had disappeared under the snow.

She looked out over the frozen lake. Doug had put Igor's cage down on the ice about a hundred yards out. He'd coaxed the eagle out of the cage and now the bird was standing in the snow, still hooded, but otherwise free. The Bronco drove into view at a breakneck pace, snow flying from under its wheels.

"Hurry," Carrie said through stiff lips, but this time it was a whisper, a prayer.

Doug tugged the hood off the eagle's head. Boy and raptor watched each other for a long moment. Then Igor lifted her great wings and flew, just as four men jumped out of the truck. They were all wearing camouflaged snowsuits, just as they'd been last night. Except for one. He was wearing jeans and a hooded sweatshirt and watch cap. He looked cold and miserable and scared. Carrie had no idea who he was.

One man carried a gun—the same man, Carrie was certain, who'd attacked Micah the night before. Today, none of them bothered with masks.

"I told you it was the China-boy and the woman," the man who'd been driving the Bronco crowed. "How about that for luck, eh, Lance?" Hank Kisabeth, Carrie guessed, and the man with the gun, his cousin.

"We couldn't have planned it any better if we'd been drivin' around all day just lookin' for 'em."

"Shut up, Leon, Hank," Lance ordered. He swung the gun around, not quite pointing it at Carrie. "Looks like your car's stuck pretty good."

"We'll get it out."

"Not without a tow. Where's the half-gook?"

Carrie just stood there. It was possible they hadn't seen Igor's cage in the back seat of her car. She wasn't going to make it easy for them. Every second counted. "He's practicing his snowshoeing."

"There he is," the one Lance had called Leon hollered. "I told you I seen a cage in the car." He pointed in the direction of the lake. The man with the gun whirled around. Doug was coming up behind the car carrying the cage. Carrie didn't dare look up into the sky.

"Where's the bird?" Lance demanded.

"Gone." Doug glanced at the mired car with a frown. "You can't get her now."

Lance shoved him aside roughly. He stumbled against the car. The older man threw his rifle to his shoulder and scanned the twilight-blue, cloud-studded sky. Carrie couldn't help herself. She did the same. For a long moment she couldn't find Igor. Then she spotted her, high above, circling higher, heard her faint, triumphant cry as she found her bearings and headed off toward the south and east.

"She's gone. Back where she belongs." Doug stood up, kicked off the snowshoes. "Get out of here and leave us alone. I won't turn you in. Neither will Carrie."

Lance didn't even bother to glance in Carrie's direction. "You're lying, gook. You'll run to the cops the minute you get back to town. Except you ain't gonna get the chance." He indicated the disabled car. "You're gonna be stuck out here forever."

"Lance. No." The man in the hooded sweatshirt moved forward. He was shivering in the cold. His eyes were sunken. He looked old and beaten, yet he couldn't be more than two or three years older than Doug.

"You can't shoot us," Doug said, moving to shield Carrie with his body. "You aren't that goddamn stupid." The sun was gone behind the ridge of pine trees across the lake. The sky was turning dark blue above their heads. In a few minutes it would be dark. The perfect time and place for a violent crime, Carrie thought with a shiver that ran up and down her spine and had nothing to do with the cold.

"Don't have to shoot you, greenhorn. The little lady, here, already got you killed, both of you. It's gonna be a real tragedy when they find you both froze to death in the morning, eh?" He laughed and when Doug lunged for him, he jabbed him hard in the stomach with the barrel of the gun. "Stay put," he growled. Doug slid to his knees, breathing heavily. Carrie knelt in the snow and put her arms around his shoulders.

"McKendrick knows where we are." She made herself look him straight in the eye. She saw a ruthless, desperate man staring back.

"Sure, he does," he scoffed. "Your crazy eagle man ain't so stupid he'd have let you two come out here dressed like that if he knew." He gestured derisively to Carrie's jeans and light boots, Doug's fatigue jacket and sweatshirt. "He ain't clear crazy yet. Him and his sister are gonna be so worried about what become of you they won't even notice one of their precious falcons is missing tonight until I'm long gone. It'll make a good substitute for the eagle. How long you been keepin' them things a secret out there?"

"None of your business. I'll get you for this, Lance," Doug said, his voice hoarse with pain as he struggled to his feet with Carrie's help.

"I'm shakin' in my boots, eh? And don't think if you do manage to keep from freezin' to death that it'll do you any good to go to the cops. Hank and Leon will alibi each other. We been deer huntin' all day. Plenty of people saw us. Willie, here, he lost his job again. He's goin' south with me. Aren't you, Willie?''

"Yeah," Willie said, looking at the ground. "I need work."

"You can't leave us here, man." Doug took a step forward. Lance waved him back with the gun.

"We ain't leavin' you here. We never been here."

"Willie?"

Willie refused to look at him, turned on his heel and climbed into the Bronco.

"Take it easy," Lance said with a laugh as he, too, climbed into the truck.

"So long, sucker," Hank called out the driver's window. They drove off. Carrie's heart beat high and fast in her throat. No one knew where they were. They were stranded and alone and miles from help. *Robbie.* Would she ever see her baby again?

"God, I'm sorry I got you into this." Doug raked his hand through his hair. His breath came in short, painful gasps of white frost. He clutched his stomach with both hands. "I thought Willie was my friend." He shook his head. His ears were red with cold. So was the tip of his nose.

"Let's get in the car." They couldn't risk frostbite or hypothermia in their situation. "After we warm up, we'll see what we can figure out."

"I've kept quiet all these weeks for Willie." Doug's voice was bewildered. "Now he's gonna leave us here to die." Carrie pushed him toward the driver's side of the car. The passenger door was buried in snow.

"Get in," she ordered when he hesitated. "It's my fault, too. I shouldn't have been in such a hurry to turn the car. I'm not used to driving in this much snow." She twisted the key in the ignition, praying that nothing vital was damaged. The car started with no trouble and soon warm air was blowing from the vents. They sat quietly for a few minutes. Beyond the windshield, darkness fell. Stars began to twinkle among the dark shadows of clouds.

"I'll walk out to the highway," Doug said finally. "Flag somebody down to help us."

"It's two miles over a lonely stretch of road and you aren't dressed for it," Carrie pointed out. Neither was she. What was it Micah had said all those weeks ago when they'd been stranded on the Little Fawn? *When you don't know the lay of the land, when you aren't sure of your options—stay put.*

She glanced at the fuel gauge. Less than a quarter of a tank. She'd meant to stop and fill it up after they turned Igor loose. Now it was too late. Still, if they only ran the motor as much as necessary to keep warm, they'd be all right. "We're staying here," she said, making her decision.

"But the peregrines. You heard Lance say they were going back for one of them tonight."

"Micah will deal with him." She was suddenly very sure of that. She was also sure Micah and Rachel would care for her son until her return. "He'll watch out for the peregrines. It's up to us to take care of ourselves."

CHAPTER SIXTEEN

MIDNIGHT. THE THERMOMETER outside the window read sixteen degrees above zero. It was still and clear and the temperature would go even lower in the long, cold hours before dawn.

Where was she? Where was the boy and the eagle? Were they hurt? Were they safe? He hadn't felt so helpless, so impotent since...since the bad years when he'd been so mixed-up and confused that he knew only that something was terribly wrong, that he'd lost control of his mind and his life, and he couldn't do anything about it.

He felt like that sometimes now when he thought of Carrie and what she meant to him—out of control. And oddly enough it wasn't such an unpleasant experience. Bittersweet, perhaps, but not frightening. When you cared a great deal about someone it gave them power over you, made everything about them important to you, took you over. With a woman like Carrie to love and care for, it might not be so bad to let himself go, feel again, love again. If only he could...

"Micah, stop pacing, you're upsetting the baby." Rachel's voice was pitched low so as not to wake the dozing infant in her arms.

"He's asleep," Micah pointed out. He did stop pacing but only long enough to observe his sister holding Carrie's baby. Something had happened to Rachel the night the child was born, some cleansing, some healing of her soul that they hadn't discussed but both knew had changed her outlook, subtly, for the better.

"I'm going to make coffee. Do you want some?" She shifted the baby to her shoulder as she rose from her seat in the rocking chair close to the fire.

"No." Micah started pacing again, although he tried to disguise it by taking a poke at the embers of the fire as he walked by.

"Probably better if you don't." Rachel looked at him appraisingly. "Does your head still hurt?"

"No." But the frown between his eyes told her that it did.

"I'll get you an aspirin." He began another automatic denial. She cut him short. "Micah, two aspirin aren't going to do you any harm. That episode was twelve years ago. It's in the past. Let it be over and done with."

Micah raised his arm, rubbed the aching bruise on his shoulder. "My head doesn't hurt but my neck aches like the very devil." He closed his eyes, rolled his head back on his shoulders to see if that would relieve the strain. It didn't.

"Here," Rachel said when he opened them again. "Take him." She lifted the infant toward him. "I'll get the aspirin."

Micah caught himself before he took a step backward into the fire. His hand clenched on the poker he held. Carrie's son. Over the past month the baby had become a symbol of everything he still didn't know about himself, didn't trust. "I can't," he said, knowing his voice sounded choked and uncertain. "I'll drop him."

Rachel looked stern and loving and bullying all at the same time, all big sister. "No, you won't. You've got the surest hands I've ever seen. Why are you afraid of him? Because you love his mother and he isn't yours?"

"Yes. I mean, no." He looked down at her in exasperation and something close to panic. "You're barking up the wrong tree, Sis. If I loved Carrie I'd love her son."

"I thought so," she said, smiling a little as though he'd said the right thing. She kissed the top of Robbie's head. "Carrie can't help what happened in her past any more than you or I."

"It isn't Carrie's feelings I don't trust. It's me. What I still am inside."

"You're a caring man who won't give himself the benefit of the doubt."

"I'm a man who drove my wife to suicide. Less than a month ago I came close to assaulting Erika Mannheim."

"You should have knocked her flat on her fanny," Rachel said bluntly. "I wanted to." She let it go at that.

"I'm scared of him." Micah looked at the small body, the tiny arms and legs, what could be seen of them bundled up as he was in some kind of yellow drawstring sleeper that Carrie called a kimono. It didn't look like any kimono Micah had ever seen.

"You can't be any more scared of holding him than I was." Rachel's sudden, dazzling smile made him catch his breath. She'd smiled often in the past month, he realized, true smiles of happiness with only the faintest shadow of past sadness in their depths. "Happy, healthy babies are miracles, Micah. I'd forgotten that. Don't let your chance at a miracle get away."

"I..." He placed the poker carefully against the stone fireplace. He wiped his hands down the legs of his jeans. His palms were sweating, his mouth as dry as cotton.

"You can't hide from life forever, Micah."

"I can try," he said helplessly.

"I won't let you. I don't think Carrie will, either." No, Carrie wouldn't let him fail, not with her unswerving loyalty, her faith in him, her goodness and caring. Rachel settled Robbie in his arms. "Just hold his head like this. You're doing great."

"I can't change overnight. Maybe I can't change at all. Maybe I can never learn to trust myself, what's still inside me."

"Carrie's loving and giving and stubborn as hell. She won't give up on you...unless you give her no other choice."

"He's awake," Micah said, thrown off balance as only a big man holding a very small baby can be. "What do I do?"

"Feed him." There were smiles and tears in her words. "Here's his bottle. Just sit in the rocker and get to know each other." She backed away. Micah did as he was told. Robbie regarded him solemnly from brown eyes as large and liquid as his mother's.

"Hi, fella." His voice came out rusty and strained. He cleared his throat and tried again. "I guess we need to get to know each other if you and your mom are going to be sticking around these parts." Robbie gurgled. Micah stepped quietly over the edge and was lost.

He smiled. Robbie smiled back, a trick he'd learned just that week that seemed to please the grown-ups around him.

"So what do you think of the Vikings' chances in the play-offs?"

CARRIE LOOKED AT THE CLOCK on the dashboard. It was 2:15 a.m. She tried not to look at the fuel gauge. It would read less than an eighth of a tank. She wondered if they would make it until morning. Her hands and feet were so cold they felt like blocks of ice. The heater in the little car just couldn't keep up with the cold. Why hadn't she followed Micah's example and packed emergency supplies in the trunk when she knew she would be staying here at least part of the winter?

"Did you see headlights through the trees?" Doug asked, breaking the silence. Carrie had thought he was asleep.

"No. My window's frosted over." She took a swipe at it with her glove.

"I thought I saw something." He sat up a little straighter.

"Doug," she said as gently as she could. "It was probably a dream."

"No. There it is again."

Carrie rolled down the side window despite the loss of precious warmth. "Do you think they're coming back?'' She regretted the words the moment they left her mouth. Her voice sounded lost and scared. Doug didn't need her fear to add to his worries.

"I don't know. I can't even be the hero and tell you to run for it while I hold them off. I haven't got anything to hold them off with."

"And I haven't got anywhere to run, so we'll stay here and face whoever it is together. Okay?"

"Okay." He gave her a lopsided, halfhearted grin. "We're in this together. Thanks, Carrie."

"That's what friends are for." She could see the headlights clearly now.

"If we get out of this alive, I swear I'll go back to school and work like a slave."

"Promise?"

"Promise."

"I figured that's what you'd end up doing anyway."

"I know."

"I don't think that's Hank's Bronco," Carrie said hopefully, a few minutes later. "It looks more like a car."

"Yeah, it does." They fell silent again. The oncoming vehicle made a last turn and left the concealment of the trees.

"It is a car."

"A cop car." Doug straightened, then scrambled across the seat after Carrie. Two men in uniform hats and heavy coats got out of the highway patrol cruiser, followed by a third man, thinner, less heavily dressed. "It's the cops," Doug said unnecessarily, stamping his cold feet to bring back the circulation after sitting in the cramped little car for so many hours.

"Who's that with them?" Carrie wrapped her arms around her to keep out the numbing cold.

"Willie," Doug said, and his voice cracked. "My friend, Willie Jenks."

RACHEL CLOSED HER EYES IN silent thanksgiving as she listened to Micah's one-sided conversation with the baby. Her brother was learning to deal with his feelings, to realize the rage inside him was not out of control and would never be again. He was learning to love. He was healing.

She opened her eyes and studied her reflection in the bathroom mirror. She was healing also. In small ways. In others, there was still a great darkness, a place of secrets inside her that her present life, no matter how busy and focused, could not eliminate. She didn't want to face the dark memories inside her that had been clamoring for recognition, however faintly, since she'd told her family about her dead child. They were too painful. She hated the woman who recalled that past. She hated the things she had done to keep herself and Father Pieter alive.

Yet she knew she was going to have to take the chance of letting that other scared and weak Rachel break through her carefully constructed and maintained defenses. Something was missing, some part of her she needed to know to be herself again, whole and complete. She hadn't found that new Rachel living with her parents in Florida, with Simon and Annie in Chicago, nor here with Micah. In her heart she knew that lost part of herself was half a world away. Although she dreaded what she might find if she returned to Southeast Asia, she knew, someday, she must go back there or risk losing her very soul.

THE PATROL CAR PULLED into the compound. There were lights on in the main cabin, and the soft, welcoming glow of lamplight shining through the curtains of her small home. *Her home.* It had been her shelter and sanctuary for six months. Tonight it was also her home. Carrie blinked back a tear. She was cold and tired and more than a little confused by the events of the past two hours. She wanted Micah there to take control, to deal with the authorities, to make sure Doug's rights were protected when he gave his statement to the police. And she wanted her son in her arms again.

"You'll find Dr. McKendrick in the main cabin," she directed the older of the two highway patrolmen. "My baby—" she gestured helplessly toward her cottage "—please." Her teeth were chattering. She'd been so cold, then almost too warm in the patrol car, now cold again. It was still hours until dawn and only a few degrees above zero.

"Go ahead, ma'am," the trooper said. "Come on, son." He motioned to Doug to lead the way into the house.

"Carrie?" Doug looked tired and scared and more than a little confused. "Should I?" They'd dropped Willie off at the jail in Marquette to give his statement and make positive identification of Lance and the others who'd been picked up earlier that night. No one would tell her what might happen to Doug after he gave his statement.

"Go ahead. Micah will take care of everything." Carrie smiled at the absolute certainty she heard in her own voice. "He'll know what to do."

She turned and ran along the snowy path to her cabin, expecting to find Rachel watching over her son. She opened the door to a rush of warmth and light. "Micah?" She stopped with her foot on the threshold.

"Come in, you're letting in cold air." He stood up from the rocking chair. He seemed to fill the room with his height and broad shoulders. She couldn't take her eyes off him. Or the baby he was holding in the crook of his arm.

"Welcome back." Micah's voice was low and rough. He looked down at the baby, avoiding her eyes. "He missed you. I brought him home after the police called and said you were safe." Carrie watched as Micah's big hand soothed and comforted her son. Robbie was wearing a bright red and yellow Winnie the Pooh sleeper. He looked small and fragile against the solid wall of dark blue flannel covering Micah's chest. He fixed big brown eyes on her face. Tiny arms and legs began to wave at the sound of her voice. He smiled and Carrie had not a single doubt he knew exactly what he was doing. "We both missed you." Micah wasn't looking at Robbie anymore. He was looking at her. Carrie shut the door behind her, dropped her coat and hat where she stood and went into his arms.

"Micah, I was so afraid. But I knew." She lifted her hand to touch the baby's silky hair as she tipped her head to smile into Micah's wary blue-gray eyes. "I knew you'd keep my son safe and sound." She took the baby into her arms, nuzzling his neck, holding him tight to her breast. Micah wrapped his arms around them both, holding them safe and close. Carrie could gladly have stayed there forever in the warm silence of the little cabin, in the haven of Micah's arms, absorbing the wonder of his silent commitment to her through his care of her son.

Robbie stirred and began to whimper. "Is he hungry?" Carrie asked, having no idea what time it actually was. She was tired and cold and hungry. Her apprehension for Doug tickled the back of her mind, but she was too happy being reunited with her child in the arms of the man she loved to give it her full attention at the moment.

"I don't think so. I fed him just before we got the call from the highway patrol."

"You fed him?" Carrie smiled at the picture that flashed before her mind's eye. "I wish I could have been here."

"I'm not very good at it," Micah confessed. Robbie cried harder. "I don't think he likes his mother having cold hands." He reached out and covered hers with one of his own, taking the sting out of the words with the gentleness of his actions.

"I am cold." Carrie started to shake and was unable to stop. "I was truly afraid we'd freeze to death before someone found us."

"Don't think about it now," Micah ordered, gruff and tender as only he could be. "Let me put Robbie in his crib. He'll do fine until we get you warmed up and something to eat."

"A hot shower, food and about twelve hours of uninterrupted sleep." Carrie bent to lay Robbie in his crib. He was already quiet, sucking greedily and contentedly on his pacifier. He was such a miracle of hope and love. "I couldn't have made it through all those dark, cold hours if I hadn't known he was safe with you." Carrie knew she was repeating herself, knew she was using those words as substitutes for others, even more personal, more revealing, that Micah as yet didn't seem to want to hear, or to speak for himself.

"It's all over now." His hand on her shoulder was reassuring, and more. Tiny curls of awareness swirled in her bloodstream. She turned her head, rubbed her cheek against his shirt and the back of his fingers. His grip tightened, then gentled as he cupped her cheek with his hand. She took a shaky breath and thought of... Doug.

"Micah. The police. They want to talk to Doug. They took him to the main house. I thought... I thought you'd be there." He took her arm, helped her to rise. Robbie watched them solemnly from unblinking brown eyes. "He's so scared and confused. What if he says something he shouldn't? What if he incriminates himself in their filthy poaching scheme?"

"Don't worry." Micah's voice, as always, soothed and excited her. She'd never be able to just listen to him talk as she did other men, ordinary men, men she didn't love with all her heart and soul. "I'll get it straightened out." He would. She hadn't doubted it since the patrolmen had explained the charges to him over the phone. He brushed her hair back from her cheek, fitted his hand to the curve of her throat. "Get in the shower. When I get back we have a lot to talk about."

Fifteen minutes later Carrie came out of the closet-sized bathroom of her cabin, wrapped in a big, fuzzy pink robe. It reached to the floor, had fitted sleeves with knit cuffs and a wide collar she could turn up around her ears when the wind howled outside the cabin. He was standing at her hot plate, stirring a pan of soup.

"Are the state troopers gone already?" Her heart was beating just a shade too fast. Fatigue slowed her thoughts but not her response to Micah's nearness, or the fact that they were alone together for the first time in days and days.

"Yes. I'll call my lawyer in the morning. He'll arrange for Doug to give his statement." He poured the soup, tomato from the aroma, into the mug and shut off the gas flame.

"He won't have to go to jail, will he?" Carrie accepted the mug with a smile of thanks.

"He's a juvenile with no previous record. I guess the worst you could say was that he's an accessory. I don't know. We'll have to wait and see. I wish he'd told me what was going on a long time ago."

"I had no idea." Carrie took a sip of the soup. It was just right, not too hot, warm and familiar, like winter afternoons at her parents' house.

"I told my brother and Annie I was no good at raising teenagers." He ran his hand through his hair. Carrie held her breath. Her heart kicked into a faster pace and the sensation wasn't pleasant. She'd never been able to pull him completely out of his black moods when he grew angry and impatient with his own shortcomings, his own perception of guilt. Maybe she couldn't again but she had to try.

"Micah." She put the soup down on the table in the middle of the room. Micah was standing in front of the crib, watching Robbie sleep.

"I know." He waved his hand in the air. "I couldn't have known what was going on in his head any more than you or Rachel. The trick now is to minimize the damage, right?" He kept his back to her.

"Doug knows he was wrong. And whatever he did, his influence on Willie Jenks saved our lives." She felt more confident. "You can't make me think you failed with the boy as long as I know that. He stayed here to save Igor and the chicks. He risked his life to do that."

"He's a good kid." Micah turned around slowly. "I told him that. I told him I was proud of the way he handled himself tonight. I told him we'd stick by him all the way."

We'd stick by him all the way. Did he mean that? Was he telling her he was including her in his future? Or was he speaking only for Rachel and himself? Suddenly Carrie had to know where she stood with him.

"Why are you here, Micah?" she asked, running the tip of her finger around the rim of her mug. She didn't pick it up again but watched misty tendrils of steam curl upward in the air as the liquid cooled.

"I . . . wanted to make sure you and Robbie were all right for the night . . . what's left of it."

She shook her head. "That's not good enough."

"What do you want me to say, Carrie?"

"Why aren't you afraid of holding Robbie anymore? Why aren't you afraid of being alone with me? Here. Now." She'd skirted a meeting with death tonight. She wasn't about to let fate, or insecurity, or cowardice shape her destiny from this moment forward. If Micah McKendrick didn't want her, he was going to have to say so. In plain English. Spell it out, once and for all.

He didn't say anything for a long time, so long, Carrie began to wonder if she'd pushed him too far. He shoved his hands in the pockets of his jeans. She shoved hers in the pockets of her robe. He looked at Robbie. She looked at him.

"I've lived alone for so long, really alone, in a place inside myself that was small and dark and cold so I didn't have to feel, didn't have to consider others, didn't have to remember the things that had happened to me in the past. It was the only way I knew how to get through the nights." Still not looking at her, he walked to the window and stared out at the snowy compound.

"What changed that?"

He laughed and it sounded rusty and hollow. "Can't you guess?"

"Probably," Carrie admitted, "but I want to hear you say it."

"You have. Rachel has. Doug and the baby. But mostly you, Carrie, God help me, mostly you." He swung around and his eyes were no longer shuttered, reflecting blue-gray pools that hid his thoughts and hopes and fears and dreams. They were the windows of his soul, as the poets said. And the love she saw unguarded in their depths humbled her pride and soothed her fears.

"I love you," Carrie said simply. "I've loved you for a long time."

"I know, and love's a terrible thing to fight against." He smiled then, really smiled, and Carrie flew across the room and into his arms. "I've battled it for months. But you wouldn't let me crawl back into my cell. Every time I trotted out a sin, a demon, you looked it straight in the eye and brushed it aside. Finally, I began to believe in myself again, although I tried as hard as I could not to."

"Why didn't you tell me?" She lifted her mouth for his kiss, preferring that to words. He answered her unspoken request.

"Because I didn't realize it myself until Rachel made me face facts. I'm not going to lose control of myself again. Erika Mannheim deserved a good shake."

"She deserved more than that," Carrie said with a great deal of spirit, remembering her own jealousy. "She's a bitch."

"Hey?" Micah looked slightly shocked, then pleased when she refused to back down.

"She is."

"Okay, I won't argue." Carrie subsided into his arms once again. She leaned her head against his chest, felt the strong, steady beat of his heart, felt the acceleration as she slipped her fingers inside the open neck of his shirt to caress the warm, hair-roughened skin in the hollow of his shoulder. "Last night I could have blown all three of those guys to kingdom come. If I'd been as violent, as out of control as I always believed myself to be, I would have. I didn't. I never even considered pulling the trigger of that shotgun."

"I could have told you that," Carrie said, continuing her exploring caress. She wanted to hear him talk, wanted him to tell her things, good things and bad, but not now, not tonight. She wanted him with her, in her, filling her with warmth and love, making love together. Words were good, especially when they came from the heart, as Micah's always would. But loving was better.

"I deserve a good life. I deserve a home and a wife...." He caught his breath as Carrie began unbuttoning his shirt.

She paused, fixing her eyes on the button she'd just undone. "A family?" she said very quietly, giving voice to a demon of her own.

Micah reached down, tilted her chin with the tip of his finger. "A family. I'm not used to talking this much, Carrie. What more do you want me to say tonight?"

"Three little words," she said as his lips came down on hers. "Just three words."

He obliged as he scooped her up into his arms and moved across the room to her bed and followed her down onto the mattress. "I love you." There was more they needed to say, more he wanted to say, much more, but they had all the time in the world. For now, this was enough. He let his hands and lips and body tell her the rest of what was in his heart.

CHAPTER SEVENTEEN

BEYOND THE WINDOW OF THE cabin it was full daylight. Micah came slowly awake, opening his eyes to see Carrie's head on the pillow beside him, feel the soft curves of her body fitted against his own, and savor the reality of her at his side. He loved her and he'd found the courage to say the words aloud. Soon he would ask her to be his wife, to share the rest of his life. Soon she would be his in every sense of the word.

He had wanted to make love to her last night more than he'd ever wanted anything in his life, but he had not. She wasn't ready to make love, physically, and perhaps in some ways, emotionally. He hadn't been prepared to protect her from another pregnancy. He wanted their love to be based on trust. It was more important to him than anything else. How could she trust him, even if she loved him, especially if she loved him, if he couldn't control the most basic of urges for her sake?

Micah stared at the back of her head and smiled. Carrie was a remarkable woman. She hadn't quite seen it his way...at first...but although her response to his kisses, the caresses she initiated on her own, were all he hoped for, she was still apprehensive about sex. Evan Walsham, the bastard, may have been cavalier about birth control. Micah McKendrick was not. He could wait until Doc Sauder gave her his okay. Carrie stretched and yawned and pushed her rounded bottom against him. He groaned. Being noble was one hell of a tough job.

"Micah?" She stiffened for a moment, then relaxed against him, angling her upper body a little away from him so that she could see his face. "Good morning?" She smiled and colored prettily. Her skin was smooth and clear, creamy and faintly golden. Her cheeks were the velvety pink of a woodland orchid.

"Good morning," he said, propping himself on his elbow, still unable to completely believe that she was there beside him, that the lonely, lost years were behind him forever. "Did you sleep well?"

"Once I got to sleep, yes," she said, turning pinker still. Micah couldn't be certain but he thought she might be pouting... just a little. He didn't mind it at all when he considered what she was pouting about. "What time is it?"

"Almost nine."

"So late?" She sat up, realized she was wearing only her panties and pulled the covers up to her chin. "It's late... I'm surprised Robbie isn't up."

Soft snuffling sounds were issuing from the cradle beside the bed. "I don't think he'll sleep much longer." Micah's attention wasn't centered on the sleeping baby but on his mother. The skin of her throat and breasts was even softer and creamier than her face.

"What about Rachel and Doug?" Carrie dropped her eyes to her lap. His desire, his need for her must be showing on his face. Micah swung his long legs over the side of the bed, giving her a moment to regain her composure.

"Doug will probably sleep until noon. Rachel will already have figured us out. She's pretty savvy, my sister."

"I know," Carrie said in a very small voice. "Oh, dear."

Micah considered asking her to marry him then and there, then changed his mind. He didn't think she'd appreciate an offer of marriage while she was sitting in bed, trying not to look concerned that he was seeing her naked, for the first time in broad daylight. She was so old-fashioned in some ways, and so very open-minded in others. He smiled to himself. He'd been only half-alive for so long he wasn't sure exactly how to act with her. He was going to have to trust his heart as Rachel had suggested. His heart told him to go slow, very slow. Carrie was more like one of his beautiful wild birds than she would care to admit, or perhaps he should compare her to the fawn she'd stumbled across on that long-ago spring afternoon.

"Does it bother you that Rachel has us figured out?" He reached for his jeans to give her an opportunity to pull on the woolly pink robe he dragged up from the end of the bed.

"No." She dropped the robe and the sheet and surprised him yet again by pulling his head down to hers, kissing him fully, hungrily, on the mouth. "It doesn't bother me in the least."

"I'm glad." He wanted to say a lot more but the words weren't there. Maybe they never would be, but with Carrie that didn't seem to matter. She felt with her heart more truths than other people heard, or saw, or spoke, all bundled together.

"It sounds like Robbie decided on just a little longer snooze," she said when the kiss ended. Her voice trembled, her breath came quick and shivery between her lips. Micah's body hardened with desire, but so did his resolve.

"Why don't you take a shower and I'll rustle up some breakfast before I go feed the chicks. I don't know if Doug will remember to do it this morning."

"He'll remember," Carrie said as she slipped out of bed, stooping by the cradle to straighten the baby's blanket and smooth her finger along his cheek.

"Yeah." Micah dragged his hand through his hair. "I think you're right." Carrie gave him such a brilliant smile he felt as if he'd been hit by a truck.

"There's milk and eggs in the fridge. Don't get the milk mixed up with Robbie's formula. It tastes awful."

"I'll remember that." He watched her closely. A little frown came between her eyes as if she remembered something she didn't quite want to.

"The coffeepot and the toaster are right there on the shelf." The frown disappeared. She stood up, tightened the belt of her robe and walked around the bed to wrap her arms around his waist. "I love you, Micah McKendrick."

He kissed the top of her head. "I love you, Carrie Granger. Will you marry me?"

"Only me?" she asked in a teasing voice, but there was no answering twinkle in her brown eyes. Micah was confused. He didn't say anything. "I don't know," she went on, her tone serious, too serious, it seemed to him. "I'll have to think about it. I'll get back to you after my shower."

WHY IN HEAVEN'S NAME HAD she said that? Carrie asked herself as she toweled dry in the minuscule bathroom of her cabin. She'd treated his proposal as if it were a joke. Sometimes when she was happy she did silly, thoughtless things. And sometimes, when she was scared, she did stupid things. This time she was happy and scared, and she had done the silliest, stupidest thing of all. Micah didn't say, *I want to marry you and be a father to your son.* And because he hadn't added that all-important rider to his proposal, she'd panicked and run into the bathroom like a silly schoolgirl. Micah loved her. He loved Robbie, too. She was only insecure because there was a major problem in her life that still wasn't resolved.

Evan.

She needed to come to terms with Robbie's father so that she could look ahead to the future. Carrie wiggled into her jeans and pulled her hair into a haphazard knot on top of her head. Micah would understand about Evan if she only explained it to him. He *did* understand. He'd already told her she had to do that very thing.

A letter first, she decided, chewing her lower lip. No phone calls, yet. And then, at Christmas, maybe, after she'd savored the joy of being loved by Micah long enough to be able to deal with Evan's demands . . . then she would see him . . . discuss his place in Robbie's life. Yes, that was how it would be.

Micah was standing in front of the window, his hands pushed into the back pockets of his jeans. The coffeepot was beginning to perk on the hot plate. No other preparations for breakfast seemed to be on line. Robbie was awake but quiet in his cradle. His bottle was warming in a pan of hot water on the counter by the sink. Carrie padded silently across the room in stockinged feet. She wrapped her arms around Micah's waist, she pressed her face against his back, felt the strength beneath the soft, wrinkled flannel of his shirt, smelled the tantalizing scent of wood smoke and soap and maleness that was Micah, himself.

"Micah? I want to..." she never finished what she was going to say.

"A car just pulled in," he said. Carrie let her hands drop from his waist as she stepped back, chilled by the old familiar lack of emotion in his voice. "A man got out. He's talking to Rachel and she's pointing over here. He's not too tall, about forty, I'd guess, with reddish-brown hair and a damn big nose."

"Evan." Carrie felt panic close in on her like dark wings blocking the sun. Micah turned away from the window.

"That's my guess." His face was immobile.

"I don't want to see him." Carrie backed away as if that might help. Dear God, what absolutely rotten timing the man had. Why had he picked today of all days to waltz back into her life?

"You can't put this off forever."

"Yes, I can," she said a little wildly, kneeling to pick up her son. Robbie jerked in surprise and whimpered. "I don't want to see him."

"Carrie, he's Robbie's father." Micah's voice had softened but still she had no clue to his thoughts or feelings. *Why had she thought he'd changed? She didn't know him any better now than she had six months ago. If he loved her, wouldn't he rescue her now when she needed it most?* "You can't run away from him forever."

Carrie opened her mouth to say she could, but a knock on the door forestalled her. She looked around. Micah was dressed except for his shoes. They were lying at the foot of the bed, the unmade bed. Carrie sucked in her lower lip in confusion. Evan knocked again.

"Are you ashamed of having me here?" This time she heard the hurt and uncertainty in his voice.

"Don't you dare walk out on me," she said. Micah smiled and Carrie's heart slowed to a sure and steady beat.

Her chin came up. She'd been stupid to think he didn't love her. He did. And he was proving it by letting her handle this situation alone. He had faith in her. She only needed to have faith in herself. She held Robbie high and safe against her breast. She breathed deeply of his sweet baby scent, then stepped forward and opened the door.

Evan Walsham stood outside, hatless, wearing gloves and a green down parka. His hand was raised to knock again. "Carrie?" She wondered if she'd changed that much in eight months. He looked as if she had. "May I come in?"

"Yes." She stepped back. He hadn't changed at all. There weren't any new worry lines—remorse lines, she wanted to think of them—no tinge of sadness in his eyes. He looked just as he always had, just as Micah had described him, a pleasant-looking man, no longer quite young, not bad or weak but not strong and good, either.

He'd been looking at the baby. He didn't see Micah until Carrie introduced him. Then Evan looked around him at the unmade bed, at Micah's shoes and coat and gloves scattered around the small room, and his face hardened just a little. "I hoped we'd be able to talk in private."

"Whatever you have to say to me you can say in front of Micah." She turned her head. He was looking at her and his eyes were no longer shuttered, his face no longer wiped free of emotion. He was smiling slightly and she knew what to say next. "We're going to be married." She smiled too.

MICAH STEPPED FORWARD. He didn't hold out his hand or introduce himself, just stood behind Carrie, close enough to touch, close enough for her to know that he would be there for her from this moment on. Walsham looked at him assessingly for a moment, then glanced away. His eyes kept going back to the baby. A small jab of pain tightened Micah's gut. *Robert Douglas Granger looked exactly like his dad.*

"What do you want, Evan?" Carrie was holding Robbie so tightly he squealed. Micah touched her lightly, on the back just above the waist. He felt her relax, deliberately loosening tensed-up muscles for her child's sake.

"I wanted to talk to you." Evan Walsham looked like a man on the rack. Micah didn't feel a damn bit sorry for him. "I got your parents to tell me where you were. I tried to call here but I haven't been able to get an answer. Yesterday afternoon I just decided to come and find you." He stumbled over the words.

Carrie had said he was a professor of some sort. He looked like a college professor, myopic, smug, slightly above the rest of the everyday world and everyday people. He didn't look like the type who could attract an intelligent, caring woman like Carrie, bewitch her so completely she couldn't see through his lies, seduce her and make her pregnant, at least not to Micah's biased way of thinking.

"I would have contacted you when I was ready."

"I wanted to see my son."

Carrie stiffened again. Robbie began to whimper. Walsham looked nervous, miserable.

"You can't have him, Evan." Carrie's voice was low and soft, at odds with her tense posture. Micah didn't move a muscle. She had to do this for herself, he told himself, kept telling himself. But his heart, so newly healed, ached for her.

"Robbie and I are doing fine. Why don't you just go back...to your wife...and leave us alone." Carrie shushed Robbie in a low, crooning tone but her eyes never left Walsham's face.

"May I hold him?" Carrie sucked in her breath. Micah clenched his fists to keep from taking her in his arms. This was her terror in the night. She had to fight it alone. After a long moment she handed the baby over. Walsham took him in surprisingly compctent hands. Micah hated him a little bit more.

"He's a fine boy, Carrie. What did you name him?"

"Robert Douglas."

"Robert is your father's name, isn't it?" He didn't look at Carrie again, only at the child. Robbie looked small and fragile against his coat. He regarded his father from solemn brown eyes for a long moment, blinked, and started to cry.

"Yes."

"And Douglas?" He chucked Robbie under the chin. The baby cried harder.

"A friend."

"I see." He held Robbie's hand between his thumb and finger, marveling at its size and perfection, just as Micah had only hours ago.

"Please, give him back, Evan," Carrie said with only a hint of tremor in her voice. "He's hungry and he needs to be changed."

"Of course." A muscle jumped in his jaw. For the first time Micah felt a hint of compassion for the man. "I opened a savings account in his name. For his education. I left the information with your parents."

"We don't need your money." Carrie had stiffened again.

"Let me do that for my...your...son." Evan Walsham looked like he laughed a lot. Robbie would probably laugh a lot, too. He reached out to touch Robbie's silky hair. He wasn't laughing now. He looked like a man who was beginning to realize what he was losing. "I'm sorry for what I did to you, Carrie."

"I was as much to blame as you were. I chose to believe your lies and ignore your evasions." Walsham winced at Carrie's blunt words.

"I gave up my position at the university. My wife and I are moving back to California after the New Year. That's why I wanted to contact you now, to let you know there was no reason you couldn't return home, take back your old job if you wanted it."

"I don't want it." Micah's pulse sped up. She was going to stay with him.

"You will let me know how he's doing from time to time, won't you?"

"Yes," Carrie replied very softly. "I'll let you know from time to time."

"I'd like to send him presents, for his birthday, Christmas, things like that."

She nodded. "Of course."

"You mean that, don't you? You won't just disappear with him the way you did when you found out you were pregnant?"

"I'm not that selfish or hateful. I mean it. Goodbye, Evan." Her words were dismissal as well as absolution.

"Goodbye, Carrie. Goodbye, young Robert." He touched the baby's hair once more. If he had intended to press his claim to Robbie further, it was obvious that he had changed his mind. "Take care of them." He looked Micah straight in the eye for the first and only time.

"I intend to."

Carrie turned and smiled up into his face and he knew that was what she'd been waiting to hear all along. Evan Walsham closed the door very quietly and walked back out of their lives.

Micah held out his arms and Carrie came into his embrace as if it were the most natural place in the world for her to be. And it was. He kissed her long and sweet. They didn't stop until Robbie began to wiggle restlessly between them.

"He's soaked," Carrie said, and giggled, tears in her eyes, relief and happiness mixed in equal quantities in the sound.

"You change him." Micah made a face at the dark stain on the front of his shirt.

"Spoken like a true father." There was just the faintest hint of a question in her voice.

"Robert Douglas Granger McKendrick. That's quite a name for such a little boy."

"He'll grow into it," Carrie said with great conviction, hugging her son. "I'm certain of it."

"He looks a lot like his father." Micah could have kicked himself for saying that, but he couldn't seem to help it.

"Yes, he does." Carrie lifted her hand to lay it against his cheek. Micah looked down at her, at her son . . . his son . . . and then into her eyes. He saw love and happiness and all the years of their future in their brown depths. "Robbie may look like his father," she admitted softly. "But I want him to grow up to be just like you."

Take 4 bestselling love stories FREE
Plus get a FREE surprise gift!

PASSPORT TO ROMANCE
SWEEPSTAKES RULES

1. **HOW TO ENTER:** To enter, you must be the age of majority and complete the official entry form, or print your name, address, telephone number and age on a plain piece of paper and mail to: Passport to Romance, P.O. Box 9056, Buffalo, NY 14269-9056. No mechanically reproduced entries accepted.

2. All entries must be received by the CONTEST CLOSING DATE, DECEMBER 31, 1990 TO BE ELIGIBLE.

3. **THE PRIZES:** There will be ten (10) Grand Prizes awarded, each consisting of a choice of a trip for two people from the following list:
   i) London, England (approximate retail value $5,050 U.S.)
   ii) England, Wales and Scotland (approximate retail value $6,400 U.S.)
   iii) Carribean Cruise (approximate retail value $7,300 U.S.)
   iv) Hawaii (approximate retail value $9,550 U.S.)
   v) Greek Island Cruise in the Mediterranean (approximate retail value $12,250 U.S.)
   vi) France (approximate retail value $7,300 U.S.)

4. Any winner may choose to receive any trip or a cash alternative prize of $5,000.00 U.S. in lieu of the trip.

5. **GENERAL RULES:** Odds of winning depend on number of entries received.

6. A random draw will be made by Nielsen Promotion Services, an independent judging organization, on January 29, 1991, in Buffalo, NY, at 11:30 a.m. from all eligible entries received on or before the Contest Closing Date.

7. Any Canadian entrants who are selected must correctly answer a time-limited, mathematical skill-testing question in order to win.

8. Full contest rules may be obtained by sending a stamped, self-addressed envelope to: "Passport to Romance Rules Request", P.O. Box 9998, Saint John, New Brunswick, Canada E2L 4N4.

9. Quebec residents may submit any litigation respecting the conduct and awarding of a prize in this contest to the Régie des loteries et courses du Québec.

10. Payment of taxes other than air and hotel taxes is the sole responsibility of the winner.

11. Void where prohibited by law.

COUPON BOOKLET OFFER TERMS

To receive your Free travel-savings coupon booklets, complete the mail-in Offer Certificate on the preceeding page, including the necessary number of proofs-of-purchase, and mail to: Passport to Romance, P.O. Box 9057, Buffalo, NY 14269-9057. The coupon booklets include savings on travel-related products such as car rentals, hotels, cruises, flowers and restaurants. Some restrictions apply. The offer is available in the United States and Canada. Requests must be postmarked by January 25, 1991. Only proofs-of-purchase from specially marked "Passport to Romance" Harlequin® or Silhouette® books will be accepted. The offer certificate must accompany your request and may not be reproduced in any manner. Offer void where prohibited or restricted by law. LIMIT FOUR COUPON BOOKLETS PER NAME, FAMILY, GROUP, ORGANIZATION OR ADDRESS. Please allow up to 8 weeks after receipt of order for shipment. Enter quickly as quantities are limited. Unfulfilled mail-in offer requests will receive free Harlequin® or Silhouette® books (not previously available in retail stores), in quantities equal to the number of proofs-of-purchase required for Levels One to Four, as applicable.

OFFICIAL SWEEPSTAKES ENTRY FORM

Complete and return this Entry Form immediately—the more Entry Forms you submit, the better your chances of winning!
- Entry Forms must be received by **December 31, 1990**
- A random draw will take place on **January 29, 1991**
- Trip must be taken by **December 31, 1991**

3-HS-3-SW

YES, I want to win a PASSPORT TO ROMANCE vacation for two! I understand the prize includes round-trip air fare, accommodation and a daily spending allowance.

Name_____

Address_____

City_____ State_____ Zip_____

Telephone Number_____ Age_____

Return entries to: **PASSPORT TO ROMANCE**, P.O. Box 9056, Buffalo, NY 14269-9056

© 1990 Harlequin Enterprises Limited

COUPON BOOKLET/OFFER CERTIFICATE

Item	LEVEL ONE Booklet 1	LEVEL TWO Booklet 1 & 2	LEVEL THREE Booklet 1, 2 & 3	LEVEL FOUR Booklet 1, 2, 3 & 4
Booklet 1 = $100+	$100+	$100+	$100+	$100+
Booklet 2 = $200+		$200+	$200+	$200+
Booklet 3 = $300+			$300+	$300+
Booklet 4 = $400+	____	____	____	$400+
Approximate Total Value of Savings	$100+	$300+	$600+	$1,000+
# of Proofs of Purchase Required	4	6	12	18
Check One	____	____	____	____

Name_____

Address_____

City_____ State_____ Zip_____

Return Offer Certificates to: **PASSPORT TO ROMANCE**, P.O. Box 9057, Buffalo, NY 14269-9057

Requests must be postmarked by **January 25, 1991**

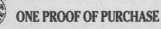

- -

ONE PROOF OF PURCHASE

3 HS-3

To collect your free coupon booklet you must include the necessary number of proofs-of-purchase with a properly completed Offer Certificate
© 1990 Harlequin Enterprises Limited

See previous page for details